The Coward

The Coward

Tom Wall

Winchester, UK
Washington, USA

First published by Roundfire Books, 2015
Roundfire Books is an imprint of John Hunt Publishing Ltd., Laurel House, Station Approach,
Alresford, Hants, SO24 9JH, UK
office1@jhpbooks.net
www.johnhuntpublishing.com
www.roundfire-books.com

For distributor details and how to order please visit the 'Ordering' section on our website.

Text copyright: Tom Wall 2014

ISBN: 978 1 78279 616 9
Library of Congress Control Number: 2014958260

A CIP catalogue record for this book is available from the British Library.

Design: Stuart Davies

Printed and bound in the USA by Edwards Brothers Malloy

We operate a distinctive and ethical publishing philosophy in all
areas of our business, from our global network of authors to
production and worldwide distribution.

In memory of Bill Robinson, who chose to farm rather than fight in 1939.

Acknowledgments

Mia, Liz, Amy, Alex, Will, Corin, Anna and Nellie for giving their time to read and comment on various drafts of this book. All narrative blunders and spelling mistakes are, however, my own.

The Peace Pledge Union and Newcastle Libraries for giving me access to their archives.

Roosa and Sami for providing welcome distractions.

And Mia (again) for putting up with me for so long.

Those readers interested in the background to this story can visit my website http://tomwall.weebly.com

TW

Like an attentive, perhaps even obsessive chronicler, Bill Rowe knows these bricks. He knows their rough calluses and crumbling lime mortar veins. He knows their dark pockmarks and dusty scars. Nothing escapes his lingering eye and grafflin hand; he knows every last imperfection and blemish.

In the dead of night, when his coughing wakes him, he runs his fingers over them, tracing the marks left by his fellow outcasts and sinners. Some have hacked mindlessly away to pass the time or exorcise inner demons. Others have painstakingly etched their own name or the name of their hinny or eked out declarations of innocence or pious pleas for forgiveness.

George McKibben 1922.

Ivy Dearlove.

I never laid a hand on her.

God loves all his children.

When Bill arrived six months ago he added his own name with the hard end of a bootlace. The waxy tip eventually bent and frayed under the pressure of his shaking hand but he didn't give up.

Bill Rowe 1941.

The voices and visions came later.

An unanswered cry for help. A man running. Flames gathering in his clothes. Skin breaking and weeping.

Two pale heads rising and falling with grey waves. The warmth leaching from their hearts and salt stinging their lips.

A heaving mob intent on doing harm to a child. Lovers perched at either end of a single bed. A constable digging his dirty fingernails into a collar bone. A pile of belongings on a doorstep. A mother turning away in disgust.

And the question always the same: why? The guns keep firing and the bombs keep dropping. And the bodies of innocent men, women and children continue to pile up in cities with familiar names and others with strange names. Coventry. Liverpool. Mannheim. Chongquin.

His fingers locate familiar lines; he explores each one, reliving those first days and nights. To begin with he liked the ritual of marking the wall each evening, it reminded him that his ordeal would not go on forever, but the more he did it, the more he realised that recording the passing of time only slowed it down.

Something wriggles in his hair and punctures the scaly skin covering his scalp. He holds it up in the moonlight seeping through the small slits above his bed. The creature's spindly, alien legs twitch hopelessly as it dangles in the air. Its tiny body is bloated and dark with blood. He flicks it towards the jerry.

He's always had an eye for detail and a way with words. As a boy he used to watch gangs of starlings peck the frozen earth in their tiny yard while Ma chopped and cooked over a smouldering cooking range. When her back was turned he'd press his nose against the steamy glass and follow their search for food. Everything else – the bitterly cold draft and the smell of sinewy meat and onions simmering – he blocked out. Their purple and green dinosaur faces and darting black eyes intrigued him.

'How do they survive the winter, Ma? Where do they go to escape the cold?'

'I haven't the time to think, Bill.'

He would stay there mulling over these questions until he was clipped round the ear by his Da returning home, with the rich, stale fug of cheap ale and baccy smoke on his breath.

'Sit down for your supper.'

Clouds obscure the moon and the cell falls dark. He turns over in search of a more comfortable position but as usual it ends in defeat. The flock mattress is stuffed with a few rags and some wool. It offers little protection against the hard board below. His bones, which these days jut out of him at painful angles, chaff on the wood.

The screws pretend not to notice he is wasting away, they insist everyone is getting the same. The truth is most men, even men who are accustomed to living on next to nothing, would struggle to survive on the rations they bring. When he feels clear-headed and brave, which is rare these days, he points out that his body is giving up, that he needs more food. They snigger behind their clipboards and say no one else is complaining.

Even the older, kinder screws cannot help. One of them, Rogers, who works in the store, advised him to ask to be moved to the infirmary when he saw his pillow case, which was speckled with tiny red droplets. But the officer in charge of the wing, Fry, a tough bastard with a squashed nose and red puffy ears, refused.

'You look fine to me, Rowe. You're just scared of a hard day's work.'

Another lie – in an age of lies. On bad weeks he cannot even make it out into the exercise yard. On good weeks he hobbles around the yard like a crooked old gadgie. He feels like a man of sixty, not a fit twenty-two-year-old who used to swim bare-buff in rivers and wander over the wild, purple-crowned Cheviots.

Moonlight again fills the cell. He closes his eyes; outside he can hear half-starved prison dogs barking and somewhere in the far, far distance the soft rumble of aeroplanes, possibly bombers. But he concentrates on the bleached, lunar interior of his eyelids. And before long he is somewhere else entirely.

*

Bare oak branches creak, and heaps of dry, brown leaves crackle in a light breeze. Bill opens his eyes and blinks furiously. It is early autumn and the sun is high in the pale sky. He is perhaps ten. The other lads are hunting for blackberries in another part of the wood or playing Cowboys and Indians. He really doesn't care because this moment is perfect. He feels part of the spongy moss beneath his head: he listens to worms churning the forest's fibrous, woody debris and watches ugly great crows strut and squawk. The city with its constables, taverns and smoky chimneys seems far away. The air here is fresh and clean, the sounds natural and peaceful.

'Bill, you there? Come on you gormless bastard? Harry's cooking up a brew. Bill? Bill?'

The shout disturbs his daydream. 'Aye. I'm over here, man. By the old oak tree.'

Len Weaver looks down at him; older, gangly, wild messy black hair, crooked teeth. The others call him Tatie-Boggle the scarecrow. He lives on the same street as Bill and goes to the same school but his parents are odd sorts. Len's father is a sometime piano tuner and journalist and his mother is a school teacher and dress maker. Their house is full of newspapers, pamphlets and vegetarian cookbooks. And the church they go to doesn't have vicars or priests – anyone can stand up and say what they like. Some of the boys at school say the whole family walk around with no clothes during the summer months.

Len grins. 'What you doing on the floor, like?'

'Don't know – just like this spot.'

Pushing their way through brambles and low-hanging branches, they head towards the den. In a grassy clearing there are two other boys: Harry Bags and Walter Kelly. A blackened metal kettle is suspended above a little fire.

Walter, his hands stained purple from sorting berries, says, 'Where was he?'

'Having a kip by that oak tree, like.'

'I knew we shouldn't have invited that dozy little clot up here. We should have left him playing hopscotch with the girls.'

Laughing, Harry passes round tin cups. He is shorter than Len but with thick, muscular arms and legs and a square jaw. There is even a sprouting of brown hairs on his top lip.

He says, 'You going to see the King open the bridge? Me Da says he coming with Queen Mary.'

Bill realises there are only three cups; Harry doesn't even offer him one. 'I've seen the posters, like,' he says quietly.

Walter ignores him. 'Might do, there'll be horses and a band, won't there?'

'Aye and probably a dreadnaught on the river too.'

Len pointedly passes his half-full cup to Bill. 'It's a lot of old rubbish, man.'

'What, Tatie?'

'I says it's a lot of old rubbish.'

Harry screws up his face. 'If me Da heard you say that, he'd clip your lug. He helped build that bloody bridge. Your family are always doing things down.'

Walter sides with Harry. 'Aye, pipe down, Tatie.'

Bill watches him closely; Len's a clever devil but he can come across as a know-it-all.

Len inspects the mud on his boots. 'I was just going to say they are a bunch of...'

'Of what?'

'Well, what does that King George do? He don't give a bugger about the likes of us.'

Bill smirks behind his hand; the cane would be used if such a thing was uttered at school.

'He does more for us than your lot—' Len shakes his head but Harry continues regardless '—go on what've you lot done for Gateshead—' Before he can finish his sentence a shot rings out.

Walter yelps. 'It must be shooting season. If that gamekeeper catches us again he'll give us a hiding.'

Harry stamps on the flames sending a plume of sooty smoke up into the sky. Walter drops the berries and starts running. Len is next up and then Bill. Soon they are all tearing through the wood, jumping rotting trunks covered with moss and landing in boggy puddles. Bill feels water seeping through the holes in the soles of his boots.

'Me boots are soaked, Len.'

As more shots ring out, Harry pushes past Bill. 'Leave him, Tatie. He's slowing us down.'

Len is having none of it – he grabs Bill's wrist and pulls through the last of the trees. 'Come on, kidda.'

The wood gives way to rolling hills of freshly ploughed, purple-brown fields. Rows of tightly packed houses line the other side of the valley. Beyond them are the dim outlines of tenement chimneystacks, church spires and dockyard cranes.

'Nearly there, Bill.'

'Me legs. They're like dead weights.'

Once they reach the Gut, Len slows down. They check along the nettle-carpeted banks and back up the hill. The others have scarpered but there is no sign of the hunting party.

'We're safe now, they'll not come this far.'

Bill sits down on a clump of earth and empties the water out of his boots. 'Sorry for slowing you down. These old things have had it.'

Len looks confused. 'Do you know where we've ended up, Bill? I don't want to go back up there and run into those shooters again.'

Bill knows from his own wanderings there is a fallen tree trunk they can get across about a mile away. He swells with pride as he points the way out to Len. It is like the story in *The Champion* where Private Jack Oil leads Flight Lieutenant Rockfist Rogan out of an enemy jungle.

When they get to the trunk, they whip down the surrounding nettles with thin branches torn from a willow tree.

Len says, 'What's your Ma feeding you? I could feel your bones through your shirt when we were running.'

'Usual.'

They inch across the silvery bark on their bottoms. The water slops underneath with its cargo of dead cats and garbage.

'What'd you have last night?'

'Ma boiled up a sheep's head with some veg.'

'Did you go to bed hungry?'

He feels a little peeved to be asked the same question again.

Isn't his word good enough? He's always been skinny – it's just the way God made him. 'I went back for seconds. Ma's a grand cook.'

They stop at the crossroads beside the King George. There are a few drinkers outside the bar doors pushing coins into the hands of a small boy working for a local bookie. The men stop to whistle and slap the bottom of a young girl carrying a basket of groceries. She escapes down a side street.

Bill nervously glances through the large windows but there is no sign of Da's narrow shoulders and dark coat flecked with flour from the bakery where he works. Len tells him he'll call for him tomorrow because Harry and the others are planning on raiding an orchard.

Bill skips along the pavement, barely able to contain his excitement; he's part of the gang. He gets home as the sun sinks in the sky leaving behind a pale orange, yellow glow – the colour of the tinned peaches he gets from the Mission at Christmas. It's pretty but the warmth goes with the sun. Leaping down the metal steps to the front door, he notices that the mist on the bedroom window is already turning to frost.

Inside, the scene is familiar: Da's slumped on his armchair near the heat of the cooking range. A copy of the *Evening Chronicle* is open on his lap and a pipe is hanging out the corner of his mouth. His chest shudders; his breathing hoarse and painful. He stares blankly at the cracked ceiling.

Ma's stirring a steaming pot of broth. She looks older than she is: her dainty face is stained with coal soot and wood smoke. A gleaming crucifix hangs around her neck. How does it stay so clean? He sits beside his little sister Peggy. When Ma's back is turned, he peeks into the pot: there is barely enough for all of them but he doesn't mind because he has been eating blackberries all day. He pushes away the ladle as she offers him more.

Da sits up. 'An-An-An...'

'What the bleeding hell is it, Joseph?'

Da stumbles over his words. They all know what he wants to say – he's going to The George – but he can't get the words out. His hollow grey-and-black studded cheeks shudder. Greasy strands of hair fall about his face. His eyes, ringed with faint red scar tissue, water. It is like he is a volcano ready to erupt.

Ma pushes his hair back into place and holds his trembling hand. Her efforts are practiced and soothing but distant – as if she is dressing a mannequin in a shop window.

'An-An-Annie, I'm off out for a game of dominoes.'

Words never came easily to Da – that's what Ma told Bill. Granda Arth, a huge beast of a Northumberland miner, would hit Da every time he fumbled for a word and call him a bloody imbecile – even though he couldn't read or write himself. Granda Arth would even pay Da's sister a penny for every new word she learnt with never a thought of his son's pride.

Da clammed up and spoke rarely until he left the family cottage to work in a bakery in Gateshead. The owner and the other bakers all thought he was dumb. They teased him and forced him to do the jobs they hated: sweeping the floors and plucking rats from the traps. But Ma, who was working in a tearoom nearby and staying in digs, befriended him and coaxed him into talking during Sunday-afternoon strolls through Gateshead.

She convinced him to jot down his thoughts when his stutter got the better of him. He found it easier than speaking and with that they managed to get by most of the time.

When it was too cold or wet for the park, they sat in Ma's tearoom as the other girls cleaned up. They talked about the Northumberland countryside, their parents and giggled about misunderstandings. Da would scrawl down compliments about her dress or hair or eyes and she would pretend not to notice before correcting his spelling. Sometimes he ran his fingers over the peaks and troughs of her knuckles under the table.

Bill always blushed when Ma told him this part of the story, but at the same time he liked the thought of them shy and happy with not a worry in the world. He only wished he still held her hand under the table.

Then the war began and everything changed. Keen to escape the bakery, Da joined the Durham Light Infantry. Ma was worried of course, but she couldn't help but swell with pride when she saw him marching in his new uniform through Gateshead. Afterward she looped her arm through his and kissed him full on the lips.

Da proposed to her one autumn evening in Saltwell Park. Ma could recite every last detail. Golden leaves were falling. The trees were swishing back and forth like dancers in the throes of passion. The sky was a dark inky blue. Da dropped onto one knee in the middle of the path.

Ma knew what was happening as he had been fretting about speaking to her father for days but she feigned innocence. 'What you doing, Joe?'

'I-I-I want—' normally Ma had to fight the urge to finish his sentences but this time she wanted to hear him speak without help '—to as-as-ask you a question?'

'Aye.'

'Will you m-m-marry m-m-me?'

She didn't have to think about it. 'Aye, I will, Joseph.'

The week after his train pulled out of the station she discovered she was blessed with a baby. He was given leave to return for a weekend and they married in the small country church, St Peters, near where she grew up. Granda Arth was too ill to come but Granda Oliver and Grandma Maude sat at the front smiling. They didn't mind Da's stutter because they saw how happy he made their daughter.

At first his letters came thick and fast: they detailed his training, the barracks, the dreadful mould-covered army bread and the boat journey across the channel. But then they stopped suddenly.

Ma became frantic with worry. Every day she would walk to the post office to check if they had been misaddressed or dropped or lost. They tried to reassure her that very few items were lost. But she grew impatient as the days turned into weeks. Exactly one month after the letters stopped she turned up at the office and refused to leave until the postmaster showed round the sorting office – she could be quite fearsome if the mood took her. She spent the best part of a day looking under desks and behind cabinets and in piles of sacks. They tried to dissuade her as she was by then heavily pregnant, but she was having none of it; she refused all offers of food and drink and insisted everybody join the search. By closing time she was so famished, she had to be escorted home.

She liked to say Bill had been a good boy because he never made a fuss even when he was inside her belly. Whereas little Peggy had her up retching every morning.

Another month passed without word from Da. At night she held her sides and sobbed into her pillow. The other wives on the street told her she would have heard if he had died and that no letters were better than an official visit. Ma, however, told Bill she wanted the truth as it was preferable to worry and ignorance. After a particularly bad night she took herself down to the local barracks and waited until the grandest car she had ever seen drew up. Without a thought to her own safety, she stepped in front of it.

She used to joke it could have been the end of her and Bill as well. But he loved hearing the story nonetheless.

The driver only just managed to skid to a halt; he honked his horn and waited for her the move. She demanded an audience with the highest-ranking person in the barracks. After about five minutes the guards tried to drag her away; she wriggled out of their holds and they were too embarrassed to wrestle a woman carrying a bairn to the ground. Eventually the government official travelling in the car got out and agreed to take her to the see General Balding.

In Balding's cold, bare office, Ma explained, 'I've heard nothing from my Joseph for months and it's not like him to keep me in the dark. Please find out what has happened to him. I want to know.'

Impressed by her perseverance, Balding sent for a clerk to check on his whereabouts. A little blond-haired man came back with a piece of paper confirming Joseph was alive and well on the frontline.

With a mean sneer, the clerk added, 'Hundreds of other letters have been sent back. Your husband must be choosing not to write to you.'

Balding indicated there was nothing more he could do. Ma left shamed and confused.

The pushing started early on Good Friday and by lunchtime Bill was born. Ma prayed for Da to return but she was forced to start planning on a life without him. She didn't mind admitting it to Bill. She knitted jumpers and socks and visited her family in the country. She found herself mentioning him less and less. Then on a wet afternoon there was a faint knock on the door. It was Da; he had been discharged with respiratory problems. She held him tight and inhaled the smell of his dirty tanned skin.

'I-I-I...'

'You don't need to speak. I love you, Joe.'

She made him a cup of tea and spent the rest of the day waiting for her husband to talk. He just sat opposite her with a blank look in his eyes. She spoke about her life for a bit and gave him Bill to hold. In the evening she made his favourite supper of liver and bacon but he could only bring himself to half-heartedly pick at it.

Later, as they lay awkwardly beside one another, like strangers asked to share a bed, Ma asked him why he had stopped writing to her. 'You can tell me anything, Joe.'

He started to speak but the words got stuck in his throat, 'I-I-I... pen?'

Ma found him everything he needed and he scrawled down a three words: give me time.

Ma pulls her hands away and wipes them on the front of her flowery pinny. It is as though she is removing something unspeakable from her skin. Coughing and spluttering, Da lifts himself out of his chair.

She observes him through narrow eyes. 'Joe.'

He covers his mouth with mitten-clad hands. 'I-I-I'm off then, pet.'

Using the walls as supports, he hauls himself down the hallway. Ma follows him and closes the door gently. Yet the wood is paper-thin and Bill can hear every word. Ma raises her voice; she is upset. Peggy leans against Bill as she has done countless times before and he rests his chin on her head. She smells of street games: damp grass, chalk and coal smoke.

'Stay with us tonight, Joseph.'

'Let m-m-me past.'

The door slams.

'I hope you perish in the gutter,' Ma snarls.

Peggy buries her face in Bill's shirt. What can he say? She needs comfort and love. But the adult world is as much a mystery to him as it is to her. Ma and Da seemed to need each other but couldn't stand each other either.

When Ma returns her eyes are puffy and dark. She scoops Peggy up and puts her to bed; Bill follows behind. The room is cold, so she piles all the blankets she can find on top of them. Then she places bricks, which have been warmed in the range and wrapped in old clothes, by their trembling feet. They lie still while she strokes their foreheads.

Bill squints up at her. 'Is Da coming home?'

'Go to sleep, pet.'

'Can you sing us a song?'

She smiles awkwardly.

'Please, Ma?'

She goes to the piano, which is wedged between the end of the bed and the wall. They wait but she just hovers over the keys with an odd glint in her eyes, as if in a trance or dreaming.

'I'm not in the mood,' she says eventually.

Bill wishes she could soothe his worries with a kiss but he's too old for that now. 'What about a story, Ma? Tell us about how you met Da? Please, Ma?'

'You've heard it so many times, Bill,' she says turning to face them.

'Please,' says Peggy.

Smiling, she runs her hand over the outline of their legs. 'Wee bairns – I was wee like you two once. I grew up in a little village in the middle of the countryside, far from this city. In the summer I played in the fields and streams but in the winter we huddled inside by the fire. Granda Oliver always got me to play that old thing— ' she waves towards the piano '—he loved a good sing song. After wolfing down dinner, we would squeeze out of our damp boots, and play hymns and songs like "Bonny at Morn" and "Sair Field Hinny".'

Peggy slaps her lips together softly in readiness for sleep. 'Did Grandma Maude sing, Ma?'

'Nah she left that to Granda Oliver. She'd sit behind helping me with difficult parts and whispering little encouragements in my ear. The looks on their faces made me so proud, Peggy. I think it went to me head though 'cos I dreamed of playing in an orchestra. At night I used to stare at this old photograph of the Royal Liverpool Philharmonic that I kept under the pillow. Granda Oliver had cut it out of the *Morpeth Herald* for me – he was a good man. Those finely dressed men and women holding their instruments seemed a world away from our little cottage, but I was spellbound.'

Ma still had the photograph. Bill had seen it her purse; it was so crumpled he couldn't make it out at first until she explained it to him.

'Go on, Ma.'

'Once I asked Granda Oliver if I was a good enough to join the orchestra. He hugged me and told me I was as bright as a button and could do anything I wanted. "All you need to do is learn how to read and write well and play the piano when you get a chance," he told me.

'So I did; I got up early and played until my wrists ached and worked hard in the classroom. But Granda Oliver was not rich and they could not afford for me to stay on at school.

'Then I had a hard choice, just like you will have one day, Bill: go into service at the Tyndall estate or move to Morpeth and find work. I remember looking at Granda Oliver, hoping he would say I could do anything I wanted again, but he wouldn't look up from cleaning his boots. So that made my mind up; in the morning I told them I would go to the big house. I can still see Granda Oliver loading up my belongings on his cart; he muttered that he was sorry he had ever given me that picture.

'But the next day he brought the piano over to the house. The head butler frowned and said it was too large. I'd never seen Granda Oliver so heartbroken. But he went on his way.

'When I came home, I was too knackered to play or sing. Instead I slept while Grandma Maud cooked supper.

'I worked in that horrible kitchen until that Lord Tyndall decided he needed to cut his outgoings because he was away in London gambling so often. I was asked to leave as I'd been the last one to arrive.

'Granda Oliver and Grandma Maude begged me to come back but I had my mind set of getting as far away as possible. Then I found work in Bridges, a grand tearoom in Gateshead. That's where I met your Da. I stopped by the back door of his bakery to ask for some old bread and he had these big kind eyes and a shy smile – I just thought it was worth asking him. Anyway he went in and got me a hot one that had come straight out of the oven. The steam was still rising off it and I had to toss it from hand to hand.'

Bill feels Peggy snoring in the nape of his neck. 'Did it taste good, Ma?'

'Aye – as soon as I was round the corner I tore a hunk off. I was ravenous and it was divine.'

Bill's own breathing deepens too. 'And the piano. You got it back,' he says drowsily.

'After your Da and I married, Granda Oliver loaded up the cart with the piano. It was a two-day round trip but there was no dissuading him. He kissed me on the cheek when it was inside and then got on his way.'

Bill is startled by the sound of the front door opening. Dirty, yellow lamplight is stealing through a rip in the curtains. Ma slips from her bed, which is opposite theirs, and makes her way into the kitchen. Bill can't get back to sleep; he waits a moment then pulls last week's *Champion* from under his pillow. It is far too dark to read so he peers for a while at a Tommy raking the Kaiser's trenches with bullets.

Da's voice carries through; Bill presses his ear to the cracking plaster. He is whimpering. 'I-I-I'm hated. I'm turning into my bastard father. None of yous lot loves me—' Something metallic is hurled to the floor, perhaps a pot or a fire poke. '—I-I-I slog me guts out to earn one pound a week and it's gone in the blink of a fucking eye. What do you do with it woman?'

Ma's reply is hesitant but precise, 'Ten shillings goes on the rent. The rest goes on jam and cocoa for the bairns and clothes and then there's the tram fares. There's the ale and all, Joseph...'

It all goes quiet. Bill slithers to the end of the bed and peeps through a gap in the door; Da is swaying in the middle of the room. Ma's sat at the table, staring at her clasped hands, which are squirming and wriggling like the grass snakes they catch in the woods.

'Please, Joseph. Sit down.'

'Leave drink…out of this. I-I-I'm an ill man. It's m-m-me one fucking pleasure.'

'You're hurting us, Joseph. Your wife. Your son. Your daughter.'

Da flings the table over and stands up blocking his view. Between his legs Bill can see Ma cowering against the wall.

'I-I-I sorry, Annie. I didn't mean to scare y-y-you.'

Before the door opens Bill crawls under the blankets and pretends to sleep. From the safety the bed, he watches Da shuffle off his clothes and flat cap and get into the empty bed. His arms are thin and the ridges of his rib cage cast dark shadows in the half-light.

After a while Ma joins him. She lifts his arm and pushes her back against his chest while he presses his face into her hair. Bill falls asleep to her sniffs and Da's coughs.

Bill wakes early with Peggy's bony knee in his side. He slips from the bedclothes and totters on matchstick-thin legs to his shorts and shirt. Sunlight has replaced the lamplight but there is still a nasty chill in the air.

The kitchen is as they left it: table upended and the pots and pans cast on the floor. So it was not a nightmare after all. There are the remains of a loaf high up on a shelf; it has been there for days but he shoves it in his mouth anyway. Beggars can't be choosers. The crust is hard and the crumbs are like salty sand. He washes it down with some cold, stewed tea left in the pot.

By the time Len knocks, Bill is ready and waiting. He opens the door immediately, startling the older boy.

'You been waiting there for me?'

'Aye. I was up bright and early.'

As they reach street level, Bill twists his neck and sees a

shadow move across the curtains. Ma will have to wake Da soon. The bakery will need sweeping once the morning batch of bread is taken out of the ovens. She could do with his help but it is not every day he goes raiding with Len's gang.

Bill trails Len as they wind their way to the edges of the city. A canvas knapsack bounces up and down on his long back. Stout boots pound the cobbles.

Bill says, 'When we meeting the others?'

'Harry and Walter?'

'Aye.'

'They didn't want to come...'

After the last row of houses, they leap over a gate and land in a ploughed field. Clumps of mud cling to their boots.

Bill says, 'Where we heading then, Tatie?'

Len comes to a sudden halt. 'Don't call me that.'

'I thought that's what the others...'

'I hate it.' Len goes quiet and they squelch across the mud. 'There's a stream I've been damming. Do you want to see it?'

'No scrumping then?'

'Nah.'

The sun melts the sparkling frost in the bushes and warms the backs of their necks as they follow the line of the hedge towards a grassy field.

Len says, 'Keep your eye out for herders and farm labourers, they sometimes bring cattle through here. They can get quite rough. Let me handle them if they show up.'

Bill smiles to himself. Len really is Lieutenant Rockfist Rogon; a brave, fearless leader. They pass through three or four fields before they reach the wood. Len ducks under some barbed wire and holds it up for Bill.

They move off in the opposite direction to the den. Dappled light plays on a blanket of leaves and twigs. Bill purses his lips and whistles a music-hall tune Ma hums sometimes and soon they can no longer see or hear or smell Gateshead. They follow faint sheep paths that come to sudden, inexplicable stops and duck under wilting brambles dotted with dried-up blackberries. A rustle makes them pause but it turns out to be a small deer feasting on some hazel nuts. It darts away as soon as it realises it's not alone.

After three or four miles they come to halt under a large, bare beech tree surrounded by mounds of tangled roots. The boys find a comfortable resting place among them and catch their breath.

Len produces an earth-encrusted swede from his knapsack. 'Do you want one of these?'

'Where did you get it?'

'I yanked it out of the ground.'

'You stole it?'

'They stole the land off us.'

'What do you mean?'

'Well, there was a time when folk like us lived off the land. Each family had its own bit and there was shared land for grazing sheep and cows and the like. The only way the gentry could get their hands on it was to bully and trick us out of it.'

'Is that what you'll tell the farmer if he comes up here with a gun?'

'No, I'll bloody run for it.'

Len peels the swede with a rusty penknife and hacks off a chunk for each of them. It tastes good: earthy sweet but slightly bitter.

In between crunches, Bill says, 'Da says there's always been rich and poor. It can't be any different.'

'And do you believe him?'

'I don't believe anybody.'

On the other side of the tree the land drops away to a grassy bowl-shaped clearing crossed by a pretty, shallow river. Len scrambles down the dusty slope, skidding on large brown leaves, and Bill follows behind.

The dam spans half the width of the river and is made from

golden stones dug out of a sandy bed. It is about two-foot high and four-foot along. 'What do you think, Bill?'

'We need to get to the other side and build it from there.'

'Well, what're you waiting for?'

Len leaps over the glinting water and lands on his bottom. Bill slips on the muddy bank as well. Laughing they pull off their socks and roll up their shorts and set about collecting stones. The cool water froths and bubbles around their sore ankles and soothes their blistered toes.

Yet as they work they grow hotter and hotter. The clearing is sheltered and the day is surprisingly balmy. Red-faced they throw their damp jumpers and then their shirts on to the grass. It's as if it is a summer's day rather than the beginnings of winter.

Once it is finished they sit on the bank and watch the water rise up against the stones. A few are dislodged by the pressure but most stay in place. Len produces some sandwiches and the remains of the swede from his knapsack. They eat nosily as the sunshine dries their legs and feet.

Afterwards Bill lies on his back and lets his eyelids droop. The grass tickles his skin and makes the hairs on his arm stand up. The thought occurs to him that he could live here quite handsomely. He could build himself a shack or put up a tent. The farmer wouldn't miss a few swedes. It was his birthright, as Len had said. He would visit Peggy and Ma at weekends. But he could never tell them where he was because they might let it slip.

'Len?'

'Aye?'

'Do you reckon we could still live off the land?'

Bill pushes himself up on his elbows; Len has finished packing and is standing over him with curious look in his eyes.

'Don't see why not.'

'I wouldn't mind living here.'

'Here?'

'Aye. I could build a shelter in the wood. They would never

find me. I could set rabbit traps and dig up swedes.'

Len's lips part in a smile. 'Sounds grand. Would there be room for me?'

There is a crashing noise from behind the beech tree. It sounds like a branch breaking. They both scan the top of the slope.

'Must be that deer again. I'll go up and see.'

Len pulls on his shirt and wades over the river. As he reaches the bottom of the slope, four boy-sized figures appear above him. Bill cannot make out their faces because it is so bright in the clearing and dark under the trees.

'What you doing, Tatie? What you doing, Tatie? What you doing, Tatie?'

The shout echoes off the different sides of the bowl. It must be Harry and Walter and some other lads from school. They could help build it even bigger.

'Dam building.'

'With him?'

'Aye.'

'He's just a stupid wee bairn. I told you not to bring him. He nearly got us shot larking around yesterday.'

Len takes a step back. He seems scared but he doesn't say anything. Bill looks around for an escape route. The slopes on his side of the river are too steep for a quick getaway.

Harry continues, 'His father is a bloody no-good drunk. Can't even speak right. Isn't that right, B-B-Billy boy?'

Bill wants to correct him: Da never has trouble with the letter B. He only gets stuck on letters like I and A.

Len answers for him, 'At least he's not a dirty blackleg like your father.'

The other boys all stop and look at Harry: he is shaking with rage. He picks up a rock the size of a small mallet head. It is so heavy he cannot lift it above his belt. The large muscles in his arms bulge and he grimaces in pain. With a grunt he drops it over the slope towards Len. It spins once before cracking into the side of Len's bare thigh. Len squeals in pain and sinks to his knees clutching his leg. Harry peers down holding another rock. There is a bloodthirsty madness in his eyes.

'Who's the scab now, Len?'

'Please...'

Bill splashes across the river and kneels down beside his friend. 'Are you hurt?'

Len lifts his hands; there is a fist-sized gash just beneath his rolled-up short leg. Blood is dripping down and he looks a little dazed. 'What?'

Harry yells again, 'Who's the scab now, Len? Who's the scab now, Len? Who's the scab now, Len?' It echoes without reply. 'Let them have it. Let them have it. Let them have it.'

Rocks start raining down on them from all directions. They hit Bill's bare chest and arms. Most are smaller than the one that hit Len but they still draw blood. Bill hauls Len to his feet and helps him towards the river. More rocks are hurled at them as they cross. Len hangs on because he cannot support his weight on his injured leg. On the other bank they collapse as they are just out of range.

Len is shaking. 'I'm done for. I'm done for.'

Harry glares at them from the slope then turns and disappears into the trees. His gang melt away with him.

Len voice crackles with fear. 'Might they come back?'

Bill knows from Da that bullies like their prey to survive so they can torment them again. 'Nah. They'd have come down if they wanted.'

'I owe you, Bill.'

Len's shorts are wet through even though the river water only came up to their shins. A fruity tang fills Bill nostrils. It reminds him of the school urinals.

'Don't tell them please. It'll be hell in class if they know I...'

He can't bring himself to say piss so Bill turns away and gathers up his clothes and the knapsack. So much for Lieutenant

Rockfist Rogon.

'You're covered in cuts, Bill. You should've run when you had the chance.'

'I hate bullies. Always have done.'

'Why's that then?'

'I've seen it close up at home. Da ain't the nicest of men.'

Len nods, although he can't know what he's going on about.

'I hate them too.'

Once Len's wound has stopped bleeding, they cross the stream and climb up the bank. Len suggests a different route to avoid running into the gang again, but he finds the going tough on his bad leg.

Bill wraps his arm around his waist and supports his weight. 'How do you know all them facts about the past, Len?'

'What facts?'

'About the gentry taking the land from the poor.'

'My family have got a lot of books,' he says, wincing with each lift of his injured leg.

'I don't think there's one book in our place—' Bill wishes he hadn't spoken so candidly and adds quickly '—course we have a copy of the Bible.'

'Well you should come over one day and have a look.'

*

Bill tentatively touches his skin: he is burning up. It is as if someone has been rubbing him with a wood file or glass-paper. Sweat runs down his forehead and stings his eyes. He wipes it away with his flannel shirt.

Damp night air lingers in the cell – dawn is some way off yet. He stands up gingerly and rests against the wall so he can see outside. The bars and the grimy glass block most of the view but beyond the gate he can just make out the rolling hills that surround Durham against the dark blue sky.

The city itself is quiet and sleepy. Usually he can see pinpricks of faint lights in windows and flickering street lamps but tonight it is all black.

A man shouts that his jerry is overflowing. But there are no officers on duty – the siren must have sounded earlier without waking him. The man's call echoes around the abandoned wing. Others join in; they complain that they are being left to die. There was a time when Bill would have taken pleasure in this little rebellion but he hasn't the strength anymore.

Eventually the cries die down as the prisoners listen in the dark for the whistle and thud of bombs. The cold from the bricks leaches into Bill's skin, so he shuffles back to the bed.

*

Ma grips Bill's hand tightly. She looks so pure away from the hellish orange and red embers of the range. Her blond hair is brushed straight and her skin seems squeaky clean.

She smiles. 'My little man.'

He skips to keep up with her brisk walk. 'What's up with Peggy?'

'She's fine, son. Just a bit chesty.'

Peggy doesn't seem right to him: she has always got a cold or a cough. Sometimes she hacks up more than Da. And her appetite is so small; she barely eats what's laid in front of her each night. She is skinnier than a girl her age should be and she's the first to be grabbed in games of catch.

He tugs Ma's arm. 'Will there be cake? Can we bring some for Peggy?'

'I don't know, pet. Let's hurry up or we'll be late.'

Saint Chad's is busy; a lot of people have made the effort as it is Harvest Festival. Bill clocks Harry and Walter outside the gates shoving each other playfully as their mothers chat with a group of women. Harry picks up an imaginary rock and pretends to chuck it at Bill. They break out into laughter but Bill just stares through them. It is what he tries to do when Da picks on him or Peggy or Ma.

As the bells ring the crowd pass under the dark stone arches, past baskets of fruit and veg and a few tins that Bill knows Ma would love to take home and cook for her family.

Reverend Pilkington, a young university man from Edinburgh, clasps the rounded edges of the pulpit. 'Welcome to our little celebration of nature's bounty. God has blessed us here in Northumberland with rich, fertile soils to grow wheat and lush grass for our cattle. But in this time of plenty we must remember those who aren't so fortunate. Think of those poor children in China.'

Few have any idea what he is talking about but his passion holds their attention. Even Harry and Walter sit quietly. The reverend sticks his square, freshly shaved jaw out and leads them through "We Plough the Fields and Scatter", "All Things Bright and Beautiful" and "Come You Thankful People Come". Bill is not moved to sing but he opens and closes his mouth to please Ma.

When Pilkington continues his sermon, Bill's mind wanders. The church is vast and solid. He loves its stony stillness, even though it is full of people. The weight of the walls and roof make him feel safe.

In the row ahead, a new father glances down at his son; the boy's mouth forms into a gummy smile. The bond between them is mysterious to Bill. Da never held him or comforted him; a couple of years back he tripped over an old rag beside the hearth and cut his forehead. The look on Da's face had stayed with him; it wasn't angry or annoyed, just blank. He was kinder to Peggy: he sometimes cuddled her and played with her when he came home early from The George. But mostly he ignored her like he ignored his son. Bill didn't resent the attention he occasionally gave Peggy; she was welcome to him.

Pilkington pauses, closes his eyes and takes a deep breath. Everybody waits for him to say something but instead he stands in front of them motionless, hands by his side. After some considerable time his nostrils flare and two streams of warm air rush out – it sounds like a football spiked on a railing.

'And now we pray.'

Bill half closes his eyes but can think only of the rumbling in his tummy. He had long given up praying for better as it didn't appear to help anybody except those who attended the churches in the smarter parts of Gateshead. Pilkington's voice starts low and slowly builds. To Bill he is no better than the barrow boys on market day; all bluff and bluster.

After the service the congregation help themselves from a spread of sandwiches, cake, sausage rolls and boiled eggs. The warden watches Bill and the other children carefully to make sure they do not go for second helpings. Pilkington is too busy attending to a pretty widow to help the unfortunate in his own congregation. But Ma gives Bill some of her fruitcake while the warden is berating Walter for pushing a girl out of his way.

'Thank you, Ma.'

'Giving to you is like giving to me because you are part of me.'

She seems happy and relaxed. If only it could be like this always. He slurps his warm, sweet tea and brushes fluffy crumbs from his lap as she runs her hands through his hair.

*

The prison is quiet yet Bill knows all the men are awake; they are waiting to discover if they will see another morning. It is an odd and desperate feeling: their lives are in danger, yet they cannot turn and flee or rise and fight. They cannot plead or beg. They cannot even break down and cry, that would be a death sentence.

He returns his fingers to the bricks, following the sandy

mortar lines that glue them together; it is hard to imagine anything, even a bomb, driving them apart. Pressing slightly harder, he feels the skin on the sides of his forefinger give way. Tiny specks of warm, pleasant blood burst to the surface distracting him from the thought of bombs and reminding him that his heart continues to beat.

*

Len is scraping a coin along the tall, grimy wall separating the girls' school from the boys' school. Bill watches from the rain-streaked corridor window. Len's head is hung low and his thick fringe casts a shadow over the rest of his face. When he reaches the locked, iron gate which opens onto the yard and the main road, he swivels on his heels and marches back along the wall to the other side of the yard, all the time dragging the coin behind him.

A clatter of clogs on the floor disturbs Bill. A group of small boys push past carrying a tin can. They are too little for proper footballs or boots. Mrs Barrett, his bent-backed school mistress, calls after them that they must get rubber corks for the sake of her ears.

'Sorry, Mrs Barrett.'

'I mean it, boys. Your headmaster, Mr Gribble, may not approve of the cane but he will use it if he must. Mark my words—' the chastened boys inch to the door trying as best they can not to make a sound '—and you, William Rowe. I don't expect a boy with such good marks to loiter in the corridor. Boys need fresh air in their lungs.'

Bill files out with the other boys onto the small gravel yard. Fine rain spits from leaden clouds and gusts of wind push his greasy hair one way and another. He waits as Len approaches; there is a tightly wrapped bandage around the top of his leg.

'How did you explain it, like?'

He doesn't look up. 'That I fell on a rock.'

'Ma didn't even blink an eyelid at my cuts. I says it was from a bramble.'

'Bill, can you leave us alone? Nobody will bloody talk to me anymore. They've all sided with that bugger Harry.'

Len walks off dragging the coin; it makes a terrible scraping sound. Bill curls his toes in his boots. He thinks about bolting but something, perhaps disappointment or annoyance, makes him hurry after Len.

'I thought you said you hated bullies too.'

'Leave me alone, Bill,' he says, turning away again.

Bill lets raindrops trickle down the bridge of his nose and drip onto his top lip. They are not going to be pals after all. It feels worse than it should because he already spends too much time on his own. The boys in his class write him off as a swot because he gets praised by the teachers. It's not his fault he's good with numbers and words.

After the break Bill takes his seat in the classroom. All the doors facing the playground are open because the headmaster believes the air will cleanse their bodies of coal dust. Bill attempts to warm his hands between his thighs but it only reminds him how cold the rest of him is.

Mrs Barrett paces up and down checking the pupils have enough ink in their wells. She dishes out a single sheet of paper each and then returns to the front.

'In a moment we will begin reciting our times table. But first Mr Gribble has asked us to do a headcount of boys with unemployed fathers. He plans to write a letter to the Prime Minister, Mr MacDonald, about it apparently. I'd prefer to teach but there you go, I'm very old fashioned—' she glances at the door to make sure she is alone '—I'm a teacher who wants to teach. He's a headmaster who wants to be a politician. So would all the boys with an unemployed father please put their hands in the air?'

Bill keeps his hands where they are. It is not often that he is proud of Da but at least he has some work. The other boys look at each other and then back to Mrs Barrett; no one raises their hands.

'Come along. We are running out of time. Norman Fairbank, stand up. I can see there are holes punched in your boots. Did you get them from the Distressed People's Boot and Shoe Fund?'

His voice is low and muffled. 'Aye.'

'Well, then your father is out of work. Those charity boots are only given to children whose parents are, well, how shall I put it politely, not capable of finding work. They would prefer to live off the kindness of this city's hardworking families. Do you know why the holes are there?'

'Nah.'

'To stop your mother and father pawning them for drink.'

Norman drops down. He hunches his shoulders and pulls his oversized, elder brother's jumper over his mouth and nose as if trying to drown himself in the wool folds.

'Now, Norman isn't the only one. Do you want me to inspect shoes and clothes?'

One hand goes up followed by another. Soon nearly half the fifty strong class are holding their arms above their downcast heads. For the most part they are the sons of shipyard workers: raggers, platers, boilermen, fitters, apprentices and welders. There is an uneasy silence as Mrs Barrett tots up the numbers. A few boys glance sideways at their pals and wonder how they did not know.

'Marvellous, children. All done. Let's hope our headmaster asks for sensible, prudent measures when he writes to Mr MacDonald, because those of us in work cannot support any more wild spending sprees. That's what got us into this mess.'

Streams of children clad in green and grey pour into the front yard as the school bell rings for the end of the day. There is little noise at first because the schoolmasters and schoolmistresses are watching but once they get into the side streets a joyful babble of shouts and cries and laughter rises steadily like coal smoke on a windless night.

Bill, however, is in no mood for football or any of the other street games. He traipses behind the throng as they make their way into the park. Len occupies his thoughts; he was not what he seemed, he wanted to be with the bullies not against them.

A hand on Bill's shoulder makes him stop by the entrance gates to the park. Len is panting from the effort of catching up.

'What do you want?'

'You're right.'

'What do you mean?'

'Harry is a bully. I don't need him or his gang.'

Bill searches Len's eyes for his motives. He doesn't want to be taken in again. 'What changed your mind, like?'

'They are never going to let someone like me into their gang. I'm an oddball like you.' Len grins hopefully at him, his lips wobbling slightly. 'Let's go to the library, I've got some books I need to return for my father.'

Bill kicks at some stones. He hasn't got anything better to do and he has never been inside of the library. 'Aye, I'll tag along.'

The library is on Prince Consort Road. Bill has seen it once or twice from the tram window. It is an impressive red brick building with two great, domed stone towers overlooking a dark, foreboding entrance. Bill tucks his shirt in while Len jumps confidently up the steps.

The librarian glances up from a box file of borrowing tickets as Len leaves his father's books on the desk. Bill feels uncomfortable as if he is committing a crime entering such a building. He comes to an abrupt halt in front of the librarian and considers turning around but Len pulls him into the lending library.

The smell of old, musty books is overwhelming. Other than

the occasional muffled cough or squeak of a metal chair being pushed back into place it is silent. They walk up and down the vast shelves with all the books perfectly lined up like soldiers on parade at a military tattoo.

Len seems to know what he is looking for; he stands on tiptoe and carefully eases some large books from a high shelf and takes them to a desk. 'What do you want to read about?'

Bill stands behind him, unsure what to do next. 'Don't know.'

'Just have a look around then.'

Bill edges tentatively along an aisle until curiosity gets the better of him and selects a book at random. Curling his finger around the leathery spine he eases it out of its tight embrace between two other books. A fine dust rises as he opens the pages. He runs his forefinger along the paper before settling on the scripted title: *Roman Irrigation Techniques*.

He flicks through the densely printed pages, astonished that there is such a book in a library in Gateshead. It makes him wonder what else he could find on the shelves. He returns it to its home and pulls another and then another and another. *Roman Law in Medieval Europe*. *The Roman Campagna and its Treasures*. *Lucius Annaeus Florus, Epitome of Roman History*.

There is so much knowledge contained within these walls. He sinks to the floor and proudly lays his finds around him. If he just could absorb all these words, sentences and paragraphs he could become as knowledgeable as Len.

'Excuse me.'

The librarian is standing over him. She is tall with a small downturned mouth. Her brown hair is tied back so vigorously he fears it may pull the skin from her bony face.

His leg starts twitching as if he needs the toilet.

She raises her grey brown eyebrows and repeats herself, 'Excuse me.'

'Aye.'

'We don't read books on the floor, young man. It damages

their backs and stitching.'

'Aye.'

'Are you even a member of this library?'

'I'll put them back, miss.'

'See that you do.'

She pulls her cardigan around her sides and glides away. Her long dress drifts over the floor without making so much as a rustle.

Len is still hunched over his books when Bill returns. He peers over his friend's shoulder: the page is covered with etchings of young men running, wrestling and throwing spears. They are not wearing much apart from thin bands around their heads.

'What's this, like?'

'Oh, it's about the ancient Greeks.' Len closes the book quickly; his cheeks are flushed as if he has been caught out.

Bill tilts his head to see the picture on the cover: a naked lad reaching towards the danglers of another naked lad.

'Do you know they took it in turns to rule over their country?'

'Must of been a right mess, like.'

'Why?'

'What do gadgies like us know about ruling anything?'

'Kings and queens aren't gods, Bill—' he pinches Bill's bare forearm gently '—they are skin and bone and blood just like us.'

'Put Da in a palace and he wouldn't know what to do? He'd drink himself to death with all that money. So would all his pals.'

Len laughs and replaces his book. 'What did you find then?'

'Books about Rome.'

'I knew you'd like this place. Do you want to join?'

'Aye. Can I?'

Len leads Bill to the counter. The librarian lays down her pen and surveys the two boys suspiciously. 'Can this pal of mine sign up?'

'As long as he learns how to treat our books.'

'What do you mean?'

'You had better ask him what I mean.'

Bill fiddles with his belt. 'I haven't done anything wrong.'

'In that case – no.'

Len frowns at her. 'We'll come back when someone else is here then.'

She picks her pen up and returns to her tickets. As they leave, Len rests his arm on Bill's shoulder and squeezes. 'Don't worry, Bill. There are plenty at our house. Would you like to come for tea next week?'

Bill worries that his family will not be wearing any clothes like in the book Len was reading. 'I don't know. People will think I'm not getting fed at home.'

Len squeezes his shoulder again like an older brother might. 'Just tell your Ma you're playing footie in the park then.'

*

Bill places his wounded finger in his month; it tastes of iron, salt and brick dust. But the pain can only distract him for a short time, his thoughts turn to the airmen in the heavens. They will never see the ripped flesh and clotted, dark blood of their victims.

In the past, soldiers faced the real possibility of seeing the broken bodies of their enemies. Yet in this war whole families, whole streets, whole cities can be erased with a push of a button or yank of a leaver.

There is a terrible humming sound. Not unlike a demented, trapped housefly. Are they circling? Are they lost? Or are they locating their target? Bill stares up into the blackness.

*

In the centre of the table is a pot of steaming spinach-and-bean stew. Beside it is a chipped china plate laden with odd-looking dark brown bread and a wooden bowl piled high with slimy raw carrots and turnip sticks.

Len whispers in Bill's ear, 'They may not look it but they are good to eat. I swear.'

Rain splatters on the window. Len's mother Lizzie, tall with thick black hedgerow hair like her son, offers Bill some of the food. He is pleased they are all wearing clothes.

'Aye I'll have a bit of the beans and that...'

'The bread? Here you go, pet.'

It is chewy but not as bad as he feared.

Lizzie continues talking as she dishes out the rest of the dinner. 'So, Bill, I hear you are a bit of a whiz at school?'

Len kicks him gently under the table.

'Nah not really, Mrs Weaver.'

'Len says you are top of the class and you even help the older lads.'

Bill squirms as Len's sister, Florence, looks up from her bowl. 'I just do my best, Mrs Weaver.'

Lizzie motions towards the bookshelf. 'Well, if you want to borrow any you're welcome.'

Face reddening, he nods. Len has gone and told her about the library and his ignorant family. 'Aye, maybe, like.'

Just then the front door opens to raised voices and laughter. Len's father Thomas shuffles in dragging his bad leg like an unwieldy sack of potatoes. His back is hunched and his shoulders curved inwards. A dapper older man with longish, parted grey hair offers him a hand and then joins them at the table.

Lizzie moves along to make room. 'Frank, sit down. Help yourself to food.'

'Thank you. I'm bloody ravenous. Your husband can talk the hind legs of a donkey. Let's hope you turn out different, hey, Len?'

Thomas gestures to Florence, who fetches plates and cutlery

for the new arrivals.

Lizzie puts her hand on her when she returns and addresses her husband, 'Why didn't you ask your son?'

Thomas sighs. 'She was nearest. Don't start an argument, Lizzie – we have guests.'

'Why should Flo serve you? My Ma didn't break those Liberal Club windows in Pilgrim Street all them years ago so you could sit on your behind while the womenfolk of this house run around after you and your pals.'

Bill cups his hand over Len's ear. 'Was your grandma a vandal?'

'Sort of, Bill,' he says with a snigger. 'She was a suffragette.'

'What's that?'

'She wanted votes for women, like.'

Thomas glances irritably at his wife. 'Give over, Lizzie.'

Frank adjusts his wristwatch. 'I should have done it myself.'

'Just make sure you clear up, Thomas.'

Thomas nods his bald head, which is still shiny from the rain. Keen to change the subject, he pulls a newspaper from his leather bag and unfurls it dramatically. The headline states in block capitals: PALMERS CLOSES.

'MacDonald has got to do something about them dole queues, Frank. It says here it's heading towards two million. Shipyards are shutting and men are being thrown out of work. I see it every day walking through Jarra.'

Frank rolls his eyes; it could be fondness or exasperation. 'Melville spoke to me about this last week...the truth is, Thomas, the majority voted Tory or Liberal in the last election. We just don't have the mandate to do anything radical. This is only the second ever Labour government and we only have a minority of MPs.'

Thomas snorts and fills his plate with stew. 'Melville. Who cares what that bloody fool thinks?'

Bill is confused again. 'Who is Melville, Len?'

'James Melville. He's the MP for Gateshead. Frank works for him.'

Thomas returns to his theme. 'It's not radical to ask a Labour government to increase the purchasing power of the working man – it's just common sense. It is the only way to increase demand and get us out of this depression.'

Frank puts down his knife and fork. 'How would you do that then?'

Lizzie frowns again – but this time at their guest. 'Well, you could start by paying more unemployment relief, thirty-two shillings a week isn't enough for a family. I see children in my classes with scurvy and rickets.'

Thomas adds, 'The Labour Party proposed forty-five shillings a few years back. They said that would support a family with three children.'

Frank rubs his face. 'We are meant to be in the same party and fighting for the same goal. You ILP'ers talk as if we were enemies. Correct me if I'm wrong but you are still affiliated to the Labour Party?'

'Aye, we are.'

Bill shrugs his shoulders at Len.

'Independent Labour Party,' Len whispers. 'It's for the real gutsy socialists, not the timid buggers in the Labour Party.'

Frank swallows some stew. 'Like I say, we will have to wait until world trade picks up before anything much can be done about unemployment. You may not like it but it is just the way things are. Now, can we get on with the meal?'

'Just so long as we're not waiting for forever.'

'For Christ sake, Thomas, we all want a socialist commonwealth. We all want to change everything. But the people aren't ready for it and the economy will not allow it.'

'Are you sure, Frank? The people I meet on the streets looking for work are ready for higher unemployment relief. They are crying out for it, not low interest rates—' Frank shakes his head but Thomas is in full flow now; his tone is sarcastic and contemptuous '—MacDonald is more interested in pleasing the rich and showing the establishment how respectable and responsible the Labour Party is than helping the working man.'

Lizzie slips her fingers between Thomas's newspaper-ink-stained fingers and squeezes. 'And working women.'

Frank stands and removes his sopping wet coat from the door. 'I've listened to enough of this guff. Do you know where it'll end, Thomas? Disaffiliation. Mark my bloody words.'

Thomas glares at him. 'Nonsense. The ILP is the conscience of the Labour Party. It was there at the beginning and it'll be there at the end.'

Lizzie rises to face Frank. 'We're all comrades here, Frank.'

'Are you sure?'

'Stay. Please. If not for us then for Len. He hasn't seen you for months and you are his godfather.'

The anger in Frank's eyes drains away. 'Aye, you're right, Lizzie. Have you got anything to drink?'

'Sorry, you know we don't partake in that here...'

Frank sits back down and Thomas scoops out some spinach-and-bean stew. They eat quietly until their bellies fill and moods improve.

Eventually, in-between slurps, Frank says, 'How's the teaching, Lizzie?'

'Good enough,' she says quietly. 'But it's really the tuning business that's keeping us afloat, like.'

Thomas mops up the last of the stew with some bread. 'Aye, the rich folk still want their pianos tuned. They're not cutting back.'

Frank waves at the small piano against the far wall. 'Will you play for us, Thomas? I think we all need cheering up.'

'There's not a lot to be jolly about.'

Len looks disappointed. 'You never play?'

'Like I say, son, I'm not in the mood.'

While Frank and Len carry out the plates to the scullery, Bill helps Florence get some coal from the store in the yard. The rain has slowed to a fine drizzle but a wind is now blowing in from the coast.

Florence is two years older, nearly fourteen. Her nut-brown hair is pinned back and her freckle-dashed cheeks are red in the salty breeze. There are two small bumps pushing against her white dress.

Perhaps sensing his thoughts she pulls her grey cardigan together. 'It's over here.'

Bill hugs the jumper Ma knitted him to his chest as they walk. 'Do you lot always talk about that stuff?'

'Aye.'

'Are you an ILD'er then?'

'ILP,' she says curtly.

'ILP,' he repeats.

'I am.'

'And what do you want?'

'More than this.'

Bill recalls Reverend Pilkington's sermon even though his mind was wandering. 'Why? We've got food, which is more than they have in that China.'

'It could be better. That's all.'

Bill bends over the coal; she stands behind playing with her wet hair. He can feel her eyes on him as he scoops. Neither of them utters another word. Bill's whole body tingles and the hairs on his arms stand up as rainwater runs down his spine. He has never felt like this before; it is exciting and strange. Is this, he wonders, why men and women marry?

Another scoop, the sack is nearly full. He cannot resist, he glances back at her. She holds his gaze for a matter of seconds then turns and wanders back to the house humming something quietly to herself.

*

The low drone fades; the planes must have been lost. There is nothing worth bombing in Durham anyway. Unless Hitler fears a castle, cathedral and pair of bridges.

Bill reaches under his mattress and locates a dog-eared poetry book. From the inside of the cover he removes a match he obtained from the wing cleaner, Bradley. He expertly probes the wall with his hands until he finds the right brick; rough and grit-encrusted like a striking strip. The match goes straight up giving him some precious moments to read.

*

The embossed gold title on the spine of the book is faded and worn: Charles Dickens *Great Expectations*. Bill turns it over and over as if he were a pawnshop owner inspecting a precious jewel or wedding ring.

He runs his forefinger along the sentences like he did in the library. Soon the story has him enthralled: a boy named Pip is in a churchyard near a marsh where his mother and father are buried. A stranger grabs him and threatens to tear out his heart and liver if he doesn't bring him a file and some wittles in the morning.

Something enters the outer edges of Bill's vision but he is completely lost in this new world. Pip has been brought up by his sister and her husband. He doesn't mention the stranger and she scolds him for returning late. Without her realising, he slips some bread into his trousers.

There is a flash of light – the pages are on fire. Bill drops the book and looks up: Da is looming over him, his thin face contorted in rage. A burnt match lies on the stone floor beside the charred book.

'That'll teach you for ignoring your old Da.'

Bill's pulse quickens; he feels like grabbing Da's shirt collar and shoving him against the wall, again and again and again, until he is limp and lifeless. Instead he holds his father's gaze – he knows the old brute still has it in him to give him a hiding. 'Sorry, Da. What do you want?'

'What do y-y-you want? What do you want? I-I-I want you to listen. I says how are you the day, lad?'

'I'm just dandy,' he says without much conviction.

'And what's that y-y-you reading?'

'A book Len's Ma lent me.'

He leans in close: eyes bloodshot and skin covered in a thin, shiny film of alcoholic perspiration. He speaks through gritted yellow teeth, breath wet and caustic. 'That family is trouble, son. I-I-I've seen them on the street preaching against hard work. Saying the war achieved nothing. It's a-a-a buggering insult to all them what died.'

'It's just a book.'

Da's jaw shakes and he raises his arm. Bill tenses and waits for his hands to slap his arms and head. Before he can do anything Ma steps through the back door carrying an enormous bundle of washing.

'Give us a hand, Joe.'

'Aye.'

Ma has saved him again. But she is not about to take sides. 'And, Bill, stop winding him up.'

Da lifts the book up high and drops it onto his lap. It slaps the bare skin between his shorts and woollen socks; his eyes water but he doesn't blink.

His father smiles cruelly. 'Good lad. Now go out a fetch m-m-me the paper? There was talk in The George of M-M-MacDonald buggering off.'

There is a long queue for the *Evening Chronicle*. The seller wipes his weatherbeaten forehead as his son adds more papers to a pile balanced on some crates. Every now and then he jerks back his head and hollers at the passing crowds of workers.

'Evening special. MacDonald joins the Tories to save the country from bankruptcy. Evening special.'

Bill notices Len near the front. He is shuffling from one foot to the other impatiently.

'Do you want me to get you one? It'll save you queuing.'

Bill had hoped he wouldn't spot him; he acts as if he's surprised to see him. 'Aye.'

'So you got sent out and all? Thomas won't rest until he's seen it in black and white.'

'Seen what?'

'The government's fallen. There's going to be a new one, like.'

A woman with a red, blotchy face and blond hair turns on her boots to face the two boys. 'Mr MacDonald's gone and done the honourable thing, laddie. He's put the country before his party. We can't go on spending if we haven't got any money.'

Len lifts and drops his shoulders. 'Don't believe everything you read.'

The seller hands her a paper and points over at The George. 'All them gadgies over there are going to get their dole cut. It might make them think twice about boozing and smoking all day.'

'I wouldn't bet money on it, pet. They would murder their own family before giving up drink.'

Len and Bill pay for their papers and part as usual by The George. Bill half wishes he could go with Len but he knows Ma and Peggy need him. He trudges home hoping Da will be asleep.

*

Before the match light fades and dies, Bill squints at the book. Each page is decorated with spidery handwriting. He traces it and tries to imagine the soap-scrubbed scent of her body and the cool silkiness of her skin. She has circled one line: *fear not the future, weep not for the past.*

If only he had listened to her. She knew his sacrifice would be in vain. What a fool he had been to think a few rebels could change the course of history? They were like pebbles tossed into a fast-moving river; gone and forgotten in a plop and splash.

The all-clear siren rings out. Perhaps the bombers are over Tyneside now? He shivers and thinks of his family holed up in a dank shelter in the back yard. Peggy would be tearful and Ma would be stroking her crucifix. Da would be laying in a stupor in bed, indifferent to their pleas and calls. His name would not be mentioned. To them he was already dead.

The landing lights flicker back on and soon he hears the soft padding of the nighttime screw's slippers. It seems odd to encounter such a homely sound here but prison is an eccentric as well as a cruel institution.

The screw pulls back the grate in each cell and peers in – presumably to check if anyone has hung themselves or expired from the stress of being stuck behind double-locked iron doors during a bombing raid.

Stifling a yawn, he opens the grate. Bill feels like saying "before long you will be back in the warmth of your office and not a soul will notice if you sneak some cheap scotch into your cocoa mug." But he stays schtum and the screw pads off down the landing.

The man with the full jerry complains again and the screw responds by threatening him. 'Shut your gob, McCarthy. I'm not having you disturbing my night.'

'Guv, I need to go again and it's full to the brim.'

'I says shut it, man. Once more and I'll be back mob-handed.'

*

Ma lets the curtain fall back into place with a sigh. She has been gazing up at the street for hours, waiting for Da's familiar wheezes and curses, as he tumbles down the steps to the front door. She collapses onto the bed behind.

Bill wraps his thin arms around her bowed shoulders, mimicking the couples he has seen queuing outside the pictures. Yet they are not long enough to provide much comfort or warmth. She pushes him off irritably.

'Ma, do you want me to go find him?'

She snubs him and goes to the piano. With a grunt of frustration, she sweeps away clothes piled on the stool and lifts the smooth lid revealing yellowing keys. She presses down gently and listens intently as wooden hammers thump steel strings. 'I can't tune it. I've tried so many times. It's no bloody use.'

Bill follows her. 'What's wrong, Ma?'

She presses another key. 'I don't know.'

'I could ask Thomas to have a look? He's a proper piano tuner, Ma. He won't want paying.' Bill regrets his last claim as soon as he utters it but he is desperate to avoid seeing his mother in tears again.

Ma blows her nose and returns to the window. 'We might not have much money but we still have our pride.'

He waits for her breathing to slow. 'Do you want me to go find him?

'Who, that piano tuner?'

'Da.'

She thinks for a moment and forces a little smile. 'Aye, go on then. But be careful.'

The cobbles glint in the blue moonlight as he surfaces. Knowing Ma's eyes are following his boots, he heads purposefully down the street. A fishmonger and a stocky lad are pulling a rickety cart back towards the river. He is not much older than him and already earning his keep.

He catches them and shouts over the clatter of the rusting iron wheels, 'You seen a baker coming that way? His coat is normally all floury. He might have had a few, like.'

Without breaking his stride, the lad hollers back, 'Nah.'

The fishmonger hoots toothlessly, 'Try the pub. That's where lost souls are normally found.'

The windows are black and shimmering when Bill gets to The George. There is no sign of life inside or out. He feels uneasy but he cannot return empty-handed; Ma's depending on him. He checks the scrapyard opposite: empty apart from a mangy dog tied to a post. The side streets are deserted too.

He is about to leave when he hears a cry, 'Go to hell, y-y-you fucking tart.'

Da emerges from a doorway; he is swaying like a sapling tree in a gale. His thin legs bow this way and that yet somehow he remains upright. A dark stain covers the front of his trousers, which are only partially done up, and there are cuts and bruises on his face.

A girl with a slightly doughy face shoves him out the way; he howls and lands on his hands. Clumps of earth and bright green moss cling to the girl's dress and coiled black hair. She can't be much out of school.

She kicks Da hard on the bottom. 'You cheap old bugger. You ain't got enough for a bloody handshake.'

Da's arms give way and he dashes his chin on the cobbles. He groans once or twice and then his body goes limp.

'Joe. Joe. Joe?' She kneels down beside him and prods him with a dirty, long finger; he doesn't move. She plunges her hands into his pockets and withdraws a few coins and a tin of baccy. 'God bless you, Joseph.' Crossing herself, she hitches her skirt up and hurries away.

Bill approaches cautiously. Is he dead? The thought doesn't bother him as much as it should. He contemplates going back empty-handed; Ma would surely be better off without him. Good husbands didn't carry on like that.

He circles Da's body a few times before nudging him with the worn toe on his right boot. He doesn't grunt or protest like he does at home when sleeping off his toils by the range.

Bill bends his neck until his hair is brushing the cobbles. Da's face is relaxed: his eyelids are still and the lines around his mouth droop like heavily laden washing lines. He looks peaceful, almost innocent.

'Are you hurt, Da?'

Da's eyes twitch and he scrambles to his knees. 'Sal? Sal?'

'Are you hurt?'

His voice is groggy, 'Who's that?'

'Ma sent me.'

Da reaches out for him. Bill waits for his mittens to grab him. Instead he rests them gently on Bill's boots.

'Come here and help y-y-your old father home.'

Bill lifts him and guides him step by step back up the hill.

'Y-Y-You're a good lad.'

Bill's curiosity gets the better of him. 'Who's Sal, Da?'

He digs his fingers into Bill's collar bone and spits on the cobbles. 'None of your fucking business.'

As they near the top, Da pushes him away. He rests his hands on his knees and retches; a ball of salvia drops from his mouth.

'Let's get you in the warm.'

Da doesn't move; he wipes his eyes with his mittens. 'They've gone a-a-and sacked me, son.'

Bill is not sure how to respond. He fears a misplaced word could move Da from sorrow to fury again. 'Oh.'

'M-M-Mr fucking Bell said there was no trade, what with the yards closing. There's nowt that can be done about it, m-m-man. It's like the weather. Sometimes it's sunny. Sometimes it rains.'

Bill studies his father; he is pale and bloodied from the fall. Already he knows he will go along with whatever story he comes up with. Not out of loyalty – but to save Ma the hurt of discovering he goes with tarts.

Da chuckles to himself and straightens his back. 'That pal of y-y-yours and his family. They don't get it. They would protest a-a-against the rain.'

*

Even though the bombers are gone, Bill cannot sleep. His mind glows and lights with people and places from his past. He knows he should forget them. It is the only way to survive, but the memories keep coming, faster and stronger, like a train roaring out of a tunnel.

*

The street is wide and the houses grand. White smoke curls from chimneys and carts weighed down with deliveries hurtle along the stones. Bill is out of breath. He puts down the empty but heavy leather suitcase he's dragging and leans against some iron railings.

There is a small park opposite; a girl in a fashionable red frock and coat is pushing a pram. Is she the child's nanny or the mother? Unlike the girls on his street, her skin is glossy and pink. Her hips sway as she strolls down a path lined with flower beds and trees. He feels like he did in the yard with Florence; his heart beats slightly faster than normal.

After she goes, he lingers a while as he can hear an engine. He is desperate for any excuse not pick up the suitcase and it is rare to see a car or a lorry in Bensham. Two men wearing floppy trilby hats and dark coats pull up in a two-seater car. They get out carrying a bundle of leaflets and posters. The tallest reaches up to the notice board at the park entrance and attaches a poster.

As they walk off, Bill crosses the road. The car is a lovely burgundy colour. He runs his hand over the paintwork and inspects his warped reflection in the metal grills. There are a few hairs on his chin and fresh pimples on his nose.

'Hey you, get your dirty hands off my car.' One of the men is running down the hill, leaflets fluttering behind him like confetti at a wedding. 'What the hell are you doing?'

'Just having a look, like.'

Hat pushed up and forehead dripping, he arrives. 'There's a police box over there. Do you want me to call up the local bobby?'

'Nah. Nah. I'll be on me way.'

'Do you live around here?'

He mumbles his response because he doesn't want anyone to overhear. Truth is he feels ashamed of his errand.

'What?'

The other man calls back. 'He's a halfwit, Jonathan. Let him go.'

'Get on your way, boy.'

Bill returns to the suitcase and starts pulling again; the edges are worn and the metal banding scrapes on the pavement. Every now and then it hits a bump and clatters into his heels and calves; each blow adds to a growing purple-and-brown map of grazes and bruises and scabs. Swapping hands doesn't help. He can see the man smirking while smoking a cigarette beside his car.

Mrs Appleby is waiting for him in the porch. She is short, plump and wrapped up in a fur coat. She would look like a jolly woodland creature if it wasn't for her pinched, mean mouth.

'Hello there, young Rowe. You're lucky to have caught me. I was just on my way to town.'

'Aye'

Through her small half-moon spectacles, she looks him up and down. 'Your Ma said you would be here at twelve o'clock. It's now quarter past. I don't want to muck my sister about: she's expecting me at the Empire within the hour.'

'Sorry, Mrs Appleby. Are the clothes ready for me? It won't take a minute to stuff them in.'

'I don't want them stuffed in, Rowe. I want you to take care of them.'

'Aye, Mrs Appleby.'

Inside her well-appointed flat he slowly folds up each garment and places it in the suitcase. Mrs Appleby groans theatrically and checks her watch.

The Applebys have no children but manage to create an enormous amount of washing: there are piles and piles of shirts and dresses and socks and underwear. On the dust-free mantelpiece is a picture of Mr Appleby and Mrs Appleby together in the Lake District. They are standing beside a black car overlooking Windermere. He is carrying a picnic basket and rug. Neither of them is smiling.

'All done.'

Mrs Appleby snorts and shoves Bill out the way. Her manner is coarser than many on this street; Bill suspects she has not always lived in such splendour.

'You can get more in than that, laddie. My arrangement with your mother was one whole suitcase worth of washing a week. That's nowhere near a suitcase's worth.'

She forces more and more in until the seams of the case are about to burst. With Bill's help she jerks the slip down and fastens the top.

'I shall have to purchase one of those fancy new washing machines. Albert's aunt in Cheltenham has one.'

The top of the case bulges like the belly of a lass carrying a bairn. Bill starts to dread the two-and-half-mile journey home.

Mrs Appleby dabs her brow with a tissue and adjusts her glasses in the mirror. 'Now run along so your mother has time to wash and dry them for the weekend. Albert has an important charity function on Saturday—' before pulling on a round fur hat, she flattens her blond hair '—he's raising money for a local grammar school. Albert's very dedicated you know. Where are you schooling, Rowe?'

'Crow Road.'

'And your father – is he out of work?

Bill hesitates; he decides against telling the truth. She would probably take some secret pleasure in his plight. 'He's a baker.'

'At times like these the only option is to roll your sleeves up. That's what Albert's father used to say and he ran the tram network in this city. There's work for those that want it—' Bill turns towards the hallway with the case '—here have some pennies for your trouble.'

As soon as they part ways on the hill, Bill throws the coins in the drain. They fall into the water with a satisfying plop. He would rather starve than rely on her goodwill. The case is now even harder to pull: he can feel the sinews in his arm stretching with every lurch. He wishes he could tip the clothes into the gutter as well.

The poster on the notice-board catches his eye. Below a painting of a white-haired working man in a worn and dirty suit staring into space there is a slogan: No more socialist promises for me I'm voting for the National Government. The bottom of the poster has been hurriedly pasted over. But he can still make out the heavy black printed script beneath: VOTE CONSERVATIVE.

*

The dawn when it comes is grey but welcome. He listens to the metallic screech of a train of rusty food trolleys, carrying vats of porridge and dried egg, being pushed across the concrete exercise yard.

The night screw unlocks all the cells on the landing not long after. He recoils when he opens Bill's door. 'What the hell is that stink, Rowe? Get out of your pit and empty that jerry.'

Bill stares at him blankly in the hope he will leave him alone. He feels spent and empty from the night; lifting a finger or crying would just about finish him off.

The screw pushes his peaked cap back and leans against the

door frame. He is in a bad mood. 'Rowe, I'm warning you, man. Get up. I'm not leaving until you empty it.'

Fearful of the repercussions of defying him, he somehow drags himself in the direction of the jerry.

'Good lad, Rowe.'

*

Bill hauls the suitcase to the other side of the street as he passes Len's house. He doesn't want Florence to see him or to have to explain to Thomas and Lizzie that Ma has to wash the clothes of other women. They wouldn't judge him but he's not keen on looking like a helpless bugger; pity is almost as bad as charity in his mind.

He is about to turn the corner towards The George when Len calls from the bedroom window. Bill keeps his head down as if he hasn't heard but Len is persistent; he indicates he's coming down.

Bill curses under his breath and waits in front of the suitcase.

Len smiles. 'What's that about? Are you moving on?'

Bill thinks quickly. 'Just picking up some clothes for Ma. They are from an old pal of hers. They'll come in useful when the weather turns.'

'Have you got time to stop? Frank is here and he's got some crumpets on the go.'

In the front room Thomas and Frank are sat sipping tea while crumpets cool on a plate. There are official-looking documents with Labour Party and ILP headings strewn over the table.

'Come and have some of these, lads?'

Thomas clears a space and pours them some tea from the pot as they smear their hot crumpets with butter.

Frank ruffles Len's hair. 'So, can I count on you lot to campaign for the new candidate?'

'Well, what's he like? I've lost track.'

'That's not funny, Thomas. Herbert was only buried this month and Melville in May.'

'I'm sorry, Frank. I know Sir James was dear to you and—' Thomas laughs '—and paid your rent.'

'You can be a heartless bastard sometimes for a socialist.'

'The same could be said of them, Frank. What did they do for the working man?'

'Here we go again.'

Len interrupts before their playful banter turns into a row, 'Who's the new candidate, Uncle Frank?'

'Someone I think we can all rally around, a trade-union leader and Labour man through and through, Ernest Bevin.'

Thomas's tone turns more serious. 'Bevin will have our support. But what the working classes of this town want to know is how are we going to avoid another MacDonald?'

Frank sloshes the tea around his cup with such force that some spills over the rim. 'Don't mention his name, Thomas. He's a shameless traitor. But he's a one-off. We won't see his like again.'

'Tell me what would happen if New York bankers again withheld loans until cuts are made? Will Bevin side with the unemployed? Or just say he hasn't got a choice like MacDonald?'

Frank looks up at the ceiling. 'I don't know, Thomas. This has been a hard two years for us. But I do know that if this National Liberal Party chap, Magnay, wins, he will do his best to make life harder for the working man.'

'On that much we agree.'

'Good, because we have got a real fight on our hands. MacDonald is going around telling the press the Labour Party are Bolsheviks gone mad and that we plan to take everybody's Post Office savings and give them to the unemployed.'

Bill wants to stay and listen to more of their conversation. But he knows Ma will be expecting him back soon. He winks at Len and they both make their excuses and go into the hall.

'Ma will be wondering what's happened to me,' he says.

'And her clothes, Bill?'
'That and all.'

*

The landing, which is three stories up, is full of shuffling, bedraggled men carrying their jerrys. Bill takes his place behind the wing cleaner Bradley, who glances back and nods. His small rodent eyes twitch and flicker nervously. Bill can tell he is desperate to talk to him or offer him something but daren't risk the wrath of the others. The line edges forward as each man takes his turn emptying his pot into the toilet bowl. Talking is banned, but a few brave souls share a breathless joke when the screw is looking the other way.

One stocky man, who he doesn't recognise, approaches him on the way back to his cell. Bill doesn't see the punch aimed at his ribs until it is too late. He crumples to the floor clutching his side.

His assailant bends down as if he has come to his aid. He puts his fingers under his arm pits and rests his chin on his shoulder. With his clammy lips close to his ears, he whispers, 'That's just for starters.'

He lifts Bill roughly to his feet and dusts him down. Unbelievably the screw thanks him and then waves him on. Bill feels like breaking down and weeping – more in desperation than in pain. Yet he can feel the line is watching him: his survival instinct kicks in and he holds his nerve. If he shows too much weakness they will come for his meagre belongings and then, perhaps, even his life.

The closer he gets to the recess the worse the smell becomes. The toilet often gets blocked but on this occasion it appears to be flushing. Bill empties his and then swills it under the drinking water tap; he hates doing it but he has no choice.

At the back of the recess there is a narrow window about two feet wide and five feet from top to bottom. A thick horizontal iron bar prevents anyone thinking about escaping. He is often drawn towards it because it is the only open window on the landing.

The screw is elsewhere and other prisoners are more interested in getting back to their cells in time for breakfast. Bill takes his chance: he places his head between the stone frame and gulps down mouthfuls of the dewy morning. It tastes of rotting leaves and hedgerows. He lets it soothe his aching lungs for as long as he can before moving on.

Back on his bed he pulls his shirt up and inspects the damage from the punch. Already there is a milk-chocolate-coloured bruise growing on his ridged side. With a sigh, he lets the shirt drop.

'He gave you a right wallop didn't he?' Bradley grins, his teeth are dark and jagged, like broken ale bottles. After checking both ways he steps inside Bill's cell door. 'That weren't right. I told the lads that you're not all there.'

'What you mean, man?'

'That you mentally you know in...capaci...tated.'

Not once does he maintain eye contact.

'There's nothing wrong with me.'

Bradley pauses. 'Why didn't you sign up then? '

'That's none of your business.'

'I'm trying to stick up for you but you're not doing yourself any favours.'

'Why are you in here then?'

Bradley puts a finger to his mouth. 'Quieten down, marra.'

'Selling rationed meat on the black market? Not exactly the work of a great patriot.'

Bill starts coughing. He catches something wet and slippery in his hands. Scared of what he might find, he wipes it on the blanket.

Bradley grimaces. 'You ought to get that looked at, marra. But that ain't the reason I came here: if you want any more matches

I'll need some more help writing them letters.'

Through a barrage of coughs, Bill tries to tell him to go. But he struggles for breath and no words come out. Instead a glistering spray of fine red droplets land on the wool blanket. They wobble and then collapse into the fabric leaving behind dark stains.

Officer Fry swaggers up behind Bradley holding a clipboard. He stamps his foot and Bradley scuttles away to safer parts. From his chewed, puffy ears, he pulls a pen. 'Stop that now, Rowe. We all know how sick you are. Well done. Round of applause. Can you drag yourself to the workshop today?'

Chest heaving, Bill looks up. 'Nah I've had it for the day.'

Fry turns his tree-trunk neck and shouts down. 'Right, Mr Trudgill, can you bring some mailbags up to Rowe here?'

*

The kitchen is draped with the Applebys' clothes. Shirts, socks, ties, florid dresses, blouses, silk pyjamas, nightdresses, woollen tights, jumpers and jackets hang from every bit of furniture. There are also a couple of racks and three or four lines hung across the ceiling. The range is roaring away, the coals glowing white hot. It is so steamy Bill can hardly see to the other side of the room.

'Ma?'

'Aye. I'm here, Bill. Can you lend us a hand? Peggy's been grand but she can't reach up to this one.'

The steam parts: Ma is standing on tiptoes on the one chair free of clothes. She wobbles precariously as she ties to peg a pair of trousers to the line.

'Let me do it.'

Ma gets down and wipes sweat from her red brow. 'God, haven't you grown up quick. You'll be a man soon.'

Da grunts and Bill realises he is sleeping on his chair behind them. Bill can hardly bear to look at him. His drool-drenched chin and filthy hair turn his stomach. The *Chronicle* is on his lap and his belt is undone. He can just about make out the headline: National Liberals beat Labour in Gateshead.

'Has he been out looking today?'

Ma shakes her head. 'He glanced through the paper and called in at a few places. Came back drunk, about two hour ago.'

'Oh.'

Ma hands him some dry washing to fold up. 'If only more men in this town were as hard working as you, son, we wouldn't be in such a mess.'

'It's not all their fault, Ma.'

'There's work for those at look hard enough, Bill. Granda never missed a day out in the fields. He died on the plough, do you know that?'

'Aye, Ma, you've told me the story before. But there ain't enough jobs to go around. Can't you see the yards are closing?'

Suddenly Da is awake again. 'I-I-I told you about listening to more of that claptrap.'

Bill snaps, 'I'm just saying that there ain't enough work. You of all people should be able to see that?

'Is that what Thomas Weaver tells y-y-you?'

Bill bridles at the suggestion that he has no mind of his own. The fact is Da can't stand the thought that his son might perceive things differently than him. 'I can see it with my own eyes, Da. I don't need the Weavers or anybody else telling me what to think.'

Da waits and then changes tack. 'I-I-I've been Labour all me life, son. But this shower. They've bankrupted the country. At least the Tories and Liberals know how to handle m-m-money.'

Bill suddenly realises where this is leading and recalls the conversation about Magnay. 'Did you vote Liberal?'

Da grunts.

Bill mutters, 'Bloody fool.'

'What was that y-y-you…'

Ma puts her hands up. 'Leave him be, Joe.'

Da eyes her suspiciously and slumps back into his chair. 'What does he know about life?'

'He'll find out the hard way.'

Bill hates the way they talk about him as if he wasn't in the room; he's not a boy anymore. 'What will I find out?'

'That you have to fit in and it ain't no good ranting and raving about what should happen. That's for oddballs with too much time on their hands. Our world is different,' says Ma.

Bill storms into the hall. He can't contain his feelings any longer. Da can beat him all he likes but he can't make him think like him. 'I hate our world.'

Da stumbles after him but Bill is half out of the door. His eyes are bulging and his fists shaking. 'Don't cheek your M-M-Ma. We work hard for this.'

'Let him go, Joe. He'll see things differently when he starts working.'

*

The ball of wax is the size of a baby's head. Bill runs a length of thread through it and starts stitching the mailbag. He has done this on countless occasions but he struggles to concentrate. His mind is heavy with tiredness and hunger; his eyelids keep dropping and his head keeps lolling forward. Sleep tempts him with its promise of warm oblivion.

White sunlight runs down the bed in long strips. He puts down the wax and listens: wind rattles the loose slate tiles on the roof and iron drainpipes creak. He might have time for a nap? The others would still be at the workshop, sitting in silent lines, some coating the thread in wax, others sowing the hessian together and collecting up the finished mailbags.

The light reaches his head. It is warming and healing. A smile crosses his hollow face: Fry cannot hurt him anymore, he is dying. What can he do to a dying man? Letting the mailbag fall from his hands, he leans back against the wall.

*

It is dusk. Chimney stacks cast long rectangular shadows across the road. Len offers Bill a bag of steaming chips dripping with malt vinegar and fat.

'Do you want some birthday chips?'

Bill scowls darkly; he wishes he kept it to himself instead of mentioning it to Lizzie. 'Nah.'

'So you're fourteen...why didn't you tell us?'

Bill accepts the chips. 'What've I got to celebrate? I'm ripe for work now. The school can't stop them taking me out.'

'Are they going to? Have they said anything?'

'Nothing yet but they can't afford to keep me there that's for sure.'

Bill hangs back and tips the last of the golden chunks of fried potatoes into his mouth. When he's finished, he tosses the greasy bag into a well-kept garden.

'This is Appleby's mansion block. Ma cleans her dirty clothes every week.' Bill pauses and gazes up at the glowing windows. 'She refused to pay her last month, said her clothes "smelt of damp".'

Len scratches his head before making the connection. 'That explains all those suitcases. Why didn't you just say, like?'

Bill glances down the street and kicks at a loose cobblestone until it comes free from its sandy home in the road. He is not in the mood for explaining or apologising to Len.

'She said she could smell the filth in our house. And she is right, you know, it is filthy. She keeps threatening to order a machine for washing from London.'

Len looks nervous suddenly. 'What the hell are you doing?'

In one smooth movement Bill gathers the stone and hurls it at the window. The glass shudders then splits into four triangular shards, which explode into glinting shrapnel as they hit the steps.

The boys dart behind a line of moss-covered bins. They huddle in the shadows holding their noses against the ammonia-laced stink of fox urine.

A light goes on in the porch and a man's head pokes out. It is Mr Appleby; he is wearing a red-velvet smoking jacket and smart pressed trousers.

A trembling voice from somewhere inside the block asks, 'Who's there?'

'I don't know, dear.'

'What do you mean you don't know?'

'The street is completely deserted.'

The door shuts and Len yanks his friend's coat. 'Right let's go.'

They creep away but Len's trailing arm catches one of the bins. It topples over, spilling bones, rotting potato peelings and tin cans over the pavement.

Mr Appleby appears above them; he squints into the darkening street, his eyes unaccustomed to the fading light. 'The constable is on his way and he'll beat you scoundrels black and blue.'

Bill snorts and Len puts his hands over his friend's mouth; his eyes are wild and fearful.

'I heard something, Albert. There's something down there by the gate. It sounded like a boy.'

Mr Appleby steps forward. He is holding a large hammer in his quivering right hand. Instantly, he is transformed from a clownish figure of fun into something darker, and more violent. 'Right then, you little buggers.'

Bill and Len make a dash for it but Mr Appleby doesn't give chase. Instead he shouts at the top of his voice, 'Help, help, help, they're getting away.'

As the boys steal into the nearby park Bill feels like laughing and he does, loudly and raucously.

Len jabs him in the side painfully. 'What's got into you?

'I thought you lot wanted to change everything?'

'Aye, but this won't change a jot. We need to convince people. Not smash windows.'

Bill shakes with annoyance – Len can be so arrogant. 'I need it to change now. I want to stay at school. I can't wait before you convince Da and all his pals not to vote for a rich bastard with a nice smile.'

'What choice do we have?'

'No choice – that's my point.'

'If we get a decent Labour government with enough ILP MPs then we can put the dole up and tax the rich in this street.'

'What do you know about the dole? You've got money coming in, haven't you? You have milk and butter and jam every day. You can lecture me when you know what it's like to watch your Ma washing other people's clothes just so she can buy some bait.'

Len shrugs and walks quickly off into the park. 'That's a load of horseshit, Bill. You can spend the night in the cells if you want.'

Behind them the street comes alive: residents in dressing gowns and night dresses emerge shivering on the thresholds, shouting and calling.

*

The world is at strange angles and his vision is blurred; the mailbags lay unfinished on the ceiling. He reaches out and knocks over a jug of water, water runs up the walls, gushing down the dry mortar beds.

*

Da pushes carrots and potatoes aimlessly around his broth. Ma cuts a slice of stale bread she got for one penny from Da's old bakery and smears it with oily, yellow margarine.

'There you go, pet.'

He continues stirring. 'Is there any meat in here, like?'

'Aye, a little. I got it from the slink butcher this morning. It's a bit of broxy.'

'I-I-I not a bloody stray. I-I-I ain't eating diseased sheep.'

There is a tense silence. Peggy wipes her nose and tries to raise their spirits. 'It's lovely, Ma.'

Bill forces a smile as he pushes the rubbery meat from one side of his month to the other. 'Aye, Ma, it's good.'

There is a loud series of impatient rat-a-tat-tats at the door. Ma stops and Bill immediately worries it is the constable. Could Len have snitched about the window? They hadn't spoken since parting in the park. Or maybe Mrs Appleby recognised him from his snort?

'Ma it might be...'

Da interrupts, his breath panicked and gasping, like a drowning man, 'I-I-I-I-I know who it is. It's them m-m-m-m-means inspectors.'

Ma looks shocked. Her face empties of colour. 'Why didn't you say anything, Joseph?'

'I-I-I-I...' Da gives up and goes to the steamed-up window.

Bill waits for an outburst of violence or cruelty; usually he takes his troubles out on his family. Instead he stands there motionless, staring hatefully at his own reflection in the dark glass.

A man shouts through the letterbox, 'We're from the Public Assistance Committee. Open up. Your money will be cut off if you don't let us in. It's only yourself you're hurting, Mr Rowe.'

Ma pushes her hair back and straightens her pinny. 'Peggy, sweep up in here. And, Bill, get up and make yourself presentable.'

The inspectors squeeze into the narrow corridor. The older one, with a neatly trimmed ginger moustache, fills the doorway into the kitchen. The taller, younger one, peers round him, eyes bulging like a hungry dog in a butcher's shop.

'Evening,' says the older one. 'I'm Mr Cartwright and this is my assistant, Sid.'

Ma stands with a strained smile. 'Would you like a cup of tea?'

Mr Cartwright beams back with what could be politeness or derision. 'You know what this is all about don't you, Mrs Rowe?'

'No, sir, I don't?'

Mr Cartwright glances over to where Da's standing; he still hasn't turned or acknowledged them. 'Mr Rowe?'

Da's shoulders tense and neck veins bulge as if he is preparing to confront them. He starts to turn and the corner of his mouth shudders in readiness. What will he say? Despite everything, Bill wills him on – he wants him to give these invaders hell. But his muscles relax and he drops his head in defeat.

Ma says falteringly, 'He's not well today, sir.'

'No bother. We have most of what we need. But perhaps I should explain the ins and outs to you?'

Sid, who is already craning his long neck so he can see into the bedroom, smirks in anticipation. Bill half expects him to howl with delight.

'Last year the government decided that unemployed men are only allowed to claim unemployment benefit for twenty-six weeks. After that point it is deemed that their contributions have been exhausted and they are transferred to transitional payments.'

'I sorry, sir, what does it...'

'I'm coming to that, Mrs Rowe. The PAC then assesses what kind of assistance is required. That's why Sid and I are standing in your kitchen.'

'Oh aye.'

'So if you don't mind we need to go through a few things? We can fill out these forms while Sid here checks everything is in order.'

Mr Cartwright plants himself on the chair Bill had been sitting on. He pulls some paper from his leather case and pushes the cooling broth away. 'Name and age?'

Ma sits opposite him; a worried, resigned expression creeps across her face. 'Ann Rowe. I'm thirty-two.'

'Income?'

'Well, I look after the bairns.'

'Please be frank with us.'

She strokes her crucifix and waits for what seems like a long time before answering. 'I wash some clothes for another woman.'

'How old is your son?'

'He's fourteen—' she says before adding quickly '—but he's not working yet.'

Sid slips into the bedroom and Bill follows behind him unseen. If Da won't do anything then at least he can keep an eye on these men. The stranger strides around pushing at blankets and boxes with his shiny black boots. He looks under the pillows, behind the wardrobe and runs his finger along the piano. Bill detests his manner: his investigations are quick, careless, violent almost; he is not really looking for anything, just flaunting his power over them.

The drying rail draped with Mrs Appleby's clothes draws his attention. He lifts up a lace bra and pair of knickers, rubs them between his finger and thumb like a market trader trying to judge their worth and then stuffs them into his coat pocket.

Bill can take no more; he knocks a rusting iron from the edge of bed on to the floor. It spins on the floorboards and ends up at his feet.

'Alright, kidda?' They lock eyes. 'Don't interfere in official business, laddie. Go back to your Ma.'

Bill doesn't let his fear show; he is just another bully. 'I'm watching you in case you pinch anything.'

Sid grits his teeth. 'Did you hear me, laddie? Get out or it'll be worse for your family.'

Bill holds his ground so Sid grabs his collar roughly and marches him back to the table. He reeks of cigarettes and corned-beef sandwiches. There are crumbs around his mouth and on his jacket lapels.

'Caught this fellow spying on me.'

'Get off me.'

Ma appears annoyed with Bill. 'Come here.'

Mr Cartwight takes Sid's notebook and contemplates the information for a few minutes. Then he clears his throat with as much drama as he can manage and says, 'Thank you, Mr and Mrs Rowe. We will have a decision for you when you come to sign on.'

Ma says, 'You won't cut his dole, will you?'

'No decision has been taken yet, Mrs Rowe.' Mr Cartwright gets himself ready to leave.

'I'll show you out.' She holds the door and bows her head like someone might do in church.

Sid leans towards her as he passes. 'It don't look good, sweetheart. That piano has got to go and your wages more than cover your living expenses. And anyway you can afford kinky underwear.'

'The piano? It's all I've got left of Granda.'

Once they're gone, Ma sinks to the floor and puts her hands over her face. She stays in the same position for a while and then explodes in anger; her wrath is muffled but clear enough, 'You useless bastard, Joseph. Sometimes I wish you'd copped it in Verdun. You're not the man that got down on one knee in Saltwell Park. You useless bastard. You useless bastard.'

Da comes out of his trance at the window. He picks up his long wool coat, turns the collar up and pulls his cap down – it is as if he is trying to shut the world out. He glances over at Bill and Peggy. 'Look a-a-after her, Bill.'

As he passes, Ma reaches for his hand. But she is left holding one of his mittens. 'Joseph, wait. I spoke out of turn. I'm sorry.'

Bill leads Ma back to her chair as the door slams. He removes the stinking mitten from her tightly clenched fist and strokes her arm. 'Calm yourself, Ma.'

'I don't want to lose him, Bill. He ain't the easiest of men but he's all I got. You'll understand when you're older.'

Peggy is still at the table. Tears are falling into her cold broth.

Bill wants to ease their pain. 'I'll go and fetch him, Ma. I did it before, didn't I?'

She runs her hand up his arm as if to check he has the muscles to bring him back and nods her agreement.

Outside, it is raining and dark. Da's shadow flicks over a deserted tramway waiting room and a flaking OXO advertisement at the end of the row. Bill knows where he is heading: The George. He runs down the middle of the road, skidding and sliding on the wet cobbles.

The front bar is full of unshaven men with leering expressions. They all look alike in the gloom: like the gargoyles on the church brought to life for a night. They are tottering on stools, leaning against walls and each other, slumped on floors and over tables. Some are playing cards, others dominos.

Da is counting his coins out at the bar. The feelings Bill has swallowed for years rise like sour bile from the very bottom of his stomach. He sees the tart going through Da's pockets. He feels Da's bony hands slapping the backs of his hairless legs. He sees the burnt book on the floor. Da's no more a father than a husband. He is a selfish old bastard.

Bill drops his shoulder and charges into him; Da's body offers no resistance. It is as if he is just skin and bone underneath his coat. As he tumbles his coins and keys spin in the smoky air – everybody nearby stops drinking. Then his head cracks on the stone floor with the sound of a dry stick snapping.

Some of the men laugh and point. A grinning man with a thin red face pushes to the front to get a better view.

'You can't let him get away with that, Joe,' he says spitting on the floor. 'Sons need to fucking respect their fathers.'

Bill waits for Da's reaction: for punches and kicks; for shouts and insults. But they don't come.

Instead Da puts his hands up and pleads, 'Son, not now, I-I-I love y-y-you all.'

'Why didn't you stand up to them inspectors then?'

'What can I-I-I do, son?'

Bill snorts in disbelief. 'Tell them they can go to hell with their means test. Tell them they can't have our piano. It's all Ma has got to remind her of Granda.'

'They would just take it anyway and have me bloody arrested, m-m-man.'

'Coward.'

Bill retraces his steps; the other drinkers part, allowing him to escape into the night.

Raindrops hammer the cobbles and the overhead tram wires flap in the wind. He cannot bear the thought of returning home just yet. Instead he wanders the deserted streets. Lamps are on in some of the houses and he can make out figures sitting in chairs and smoking pipes and hanging wet clothes around fires. He tries not to imagine the scene at home. He plods on passing dark, boarded-up grocer shops, funeral parlours, pawn shops, guest houses and chained-up fruit-and-veg stalls.

As the night grows cold, he finds himself heading to Len's house. They haven't spoken since their argument in the park but he can't think of anywhere else to go. Thomas answers and ushers him in immediately. Lizzie and Len are huddled around the glowing hearth playing cards.

Len offers him his chair as Thomas goes to make some hot cocoa. 'Sit down by the fire, Bill. You look chilled to the bone.'

Bill accepts gratefully – he is pleased there are no hard feelings between them. The truth is that he feels more at home here than he does with his family.

Len clears away the cards. 'What happened, like?'

As Bill sips his warm milk, he wonders if he should tell them the truth. Would they understand? Or would they judge him? Ma always warned him about airing their dirty linen in public but he had already done much worse than that; he had attacked Da in front of all those people in The George.

Len repeats himself softly, 'What happened? You have nothing to fear from us, Bill.'

Bill feels a little sick; he gasps the arm rest for support. They are gathered round him, waiting for him to speak, yet, as far as he can tell, they are not interested in acquiring some local gossip; there is nothing but quiet concern in their faces. He takes a breath and retells the story of the inspection, chase and fight. He ends with a thought that has been growing since he left the pub, 'I should have left him to drink. He's got nothing else.'

Len takes his hand and holds it tightly. 'You had your reasons, Bill. He is not right in the head.'

Bill feels his voice waver. 'I hate those bastard means inspectors. None of this would have happened had they not come calling on our door.'

Thomas adds, 'MacDonald has a lot to answer for.'

A few years ago Bill might have found his remark a little peculiar, not to say confusing, but it makes sense to him now. He steadies himself and wipes his nose. 'Well I've had it with Labour. I want to join the ILP.'

Thomas squeezes Bill's shoulders. 'I'll go and get the papers.'

Lizzie stokes the fire. 'Well, let him think about it, Thomas.'

Thomas hovers by door.

'No, I want to sign up now. I'm sick of the way we are treated. Len, you're right, we need to organise ourselves, get elected and change things.'

Lizzie sighs. 'Do you know what you are letting yourself into?'

'I'm not a kid anymore, Lizzie.'

She relents. 'Would you like to stay here tonight, pet? Len, can get you some blankets. You can sleep on the chair?'

In the night Bill wakes from frightening, unruly dreams. Fumbling in the gloom he finds the back door and relieves himself in the chilly toilet. He closes his eyes for a moment but all he can see is Da sprawling on the floor of The George. How did he end up like that? Was he always such a miserable bastard? Had his own mother looked down and seen only meanness and anger in his eyes? Had he been like that when he slid a ring onto Ma's finger?

There must have been a time when he looked like Peggy when she squeezed out of Ma that October night: pink and pure-smelling with doll-like toes and hands. What had happened to him since then? What had happened?

Bill winces as it occurs to him that he is no better. He has taken his troubles out on the weak; he has thrown an old man to the floor.

When he returns to the front room, Florence is curled like a cat on the other armchair reading a book. Her wavy hair hangs about her shoulders. She is wearing a thick cotton night dress.

'I heard the door. You woke me.'

'Sorry. I needed to go...'

She turns a page without looking up.

'What're you reading?'

'This? Percy Shelley.'

Shadows cast by the furniture envelop her as she moves her head. Her features slip in and out of sight.

Bill is at a loss as to what to do next. The age gap seems to widen each time they meet. 'I like Dickens.'

She tilts her head, acknowledging his comment. The moonlight illuminates the tiny, normally unseen hairs on her brow and lips.

'Are you staying on at school?'

'Mrs Barrett says I could get a place at Gateshead Grammar School if I work hard. But Ma has different ideas.'

'That's where I go.'

'I know.'

She yawns. 'Would you like to borrow it?'

'What?'

Her mouth tilts upwards into a half smile. 'The book, Bill.'

Bill blushes at his confusion. 'Aye.'

She unfurls herself leaving the book behind and disappears up the stairs. He listens to each creek on the steps as she returns to her still-warm bed. Trembling with the cold and excitement, he slumps in her chair with her book. Why did she come down? Did she expect something from him?

He reads until the cold gets too much and the sky starts to lighten. Ma and Da would still be in their bed and Peggy would be beginning to stir from her slumber. Despite everything he feels guilty about staying at the Weavers'. Eventually he unlatches the door and makes his way home.

*

Like the captain of a reeling, stricken ship, Bill attempts to right himself. His whole world is spinning. Before he can find his bearings the metal landing starts vibrating: it is the sound of hundreds of boots clattering down the wing.

There will be trouble if he is found like this: laying in a stupor on his bed. They might beat him or put him in the hole: the isolation cell at the other end of the wing. The blissful defiance he felt earlier gives way to fear: he doesn't want to die here after all.

Fighting waves of sickness and double vision, he pushes himself up, straightens his dribble-streaked shirt and kicks the unfinished mailbags under the bed. When the line of prisoners passes, he is sat on his bed. They pass without a word flanked by guards.

He stiffens when he hears footsteps returning. The stocky prisoner, who attacked him in the morning, is taken to the neighbouring cell.

Fry stops and ushers him in. 'Is this alright for you, Purse?'

'Aye.'

'Shame about the rat next door.'

He laughs. 'Aye.'

'Hopefully he won't be bothering you for long. He looks like he's at death's door.'

*

Da, dressed only in a vest and trousers, is hauling a sack of coal across the yard. With each wrench his back arches and scraggy arm muscles contract. Starlings scatter and window sashes are swiftly pulled down as he swears and curses his lot in life, 'B...b... bugger this bag.'

Bill observes his plight from the kitchen. Da collapses on his knees as he nears the back door, chest heaving and dripping with sweat. He looks up to the heavens in search of an explanation or perhaps an intervention from the God Ma prays to every night.

'Do you need a hand with that?'

'Have y-y-you been standing there all this time? I'll take me belt to y-y-you, son.'

The truth is he has not laid a finger on him since he threw him to the floor in The George. 'Do you want a hand or not?'

'A-A-Aye. But I'm warning y-y-you.'

Together they lift it into the house.

Da leans on the door frame. 'That's the last sack and the last of the money. Them chairs will have to be burnt this winter unless one of us can find a job.'

'I know, Da. But I'm still at school.'

'Fourteen is old enough to start work. That's what the law

says, like. I-I-I never even seen a bloody classroom.'

'It's different now, Da.'

Bill remembers when the chairs were burnt last time. He must have been six or so. They had to sit on their beds until the vicar took pity on Ma and gave them three unwanted chairs gathering dust in the vicarage hallway.

Da mops his brow, which still bears the red indent of the flagstone in The George. He told Ma he toppled and fell. Bill could have corrected him but decided to leave Da's pride intact.

'And I-I-I'm not long of this world.'

Bill feels strange pangs of not quite love but respect for the old man. 'Nonsense, you're tough as old boots.'

He totters to his chair by the range. 'I-I-I used to be, son, before the—' His voice trails off.

'The war?'

His eyes focus on some distant point beyond his son; it is like he is looking through him, at ghosts or lost worlds. 'Aye.'

Bill is intrigued; Da never spoke about his time in the trenches. Ma told him of life before it broke out as if it was a happy, carefree time. He wishes he had known his father then. But before he can ask another question Da is asleep, tongue lolling lazily from his cavernous mouth.

It is dark by the time Ma returns. She is carrying a sleeping Peggy in her arms; her body looks limp and heavy. Bill puts down the book Florence lent him immediately.

'What happened?'

He puts his palm against her small mouth, he can feel the damp tickle of her breath.

'She came on with a fever in the market. We had to get a tram on the way home and she fell asleep. I couldn't wake her.'

'We've got to get her to a doctor, Ma. There's always something wrong with her.'

Ma's eyes dart back and forth. 'She's not strong like you, Bill.

When she was a bairn she was too lazy to even feed on my breast.'

'She's getting worse, Ma.'

Ma carries her into the bedroom and Bill follows. 'Your Da hasn't got any insurance now he's not working, and we can't afford doctors' fees.'

'What about St Thomas?'

'They can't take anymore. There are queues every day. And they'll probably want paying and all if they find out I'm washing clothes.'

Bill is becoming desperate; if anyone is blameless in this family it is Peggy. 'Can we cut back on food?'

'Keep your head, Bill. She'll be right as rain by the morn,' she says, tucking Peggy into bed.

Bill stays with his sister watching her nostrils flare with each rise and fall of her chest. She draws her legs up instinctively and clutches her arms to her body like a baby in a womb. Her eyelids flicker for a moment and Bill wonders if she might wake up but she just turns over to face the wall.

As the moon glows in the sky, Bill peels blight-scarred potatoes with a rusty knife and Ma loads the range with the coal from the sack.

'I'll have to find work, won't I? This can't go on.'

She gives him an odd look of sadness mixed with relief. 'Daniels Metals are looking for apprentices. Some of the lads in the market were going on about about it. You should get yourself down there tomorrow.'

'What about the means test? Won't they cut Da's dole if I start earning?'

'We'll find you some digs if it comes to it.'

Bill stops peeling – all the strength in his body suddenly drains away. He can see his future: a life of hard physical labour ending with a broken body and mind. What a fool he was to think it could have been any different.

'So that's it for me.'

Ma studies his face. 'I know you're thinking, Bill. Fact is we've all had to make sacrifices for other. I dreamt of all kinds of things when I was bairn. I thought I could play in an—' she snorts '— orchestra.'

Mr Daniels is facing an oil painting when Bill is ushered into his small office. It is of a handsome blond-haired man sitting awkwardly by a fire in a bare, unadorned room. Mr Daniels doesn't stir so Bill takes a seat opposite a wooden desk with two neat piles of papers, a fountain pen and a large well-thumbed Bible.

'My father built this from nothing. There were some who warned him about coming to Newcastle but he was not deterred. Not for a moment.'

Mr Daniels' voice startles Bill; it is deep and mannered, like a gramophone recording from another place and time. The glass in the picture frame and the paper on the desk appears to vibrate as he speaks.

'It's true there have been up and downs. That's the nature of the trade cycle. But the Daniels family has kept its faith in this workshop and the people of this city. And do you know what? We have all benefited. This factory has given work and purpose to four generations of Tyneside men and by doing so has paid for wholesome food and good clothes and housing for their families. Not to mention doctors, and beanos to the seaside. It has also allowed my family to live comfortably, although I should add, never extravagantly.'

At last Mr Daniels turns from the painting. His narrow baldhead is ringed with a band of faded tufts of blond hair, the colour of summer grass burnt white by the sun. He has a long, perfectly straight nose and small bright blue eyes, like glinting little marbles.

The monologue resumes, 'Now times are hard. I've had to lay

off men to ensure that this factory survives and continues to benefit future generations. I've done this with a heavy heart. I've seen men whimpering in this office, too scared to tell their wives. But He has not forsaken us. Government orders have started to come in and as a result I need a couple of apprentices. As ever it will be a beneficial relationship; I'll train you up to be an engineer and you'll work hard in return.' Mr Daniels stops to draw breath and grips the back of his chair.

Bill realises it must be his turn to speak; he clears his throat. 'Aye, that's why I'm here, Mr Daniels.'

'Tremendous. What's your name?'

'Didn't they tell you? Rowe. Bill Rowe.'

'Well, welcome, Bill Rowe, to the Daniels family. I like to think of all my employees as members of my extended family. There are a few other matters I should tell you about our family. We are Seventh Day Adventists. This means we do not work on Saturdays. Nonetheless we do believe in the holiness of work. It cleanses men of the sins of sloth and idleness. So we work extra hours in the week to make up the difference, six until seven. I trust that will be agreeable to you, Mr Rowe?'

The hours will leave him little time for reading or studying but Bill keeps his thoughts to himself. 'Aye that's grand.'

Peggy is playing with her friends on the street when Bill makes it back. He holds off and watches: she must have recovered from her fever. Shrieking with joy, the children skip over chalk marks carefully dubbed on the paving slabs and chase each other around lampposts. He feels sad he is leaving his childhood behind but maybe Ma had a point: it was time for him to make his way in the world. The children race back towards him. Peggy is slower than the others and keeps falling over; her knees are grazed and grimy.

'Better then?' He kneels down to her height. The edges of her eyes are the colour of egg yolks and her hair is tangled and sweaty.

'Aye, Bill. It was just a funny turn.'

'I got the job.'

She hugs him. Her skin smells sickly like rotten fruit. 'Ma will be chuffed.'

Taking him by the hand, she leads him down the steps into the basement. Ma and Da are sat at the table eating bread and margarine. For once they look peaceful and happy.

Somehow Ma knows and pinches his cheek. 'I prayed and prayed for this to happen.'

Bill is not in the mood for celebrating but he musters a smile. He is pleased she at least is relieved.

Ma pulls Peggy close. 'There will be enough for milk and grapes for you and we can save up for a visit to the doctor.'

Da looks oddly happy. 'Don't get carried away now,' he says with a smile. 'How much y-y-you getting paid, son?'

'Eight shillings a week.'

'That's wonderful, son.'

*

Bradley presents Bill with a thin package after the doors are opened for dinner. 'One more for you, marra.'

The familiar handwriting and the size suggest another copy of the *New Leader*, *Picture Post* or *Manchester Guardian*. Bill tosses it into the corner, where it lands on a pile of mail.

'Pal of yours?'

'Someone I knew once.'

Bradley scratches his small head. 'Could I take some, marra? We are running a bit low on bumf paper. I could get you something in return.'

Bill agrees immediately. He quite likes the idea that the work of the nation's finest war correspondents will end up unread and covered in shit. He knows well enough Hitler's empire is spreading across the continent like a vile growth and he knows people are slaughtering each other because they were born under different flags.

Bradley studies the mail. 'Is it the same chap who sent all these? The R is the same on the address. It curls round like a tail.'

'Aye, he got me banged up. But he can walk the streets and hold his wife close at night. Look at me.'

'We've all got our crosses to bear, marra. At least you got a pen pal. None of the bastards I used to knock about with bother to visit.'

One of the screws bellows below and Bradley backs out with his arms full of unwanted mail.

'Grub's up, lads.'

*

The landlady waddles along the narrow hall and lifts herself onto the first step of the staircase with a grunt. She uses her arms as winches as her left leg is devoid of strength. Her ankles are thick and laced with knobby blue and purple veins.

'Are you next door to the lunatic asylum?'

She ignores Bill's question and grunts.

'Is that the asylum over there?'

She narrows her eyes and says, 'I've not sure of its purpose, laddie. Where's me stick? I can't get up these bloody stairs.' She grunts again but this time with anger rather than exertion. 'Eric? Eric? Where's me stick? Wake up? Eric?'

There is a muffled reply and the sound of boxes being moved. After a while a door opens and a stick is hurled in her direction.

Ma picks it up and passes it to her. 'Here you go, Mrs Bradshaw.'

'You'll get used to the steps but the view, well, it's a delight. The last lodger said it made him glad to be alive every time he woke up. Eric and me would live up here if we could. But our legs aren't as young as yours, laddie.'

The stairs wind up though the house. Damp plaster falls from the walls as they follow Mrs Bradshaw. She points out the lodger's kitchen and gestures coldly to a small man making a pot of tea, who nods his head timidly at them.

At the next landing Ma brushes her arm of dust and makes to return the plaster pieces to a hole as if Mrs Bradshaw is going to chastise them for damaging her property.

Bill catches her arm; he doesn't see why they should make any effort to maintain her home as she hadn't lifted a finger in years. 'Leave it, Ma.'

'What was that, laddie?'

Bill whispers to Ma, 'I don't want to live here. Couldn't I just pretend to live somewhere else?

Ma is unmoved. 'There is no way. They would find out.'

At the very top Mrs Bradshaw opens a thin painted door, which is hanging from a single hinge. The room measures about nine feet by nine feet. She sits on the bed and leans forward resting her chin on her stick. The sheets are wrinkled and imprinted with the bodies and stains of countless strangers.

Ma yanks apart the thick curtains releasing a cloud of dust but at least letting in the midday brightness. 'Look at that, son.'

Bill glances over her shoulder. The view is not as spectacular as Mrs Bradshaw promised but you can still see the bridges and the river over a patchwork of roofs and chimney stacks. 'Aye it's good, Ma.'

'Told you, laddie. Told you it were nice.'

Mrs Bradshaw pushes three long strands of sweaty grey hair from her glasses and flattens them to her head. He can see her glistening, blotchy scalp despite her efforts. She is almost completely bald.

'So are you working, laddie? I told Eric I'll only have working lodgers here. This is a working household.'

Ma answers for him, 'He starts at Daniels Metals next week as an apprentice.'

'What's that, love?'

Ma twitches; she is starting to lose her patience with the old woman as well. 'He's working. How much do want for the room?'

Mrs Bradshaw pulls a pen from her pinny with her surprisingly nimble podgy fingers and notes down a figure on a scrap of paper for Ma.

'Aye, he can make that.'

'When's he want to move in?'

Bill answers for himself, 'Sunday.'

'What's that, laddie?'

Ma repeats it, 'Sunday.'

*

Bill waits for his new neighbour Purse to leave his new cell before joining the hordes heading down the stairs to the canteen. He hobbles onto the landing and hugs the rail overlooking the trolleys.

Fuggy steam from the tubs of broth and the ever-present stench of the overflowing toilets mingle in his nostrils; he feels like chucking his guts up. The others don't seem that bothered, they barge and jostle each other for the best position in front of the men dishing out their watery supper and dry bread. Bill spots Purse deep in conversation with Bradley.

Rogers, the screw from the store, notices him on the rail and beckons to him to come down. Bill inches along the metal, a step at a time, until he can go no further. His head is pounding and his legs are about to give away.

He slides down to his knees. Rogers is too far away to help and no doubt distracted by the hungry mob in front of him. Bill crawls, wheezing and coughing back to his cell, like some monstrous baby.

*

The bark is rough and the ground is still damp from the morning dew; Bill can feel the wetness seeping into his shorts. He looks across the valley towards Gateshead; the first light of the day catches on glass, wet slate and steel tramlines. He had woken early to walk up the hill in time for sunrise; there was no better place to mull things over.

He had always imagined he would do things differently than Da; he was good at school whereas Da, as he liked to remind everyone, had never seen the inside of a classroom. Bill got top scores for spelling and mathematics; he loved reading; he loved stories; he loved learning.

The glittering city comes to life below. Men with work fill the streets and then men without work are joined by women and children. Market stalls come to life and bookies open their doors. A few large ships chug down the river and warehouse gates are hauled open. He loses himself in the relentless but pleasing motion of the city until he hears the approaching squelch of a boot in mud.

Len rounds the tree and grins broadly. 'I thought I might find you up here. Peggy said you'd "gone for a walk". I knew it would be this spot.'

Bill blinks; he resents the interruption however well-intentioned. 'Well done, Constable Weaver.'

'I didn't mean to disturb you, like.'

Bill turns back to the city. 'I'm starting work at Daniels Metals on Monday.'

'What about school?'

'Mr Gribble has agreed to it. Ma told him we didn't have a choice.'

Len runs his finger down the tree trunk while he thinks. 'There are plenty looking for work. It can't have been easy.'

'I wanted more than this, Len. You more than anyone should

have known that. I wasn't borrowing those books just for fun.'

Len offers his hand to pull him up. 'I didn't mean anything by it.'

Bill keeps his fists in his pockets. He knows Len means well but he envies his life. 'Let's head back before the weather turns.'

They walk towards Gateshead as dark clouds smother the early brightness. Bill can tell the silence is making Len uncomfortable. He starts to regret his curtness; Len wasn't to blame for the means test or his new digs. The truth was, he had come to find him whereas no one else would have bothered.

'This is why we fight for a better world, Len.'

'I just wish you could of stayed on a little,' he says.

Fat raindrops begin to fall as they reach the barley fields on the far side of the valley. Water runs down the emerald and golden stalks and forms brown little streams, rivers and lakes in the mud.

Bill brushes curls of wet hair from his face and watches Len trudge ahead down the path with his coat pulled over his hair.

'Will you be going to the grammar school?'

'If I can,' he calls back.

Nearing The George, Len tugs Bill's shirt. Harry and an older man are sheltering from the downpour in the doorway. Len hangs back but the older man spots them; his voice booms across the street.

'Hold up, red Len.'

Len eyes a side road. 'Let's go down there. It's Archie – Harry's Da. He's got it in for me.'

Yet Bill is in no mood for running away: why should they get wet to avoid a pair of drunks. 'We have a right to walk these streets, Len.'

They move in a straight line, focusing on the terraces beyond. Archie lurches drunkenly out of the doorway, blocking their path. Rivulets of rainwater pour down his wind-burnt face.

Bill recognises him from The George. He was the one who had a go at Da when he barged him over by the bar.

Archie opens his tiny mouth displaying a craggy ridge of yellow teeth in what could be a smile or a grimace. 'What's the rush? Don't you want to talk to your uncle Archie?'

Len looks him dead in the eye. 'Let us pass.'

Archie laughs and spreads his arms out. 'Nah.'

'Go and have another drink, Archie.'

Len steps to the side but Archie follows him so they are eye to eye again.

'You'll all the same, you reds. You say you want to help the working classes but you won't do nothing about them dirty, stinking Yids making all the buggering money, whilst we rot.'

A crowd of men congregate in the doorway despite the storm; they like a good punch up. Bill catches a glimpse of Da milling around near the back.

Len steps back and repeats his advice, 'Go and on, Archie, have a drink. It will do you good, man.'

'Don't tell me what to do. Like a bloody constable you are...telling people what to fucking do.'

Archie lunges at him; Len avoids his fist but slips on the wet cobbles and lands on his back. Archie pulls back his foot and aims at Len's grazed rib cage where his shirt has ridden up.

Bill has got to do something; it is his fault they didn't turn and run. He digs the old man hard on the nose, drawing blood; Archie swings round in the middle of his kick and collides with his son. The pair of them crumple on the cobbles and Archie starts throwing his arms about battling an invisible enemy. One or two blows strike Harry before he grips his father in a bear-hug.

'Calm fucking down,' says Harry, with what looks like embarrassment and fear.

Archie's jeering drinking pals start advancing from the

doorway of The George. Da is nowhere to be seen.

Bill doesn't fancy their chances much. 'Let's get out of here.'

They spirit down the side road back towards the safety of the valley as the rain slows to a fine spray and the clouds part revealing the sun. Once they are sure they are alone they stop by a coal-dust-coated stone wall to let their clothes dry out.

Bill washes Archie's blood from his knuckles in the filthy river. 'How's your head feel?'

Len looks a bit embarrassed that he had to rely on the younger boy again. 'There's a bump the size of football coming up.'

'What was all that about?'

'I don't know, Bill. I guess it all goes back to that dock strike a few years ago. Archie was a union steward. He was respected by the men. Thomas knew him well too. But he sneaked back on the second week – he justified it by saying his family was hungry. The strike petered out and the other union men were sacked. Archie got made foreman and now he knocks about with the brown shirts.'

'Is that why Harry hates you?'

'He was alright at first but his Da has filled his head with poison.'

They follow the bank of the Gut so they can get back home without running into Archie and Harry. It is getting dark by the time they reach Len's house.

'Thanks for standing up to him, Bill. He could of done me in.'

'I told you, I hate bullies.'

'Do you want to come in for cocoa?'

'I need to get home. Peggy is not well.'

'Don't be a stranger, Bill,' he says opening the door.

*

Rogers peers down at Bill: he is curled on the landing. He hasn't even the strength to ask for help. All the other officers are on the ground floor, so Rogers has no choice but to drag him towards his bed. He is perhaps fifty or sixty years old but still strong as an ox.

'Easy does it. Let's get you back in here.'

Bill is almost moved to tears; acts of kindness are rare in this place. He forces out some words as he lifts him onto the bed, 'Thank you.'

'Just doing my job, Rowe. Whatever you did, whoever you hurt, you were made in God's image. That cannot be denied. Now, have you mentioned your health to Officer Fry?'

In-between breaths, Bill says, 'Fry said I've "got nothing to worry about".'

Rogers drops his eyes and voice. 'Well, he is in charge.'

Bill guesses that he has only survived by keeping his views to himself. Yet he feels no resentment to Rogers; maybe even a little pity at what such a brutal workplace has done to the spirit of a naturally kind man.

'I'd better get back downstairs, they may need me,' he says resigned.

*

The howl is terrible, it sounds like the last gasp of an animal before it is torn apart by a predator. Bill climbs out of his new bed and pulls back the curtains. His vision is heavy with uneasy dreams but he can make out figures clambering over the flat roof of the asylum.

The warders are chasing a young girl. She looks a little like Florence, thin with thick hair. Before she reaches the edge they grab her and bundle her to the floor.

Mrs Bradshaw leans out of a window below and hollers at them to keep it down. The girl shrieks again as they try and force her through a hatch. She digs her nails in but they prise her off finger by finger.

Bill returns to the warmth of his blankets. He feels a strange kinship with the girl: his situation is as hopeless as hers; his wishes, like hers, count for little. He stares at the tin clock on the wall. Only four hours before he has to get up and walk the six miles to the workshop.

His worn boots slide and skid on the worn paving over Tyne Bridge. The mirror-flat river is close to perfect in the early morning stillness although he doesn't have much time to enjoy the view. On the other side, he descends winding steps towards the salty murk of the docks. He only glances the edges but he daren't slow down. In an oily puddle at the bottom he glimpses himself; his restless night is written all over his face, he is grey and hollow-eyed.

The foreman is standing by the entrance leisurely smoking a pipe when Bill hurtles through the moss-covered yard.

'I'm starting today. Where do I go?'

'Just get in there before old Bob sees you, laddie. He's on the prowl for idlers today. He says the Devil has got into the factory.'

The workshop is alive with the roar and bark of heavy machinery. Sparks fly off grindstone-wheels, hammers crash on anvils and rivet holes are drilled into sheet metal. Bill doesn't know what to do so he approaches an old man in a vest unloading boxes of screws. His freckled, muscular back arches with each lift.

'Where do the apprentices work?'

The man looks over his shoulder; his face is crossed with a long purple scar. White hairs poke out of his chin like the bristles of a brush. 'You stole Ned's job.'

'What do you mean?'

'Boys are cheap. Men are expensive. Now sling your hook.'

Bill retraces his steps, fearing a confrontation. He bumps into the foreman, who is packing his pipe with dark, richly scented tobacco, and chatting to a group of panel beaters.

'What did I tell you, son? Bob is on the look out today so don't be shirking your duties.'

'He told me to sling my hook.'

'John? He's still sore about the sackings. Take no notice.'

'So what do you want me to do then?'

The foreman pats his tobacco gently with his large flat thumb, which looks as though it has been thumped by countless hammers, and glances at the welders. 'Go to the store and fetch us a rubber spanner and some tartan paint?'

The foreman gestures to a door on the far side with his pipe. Bill trots off obediently and they burst into laughter.

*

Bill wakes in hunger; he wishes he had eaten something before sleeping. The door is locked but it is still fairly early because he can hear Purse doing what sounds like sit-ups and press-ups in his cell.

Without warning, Bill's chest and throat begin to tighten. He knows what is coming next but there is little he can do: he rears forward and coughs. Mucus and blood land on the blanket.

*

The driver of the flat-backed Thornycroft lorry runs his hand along the still-warm shiny, green bonnet with pride as the foreman looks on admiringly.

'She runs lovely, really smooth, like. This is the future, Jim. This is the way goods will be moved about...when your apprentice grows up.'

The driver ruffles Bill's hair as if he was a baby, so Bill jerks his head away. It was bad enough giving up his education but he wasn't going to let them treat him like a halfwit.

The foreman snarls at him as if to say don't upset this man. 'Aye she's a beauty alright. Do you want a smoke while Bill here unloads?'

Bill screws up his face. 'The whole thing?'

'Aye, the whole fucking thing. I'll get John to help, seeing as you two get along so well,' he says with a mean titter.

The foreman and the driver stroll to his cramped little office just inside the workshop.

John emerges shortly after, scowling and muttering curses under his breath. Like the first time they met, he is unshaven and drenched in sweat. He starts tossing the boxes and packages on to a wheelbarrow. They split and rip but he doesn't bat an eyelid.

'This ain't a spectator sport.'

Bill climbs on the back of the lorry and starts moving the bigger boxes to the front where John hauls them off. They are stamped with a smudged, official-looking crest.

'This one says fragile, John.'

'What do you know about anything? You're only a lad.' He lets the box fall to the ground. Something shatters inside.

At that very moment the foreman and the driver come out of the office. 'What you playing at, John?'

'It fell.'

'I saw you bloody drop it. Are you getting too old for this lark?'

John stares at him for a moment with a fierce intensity before dipping his gaze in a gesture of submission.

'Now, you had better take more care with the others. Bob's not best pleased with you right now because you've been pestering him for days off.'

John turns and starts lifting the boxes off the truck again. The foreman points to his eyes to indicate he will be watching and returns to his office.

When they are out of earshot, Bill whispers to him, 'What a bastard.'

'He's Bob's policeman. He likes to have a joke with us but he knows which side his bread is buttered on.'

Hands on his bony hips, John stops. For the first time since they met, he looks him in the eye. 'How old are you, son?'

'Fifteen soon.'

'You're too young for this. You should be learning at school. I wish I could have stayed on, like.'

'How old are you, John?'

'Fifty-eight.'

'You're too old for this.'

John's face forms into an expression that seemed quite improbable a few moments ago: a gentle, warm smile. 'Aye.'

They unload the rest of the boxes quickly but without any breakages. When they are done, they sit with their backs against the wall, just out of sight of the office. John stuffs some chewing tobacco into his mouth while Bill closes his eyes and lets his muscles relax.

'Why did you want Thursday off?'

John moves the tobacco around in his mouth and spits some inky gunk onto the cracked concrete. 'To visit my wife—' He stops suddenly as if he is unsure he should continue.

'Go on?'

'She's not well. It's her heart, like.'

'And he wouldn't let you?'

'He said he had a big order to get through this week. He said our jobs depended on it.'

'And he's a man of God?'

Before they can get up, Mr Daniels rounds the corner with the foreman and the driver. The foreman points to the boxes.

Mr Daniels smiles and slaps the foreman on the back. His voice carries across the yard. 'Look at this. Like I told you He has not forsaken us. But this is just the start, Jim. There's a lot more coming let me assure you; the country needs to rearm and rearm quickly.'

The foreman purses his lips again and nods in agreement.

Mr Daniels is about to continue his speech when he spots

John and Bill beside the boxes. 'Why are you two lazing around?'

They both climb to their feet.

Mr Daniels' cheeks shake and his blue eyes roll madly. His expression turns in an instant from joy to anger. 'John Baldwin? I thought I told you to stay out of trouble.'

'Sir?'

'We need to stick together if we are going to weather this economic storm. Do you understand?'

John remains silent.

'Do you understand?'

John spits and then says flatly, 'Sorry, sir.'

Mr Daniels signals irritably to the foreman. 'Can I have a word?'

The three of them walk towards the door leaving Bill and John standing beside the boxes. Bill is unsure if he should leave or stay or get on with the work.

After a while the foreman returns to face them. 'That's it, John. He wants you out. Here's your wages for the week.'

John goes white; the tobacco falls from his lips and lands in a soggy heap. Bill imagines he wants to have a go at the foreman but the shock robs him of the strength to utter a single insult or curse. He staggers backwards into the boxes; his mouth opens and shuts like a pike yanked from a canal.

The foreman winks at Bill. 'Get yourself inside, Rowe. You're the lucky one.'

Bill walks away. He feels guilty but he has to think of Peggy. He turns back one last time to see the foreman drop something into John's hand and usher him towards the gate. John will be just fine; his pay will tide him over.

Inside, all the machines lie silent. There are no crashes or bangs or bawdy jokes echoing around the workshop. The men are gathered around the window watching John and the foreman.

One of the welders shakes his mop of oily black hair. 'Those bloody coins won't buy him more than a couple of beers.'

There are nods of agreement.

'It's not right, Dermot.'

'Poor sod.'

A smooth-faced panel beater steps back from the window. He licks his thin lips slowly. 'We all feel sorry for John. Of course we do. But Bob has got to look after business otherwise there will be no jobs for any of us.'

The other panel beaters clap. 'Never a truer word said, Reg. Let's get on with the day.'

The welder Dermot slicks back his hair. 'Wait up, lads. Bob has been looking for an excuse to get shot of John because he's old. He'll do the same to us when we tire and slow.'

The men wait for panel-beater Reg; he licks his lips again. 'Let's not forget that John has caused us all plenty of bother. If he ain't complaining then he's shirking.'

'That's a bloody lie. John is a hard worker.'

An apprentice panel beater waits and says, 'Fact is we don't know what went on out there. John could have hit Bob for all we know.'

The foreman, who has been listening unnoticed in the doorway, pushes his way through the circle of men. 'That's right. You don't know what went on out there. So you best get back to work before Bob catches you.'

The men start to seep away. The welder Dermot looks around for support but only three of the welders hold their ground.

The foreman paces up to each in turn. 'Didn't you hear me? Back to work now.'

Dermot exchanges glances with the welders. 'We can't let Bob get away with this. He works us until our bodies give up and then discards us like scrap.'

The foreman laughs. 'Get back to your machine, V. I. Lenin.'

Bill can keep silent no longer. He was wrong to leave John. He can hear his heart beating and blood rushing in his ears. 'I saw it all.'

The foreman cocks his head. 'Did you say something, laddie?'

Bill swallows. He doesn't want to lose his job but there is only one way to make amends for abandoning John. 'Aye, I did.'

The foreman walks so close he is nose to nose with Bill. 'Careful, laddie. This isn't a game.'

The men stop at their machines; the whole shed falls silent again. Light from the window plays on the floor by Bill's boots.

Dermot gently separates Bill and the foreman. 'Spit it out, son. A man's livelihood depends on it.'

Bill is quivering. 'His wife is in hospital. She's dying. Bob wouldn't let him spend Thursday with her.'

Dermot waits for Bill's words to sink in and then says loudly, 'Who's for downing tools?'

The foreman laughs again but this time with less pleasure. 'Let's not get carried away. This laddie is just after some attention. He's made the whole thing up.'

The welder ignores him and repeats, 'Who's for downing tools?'

'You'll all be following John down the pub with your last ever earnings if you listen to this...'

Dermot is joined by all ten of the other welders. They stand behind him with their arms crossed. He says, 'I'll have you chucked out if you interfere in a trade-union vote.'

The foreman slams the door muttering, 'There's no helping some people.'

The men raise their hands apart from Reg and the apprentice panel beater. Bill sticks his hand up too with giddy excitement.

'That's carried. You coming, Reg?'

Reg wipes his nose of his sleeve and says bitterly, 'My wife has got a bairn on the way. I'm no blackleg, mind.'

As they file out into the yard, Dermot comes over to Bill. 'What you did in there was very brave. I'll make sure nothing happens to you.'

The men are milling around the yard entrance when they catch sight of Mr Daniels. The chatter dies down as he draws close to Dermot. His manner is oddly timid and hesitant; when he finally comes to speak he cups his hands over his mouth, 'Can we talk somewhere private?'

Dermot lifts his chin up. 'Nah we can talk here in front of the lads. I'm nothing special.'

'Have it your way. Can you tell me what this is about? The orders are going to dry up unless we meet the deadline.'

'Either you let John back or we stay out.'

Mr Daniels rubs his eyes. 'This is just a misunderstanding. Jim here has got a bit confused. I told him to give him a ticking off not the sack.'

The foreman, who is loitering behind him, shifts his jaw from side to side uncomfortably. 'Aye. I got the wrong end of the stick.'

Bill enjoys the foreman's discomfort for a moment; he was prepared to take the rap to protect Mr Daniels. Why did he ever let him bully him? He was no more frightening than a small dog barking from behind his master's boots. 'So he can come back then?'

Mr Daniels fixes on Bill. 'He can come back.'

Bill is not in the least bit intimidated. He feels full of himself and celebrates with the others as Mr Daniels retreats into the building.

Dermot and other welders shake Bill by the hands. 'Well done, son. Do you want to tell John the good news? I'll wager he'll be down The Crow.'

'Aye,' Bill says with a laugh. For the first time since he arrived he feels as if he belongs with them.

*

Bill braces himself against the next coughing fit. He digs his fingers into the bricks, hoping he can exercise some control over the mucusy phantoms in his body. But it is useless: he rears forward and coughs again. His eyes water and cheeks quiver. It is as if someone is wrenching and tugging and squeezing his lungs.

*

The meeting has already started by the time Bill arrives. He tip-toes down the steps so as not to disturb anyone. The hall is small and smoky. Thomas is addressing a gathering of about fifteen comrades; there are a couple of young men in dirty slacks and shirts and some other older men and women, who look like teachers or office clerks. A few are puffing on Woodbines. He spies Len and Lizzie at the front and waves. He leans his bottom against a dusty table covered in pamphlets and a bucket for donations.

'There are less than six hundred thousand owners of land in Britain. Of those, at least five hundred thousand are small land users, cultivating holdings below a hundred acres. And the minority who monopolise the soil of their country got hold of it in some curious ways. Some large estates were granted by kings of previous years to peers who undertook care of their mistresses. Others were obtained by peers supplying the king with straw for his bed.'

Thomas's shiny forehead is reddening and dark patches are growing under his shirt. It is not so much nerves as exuberance. He throws his arms around to explain his points, only stopping to consult his scrunched-up notes in his hand every now and then. His bad leg drags as he shuffles from one side of the room to the other but he shows no discomfort.

'The Enclosure Act was more important though, comrades. It appeared the lord of the manor and the village labourer had the same rights to apply for land. But in practice the lords took virtually all of it. By 1845 no less than three hundred thousand acres of common land had been taken from the working class.

Only two thousand acres were then re-allocated to cottagers. They took the rest and have kept it ever since. This means that today the vast majority are landless. So I ask again, whose country are we again and again asked to defend?'

A lass gets up at the back and Bill takes her place.

Thomas starts talking about money. Facts and figures gleaned from newspapers and books come tumbling out of him in great gushes. He barely has to look towards the ceiling or close his eyes to concentrate his mind – he knows them so well.

'As with land, so with money. The total value of private property in England and Wales is eighteen billion pounds. One per cent of the population over twenty-five in England and Wales owns fifty-five per cent of the total.'

After he finishes speaking there is a discussion about getting Labour to address the issue of land ownership. Some say they cannot be trusted anymore. Others argue ILP MPs have no choice but to try to persuade their Labour Party comrades.

As the meeting is drawing to a close, one of the young men, who has not spoken yet, sticks his hand up and says, 'What you're forgetting is that working men are too ground down and beaten down. They are just looking for their next meal – not land reform.'

Bill thinks of the strike and how quickly the workshop emptied. He signals he wants to speak. 'Well it might seem like that at first, but take my word for it – workers can go from moaning to fighting in the blink of an eye.'

The chairman, a willowy fellow with sunken cheeks, asks, 'What do you mean, comrade?'

Bill tells them about the strike and takes particular pleasure in describing the way Bob walked, head bowed, back to his office with the shouts and cries of his men in his ears.

Thomas catches with eye and adds, 'The people of this city are beginning to raise their gaze from ground. But they cannot stop with the factory owner, they must look towards parliament.

We need more ILP MPs.'

The young worker seems satisfied and so the chair moves on to practical matters. 'A vacancy has arisen for the role of propaganda secretary, comrades. We need someone to take charge of delivering the *New Leader* to miners on a Sunday. Any takers?'

Not one person volunteers. The chair and Thomas look pleadingly at Bill. While he only has a few days off a week, he reasons that it is an important job.

'I'll do it but I haven't got a bike.'

'Marvellous, comrade. I'm sure someone can find you one.'

*

Once the coughing subsides, Bill lets his arms drop and slides down the wall, too weary to get up and too feverish to sleep. Purse is snoring now; it is a low, rumbling, menacing sound. He imagines him on his back, nostrils flared and flabby chin glistering with frothy spit – a dragon in his cave.

*

The chain is rusty and the wheels are a little warped but Len's bicycle gathers up speed coming into Biggin. Bill ducks under washing lines draped with trousers and shirts drying in the spring sunshine and passes four little girls paddling in a sooty steam. He stops at the first house he comes to and pulls out a copy of the *New Leader*.

A small boy opens up; he can't be more than seven. 'Who are you?'

'I'm here with the paper for—' Bill checks the name Thomas pencilled in the top corner '—Mr Arthur Walley.'

'You ain't a bit like the other delivery boy. He was taller, like.'

Bill is taken aback for a moment; he is the new ILP propaganda secretary not the delivery boy. But standing there with the

New Leaders in his knapsack and his bike outside it suddenly occurs to him that the child might be right.

'Actually I'm the new propaganda secretary.'

A man's voice from somewhere inside the dark house calls out, 'Propaganda what? Who the hell is it, George?'

'It's the paper boy, Da.'

'Show him in then, George. I've got the money here.'

Arthur Walley is sat in a deep, steaming bath beside a glowing coal fire. His skin is stained black; only the pink around his eyes are visible. He looks like something you might see in a circus or carnival. His wife kneels beside him squeezing clothes over a large bucket.

'Here's your paper, Mr Walley.' Bill puts it on the table.

'Would you like a cup of tea, son? It's a long ride from Gateshead.'

Bill sits at the table and averts his eyes as Arthur washes himself.

'Don't worry about me, lad. In the socialist world to come we won't be embarrassed and ashamed of our bodies.'

Bill blushes. 'Well I didn't think of that. Sorry.'

His wife giggles and places a mug in front of Bill. 'Hadaway, Arthur.'

Arthur starts scrubbing his back with a large wooden brush. 'Last couple of months they've been driving us harder and harder. They say we got more orders or something. Anyhow, there was a little explosion on Wednesday night. A pony boy, a collier and two borers were nearly trapped. They got out unharmed but it's only a matter of time.'

Bill gulps down his tea. 'What's the mine company doing?'

'The owners know all about it. But no man wants to risk losing his home. All the houses are owned by Biggin Mines. I just want the story in the *New Leader* so if something does happen there'll be a record of it. Can you help me?'

Bill pulls out his notebook. He is glad he accepted the job.

This might be his way in to writing for the *New Leader* like Thomas. 'Aye, it would be honour.'

*

The screws have put Purse next door deliberately. For them it is entertainment; a form of sport to pass the time. Bill has seen it before: enemies put together; bullies paired with their victims; rivals made to share single cells.

On his second night in Durham he witnessed a terrible beating, which still haunted him. A mild-mannered office clerk who had been caught kissing one of his student lodgers was placed with a young pick-pocket known as Burrows. The screws teased Burrows. They said the pair of them would only need one bunk. They said Burrows had asked to be placed with the clerk. The rest of the wing joined in and made his life unbearable. At about midnight the clerk got up to the use the chamber pot. Burrows leapt up and accused him of trying to bugger him in his sleep. He beat him unconscious with a boot. It took more than three screws to pull Burrows off the clerk. Bill glimpsed the blood-covered body when it was taken to the infirmary: Burrow's heel had left neat square gashes all over his face and his eyes were swollen and closed.

*

Bill falls into an armchair opposite Len and Thomas. His body reverberates with the noise of the workshop and his mind is groggy. There are a few frayed political pamphlets on the table in front of them but Len appears to have a more important issue on his mind.

He waves a typed sheet at them. 'Have you seen the Bradford conference motion?'

Bill says, 'What's that?'

'There's going to be a vote on leaving the Labour Party.'

'The ILP?'

'Aye.'

Lizzie takes the sheet. 'This is a mistake. What can we achieve outside Labour?'

Thomas is next to read it. 'I'm sorry, Lizzie. I find myself in agreement. We can't let ourselves be compromised anymore.'

'I'm the first to criticise them but it's not all been bad. We've had more free places at grammar schools. Florence has benefited from that.'

'All true. But that doesn't excuse what they've done to the unemployed. The cuts made families destitute. You saw it in your classrooms. I saw it on the street. Then when things got worse because mothers couldn't buy anything but margarine and sheep brains they proposed more cuts. Then MacDonald...'

'I know all this, Thomas. I know it. I don't need a history lesson. I'm as furious with MacDonald as you. I just think disaffiliation is a mistake. What can we do by ourselves? We are better in a mass party fighting for socialism than outside it. Pure but alone.'

Len paces up and down excitedly. 'But don't you see, Ma, they are making it impossible for us to stay. They are saying ILP MPs will not be allowed to vote against Labour. If we agree to that, there will be no point in the ILP. Our MPs would have been forced to vote for the Anomalies Bill, the Economy Commission and the Education Bill.'

Lizzie throws her hands open. 'Do you remember what we said to Frank, that the ILP's mission is to convert the Labour Party to socialism? Have we failed? Or given up?'

Bill picks up the sheet. To him disaffiliation makes sense; what does the ILP have to gain from a party that cannot even hold on to a working-class seat like Gateshead? 'They've failed. They've given up.'

'But millions still look to the Labour Party,' says Lizzie.

Bill thinks quickly. 'Do they really? They lost in Gateshead. The fact is workers are finding out the hard way that they have no choice but to fight for themselves.'

'Strikes will not change things by themselves, Bill. We need a new government not walk outs.'

'They helped my workmate which is more than you can say for Labour.'

Len puts his hand on his mother's shoulder. 'Attitudes are changing, Ma.'

Bill picks up the empty teapot. The others barely register his exit and carry on arguing.

Florence is in the kitchen. Something makes Bill stop dead. He watches her from the hall; she is making herself a sandwich. She saws carefully through Thomas's dark bread, lays two rough slices on a plate and smears butter over them. His skin prickles with excitement, perhaps because she cannot see him, or perhaps because she has seen him but is continuing with her task anyway.

Her head moves to the side. 'Bill...'

Dust tickles his throat and he starts to cough. But he feels he should offer an explanation. 'The pot needs a refill.'

Her expression is a strange mixture of amusement and disdain. 'I thought what you did at the factory was very brave. Thomas and Len have been talking about it for weeks.'

'Thanks.'

Bill senses the conversation is coming to an end; he feels silly and wishes he had never left the fireside discussion. He searches for something else to say. 'I finished your book at last.'

'Book?'

'Percy Shelley.'

She takes a bite of the bread. 'Oh aye, I remember. Did you like it?'

'Aye.'

She lowers her voice to a whisper. 'Does all that talk in there interest you?'

'Aye it's just the pot... it needs...'

'You said, Bill. If talking could change the world the red flag would be flying over Gateshead town hall by now.'

He smiles. 'Don't you care about the ILP?'

'Thomas wouldn't have it any other way.'

'He didn't make you join.'

'Don't get me wrong I'm a socialist of the heart. But I don't want to give my whole life to the struggle. It takes over every waking moment. But there's so much more...'

'And what's that?'

Florence steps closer as if she is about to divulge a guilty secret. 'I just want to get away from Gateshead. Travel around. See different places and countries. You know Shelley wrote "Mont Blanc" during a six-week tour of Europe?'

'Is that the one about—'

She cuts him off. 'You should get out of here and all. Because you know what? All the ILP's books, pamphlets, newspapers, memos, minutes and meetings might come to nothing. The rich might hang on for as long as we are alive. All Thomas's indignation might not make the slightest difference to anything.'

'I've got too much to do here. Things are about to happen in this city. I can feel it, Florence.'

'Good for you.'

'I'm writing something up for the *New Leader* at moment. The editor might take me on a trial basis, like.'

'There's more to writing than that paper, Bill.'

Bill doesn't want to part on a sour note. 'I can picture you almost anywhere.'

'That's a nice thing to say.'

Thomas calls from the other room, 'Bill? Where's that tea? We're parched.'

Bill doesn't want to squander a chance to get to know her properly. She must like his company as she always finds ways to talk to him. 'But we could go for a walk in the valley on Sunday? It's not Mont Blanc but it's pretty.'

Florence glides around him and laughs with what could be cruelty or faint affection. 'Keep the book – you might learn something.'

*

Bill's eyes flicker as the screw unlocks the doors for morning slopping-out. He realises he must have fallen asleep. Rain lashes the window and a draft racing through the wing makes the hairs on his arm stand on end. He makes not the slightest effort to rise from the sodden sheets; he feels more dead than alive.

*

The union man shakes Bill's hand and manoeuvres his considerable bottom into the seat opposite them. His hand feels like bread dough: soft, puffy and slightly clammy.

He loosens his tie and mops his brow before speaking, 'I'm glad I've finally got the chance to meet you, Bill. Dermot here has been singing your praises.'

Bill takes an instant dislike to him; his double-breasted jacket is flashy and there is something of the spiv about him.

'That little walkout you pulled off when you started here was quite something.'

'It wasn't really my doing, Mr Pope,' says Bill.

'Call me Ted. I'm a worker like you, Bill. Now, I've just had a chat with Mr Daniels. This won't come as news to either you but this country needs to prepare for the worst.'

Bill eyes the big man suspiciously; he sounds more like a Tory than a trade unionist. 'Why?'

'You only need to look at our neighbours, man. Anyhow, Daniels has some big orders from the War Office on the books.

Keep this hush hush, but they need aircraft parts in order to keep up with the Krauts. The last thing he wants is any trouble, if you know what I'm saying. So I have his word that there will be no more sackings. All you need to do is keep your side of the bargain.'

Dermot massages the grey stubble on his cheeks. 'What's that, Ted?'

'We just need to get production back up to what it was before Bill's strike.'

Ted pulls the side of his pale blue jacket, which is caught between the armrest and his stomach, and retrieves a letter and a yellow hankie from his pocket. He mops his brow again and squints down at the letter. 'All the details are here. I've gone through them with the lads at HQ and between you and me we should have no trouble meeting them.'

Dermot looks chuffed. 'That's marvellous, Ted.'

Bill leans towards Dermot. 'Shouldn't we check them before signing up to this?'

Ted licks his lips with his large, swollen pink tongue, which looks like something you might find in a butcher's bin. 'Of course, lads, but it's just rows of figures. We're all on the same side now – even old Bob. We want little old England ready for whatever the Krauts or Frogs or Ruskies throw at us.'

Bill doesn't trust him but he can't challenge on gut instinct alone; if he could just get enough time to go over the figures. 'Could I have them for the rest of day? Run it by the workshop?'

Ted forces a smile, which looks more like the grimace of a man straining on a toilet. 'There's no need for that, lad. I've checked them myself. It's all above board.'

Dermot laughs with faint embarrassment. 'Leave it, Bill. He's our union man. If we can't trust him then who can we trust?'

Bill shrugs his shoulders. 'I didn't mean to...'

'No bother, lad. It's good to ask questions. Do you two want to tell the men the good news? Or shall I do it?'

Bill gets up and walks out. 'I need to get back to work.'

*

The stench of unwashed skin and urine makes Bradley gag. Not wishing to go any further, he beckons with his hand.

'He's sleeping – he won't put up a fight.'

Bill squints in the gloom. Purse is lurking behind Bradley; he is holding what looks like a snapped-off wooden bed leg. Bill is too weak to resist; he prays they make quick work of him. He wants it all – the aching, the fevers, the hunger and the regrets – to end.

*

Bill slings the bag of tools over his right shoulder and pushes the piano onto the cart with the help of the driver. It is heavy and awkward but his body has grown strong at the workshop. Sweat beads form on his forehead and run down his cheekbones.

Thomas stands behind clutching his bad leg. 'You're the only person I could think of asking on a Saturday.'

'Glad to help, pal,' says Bill, watching the cart trundle down the road. 'How do you cope normally, like?'

'This pain comes and goes,' he says.

On the corner of Pilgrim Street, Bill puts the bag down and waits. Thomas gets to a lamppost about halfway up and stops dead.

'I just need to catch my breath,' he calls.

Bill goes back to help; Thomas is rubbing his leg and wincing.

'Give me a moment, Bill.'

Bill puts the bag over his left arm and offers his right arm as support. Thomas clasps it and they inch forwards.

'How did it get like that, Thomas?'

'The government sent me to kill Germans and the ungrateful

bastards tried to kill me,' he says with a chuckle.

Bill doesn't know if he should laugh. 'I didn't mean to pry.'

Thomas fights through the pain. 'I got caught in a shell blast in France. The pain comes and goes. Today it's particularly bad, mind.'

'Da fought in France and all – though he won't talk about it.'

'That's not unusual, Bill. A whole generation of men my age has been silenced by what they saw.'

'How come you can talk about it?'

'I suppose it's because I want to stop it happening again. Hold on, Bill.' Thomas mops his forehead and points to a boarded-up shop down a side street.

'What's that?'

'I grew up there,' he says. 'My father was one of the best piano tuners in the city.'

As they make their way in fits and starts across the city, Thomas tells Bill about his upbringing and the war.

Thomas liked nothing more than to watch his father, Norman, in the workshop. On special occasions he was allowed to accompany him on visits to grand houses; he held his tool bag while his father fiddled with pedals and strings.

Under his tutelage, Thomas became an able tuner. But the piano business was waning and there was not enough money coming in to keep the family in the manner to which they had become accustomed. Thomas did what he could to help – working long hours with his father and knocking on doors. Yet still the shop struggled. His parents became embittered. They railed against the decline of the Great British way of life. They took it in turns to blame Keir Hardy, suffragettes and the work-shy tramps sleeping in the doorway.

When the war started in 1914, Thomas did what was expected of him and joined the Northumberland Fusiliers. But the years of practising scales and bending over dusty pianos in the dimly lit shop had taken its toll: his arms were flabby and skin pasty. The sergeant turned him away. He was forced to leave the hall head bowed with all the other sorry specimens.

Thomas's father was dejected and humiliated: his only son was too weak to fight. He pleaded with General Randolph Selby, who attended the same church, and the sergeant eventually relented.

The training and day-long marches were gruelling but exhilarating. Away from the shop, Thomas lost his boyish fat and grew into a man. Soon he was leading parades and taking part in regimental athletics competitions. Captain Weaver, as he became known, attracted many admiring looks from local girls. And he didn't have to feel guilty about abandoning the family business, because, as his mother told every well-heeled customer who sauntered into the shop, he was defending King and Country.

The farewell dinner was a wonderful occasion with large helpings of beef and endless mugs of beer. There was raucous singing and wild dancing. Thomas joined in with gusto and danced with ten or so different women.

The next day, however, he left for France. They were billeted in a desolate place called Fricourt, surrounded by rusting equipment and tents full of injured men with rotting wounds and shellshock. He spent that first night trying to work out his chances of survival as rats the size of rabbits nibbled at the rock-hard shortbread biscuits his mother had packed for him. Perhaps a quarter killed, a quarter wounded, a quarter captured? His grim calculations kept him awake all night.

Yet when his time came, he went, without protest. As warm rain fell and leaden clouds crowded out the sun, Selby wished them the best of British luck. Later, on the march, he imagined Selby and the other generals pushing bits of wood around a map and making life-or-death decisions; they were only human; they might order an advance without fully knowing what might happen; they might drink too much port at lunch and make a terrible tactical blunder; they might reluctantly elect to sacrifice a platoon to make gains elsewhere. Anything was possible.

As the men closed in on the trenches they were engulfed by unfamiliar and terrifying sounds: explosions and blasts so powerful that the earth in front of them was pulled apart and forced back together again.

Two yellow-eyed wagon horses emerged from a cloud of dust and debris when they stopped to receive orders. The horses careered towards them, legs splitting and buckling. Thomas, who had always loved to tend to horses in the street outside the shop, attempted to bring them to a halt. It was only then that he realised that where their heads should have been was a mass of severed arteries and bones. They collapsed and died at his feet.

The sight shocked him to his core but it was only a harbinger of what was to come. His platoon was sent over the top after a furious bombardment that lit up the sky. When they reached the first German trenches they discovered they had collapsed under the barrage. The men picked their away across the freshly churned earth. Most of the German's had been buried, but they found two blinded men submerged in the debris. They pleaded and cried in breathless German when they heard Thomas's platoon. He ordered his men to dispatch them because they were so badly injured. As they lifted their Lee-Enfield rifles, he stumbled away to be sick.

The German soldiers further back, however, had not been defeated. Soon shells started pounding the ground near the killings. In the confusion the men scattered. Some dived into craters, some tried to retrace their steps, others ran forward to their deaths. Thomas was blown sideways. When he came to he was laying in a mound of mud. He dug his legs out with his pistol and half-crawled and half-slithered back towards the English trenches, through smoke and under barbed wire. Miraculously he made it into the arms of a young British private sent to survey the damage to the platoon, but his leg was shattered beyond repair.

When he returned home on crutches, he informed his parents that he had become a vegetarian as he couldn't bear the sight of flesh. He told them the war was a deranged slaughter. They tried to send him to a psychiatrist but he refused and moved out of the shop. On the day he left his mother cried but his father didn't even look up from the piano he was working on. He muttered his son had become a Bolshevik. It was the last word he ever spoke to him.

The following week Thomas joined the Independent Labour Party. He admired their stance against the war. Their members – factory workers, school teachers, office clerks, dockers, university students – had been sentenced to hard labour for their ideals. He stopped attending the family church in protest at the vicar's warmongering and the presence of General Selby, who had ruffled his hair and told him he was a hero when he hobbled in with his mother on Armistice Day in 1918. Instead, he started going to Quaker meetings. He rediscovered his faith in the long, meandering silences, which were only broken when one of the Friends felt compelled to share their thoughts.

Fuelled by feelings of guilt and a dawning, painful understanding that he knew very little about the world, he resolved to devote his life to learning. In his lodgings in the city centre he read everything he could: Tom Paine, Keir Hardie, Henry Salt, Edward Carpenter, Wilfred Owen, Robert Tressel. He took a special pleasure in reading the writing of those men and women loathed by his parents.

Over time his leg grew stronger and one winter morning he managed to walk unaided to an ILP meeting. He knew he would never be that mobile but it allowed him to earn some money from piano tuning.

He met Lizzie at an ILP summer school in Letchworth outside London. She was everything he wanted in a woman: big-hearted, clever and as desperate as him to overturn the old order. Her parents were both seasoned troublemakers: her father was a shipyard shop steward and her mother was active in the suffragettes. She had followed her into the fight for women's suffrage, but became disillusioned by the upper-class women at the helm. Some of them, to her utter disgust, became flag-draped recruiters for the war. She found that the ILP was closer to her beliefs – and neatly combined her father and mother's rebelliousness.

The summer school took place on a sultry August weekend in a rented stately home, which had seen better days. Thomas first noticed her in an evening lecture about Indian independence given by Fenner Brockway, a talented ILP leader and journalist who had been imprisoned for refusing to fight during the war.

The windows were open and the air was thick with midges and the whiff of stagnant, uncared-for ponds. Thomas sat at the back beside two fat men in their early seventies. They were wearing khaki shorts and matching mauve-coloured shirts. One was reading a cut-out newspaper article by George Orwell. The other one looked like he was asleep; his eyes were closed and his mouth was open.

Brockway walked past the three of them on his way to the front. He was tall with a jutting square jaw. There was something of the noble knight about him – the opposite of his large mauve neighbours.

Brockway had the voice of a BBC announcer; warm, charming and unashamedly upper class, 'As we meet, a great man is leading a movement which may change the world. Mohandas Gandhi and the Indian National Congress have begun a campaign of non-cooperation against British rule. Their aim is to force London to take notice of the India people's desire for freedom and democracy.'

After he had finished speaking, the chair invited contributions from the floor. There was a succession of easy questions. Then Lizzie – unkempt and nervous – stood up.

She asked, 'Will Indian non-cooperation be enough to change minds in Whitehall and the Palace of Westminster?'

All Brockway could do was smile and shrug his shoulders. 'Only time will tell.'

Thomas sought her out at the end but he lost her in the throng around Brockway. He saw her again at dinner and noted with approval she had gone for the vegetarian meal: leek-and-potato soup.

On the last day, a photographer arrived and all the members present were asked to pose for a group shot at the front of the house. Lizzie sat next to Thomas. She said she had seen him at ILP meetings in Newcastle. They agreed to travel back together.

He felt instantly at ease with her: her manner was quiet and calm. She asked him about the war and he found himself reliving feelings he thought he had stashed away in the deepest recesses of his memory.

'It's easy to say now but I wish I hadn't survived. If I'd perished on that muddy field I wouldn't be haunted by the faces of those two blind German men. I'm not exaggerating to say they are with me every moment of every day. I'm the one responsible.'

'What about the generals? The politicians? The public?'

'I gave the order. I had a choice on that battlefield. To kill or not to kill.'

'Wasn't the choice to be killed or kill?'

'That's what they want you to think isn't it? That's how they get young men to kill other young men.'

Later, as night fell on the parched countryside outside, where men still heaped rolls of hay on carts, she told him about the small Quaker school where she worked and the clever working-class children too poor to buy pens or paper. He followed her eyes as they darted from him to the glimmering window.

'It's a wonderful place, Thomas. The children get the chance to learn and when they are older they come back and do things like read to blind people living round the doors. But it's not going to solve anything in the long run. We can only help a few. There needs to be schooling up to sixteen at least. And families need to know they'll not suffer if their young ones are at school.'

The conversation moved back and forth. They spoke about their different upbringings: him, the son of well-to-do shopkeepers; her, the daughter of a suffragette and docker.

As they passed York, Lizzie produced some cheese sandwiches and nuts from her bag. 'I have enough for you.'

'This is lovely. Have you read Bircher Benner?'

'Aye of course.'

Before they fell asleep, Thomas told her Brockway had asked him to write some articles for the ILP paper.

'You must do it, Thomas. It would be great to have some articles on the North East rather than just London.'

When they hauled their exhausted bodies off the train in Neville Street, Thomas knew somehow that she would become his lover.

After crossing the Tyne, Bill and Thomas go past St Leonards. Thomas stops at the large white stone memorial and runs his hands over the engraved names.

'Local people raised money to build them after the War Graves Commission decided they couldn't repatriate all the bodies.'

Bill places the bag at his feet and stands panting. 'How many died?'

'Hundreds died and hundreds more came home...broken and crushed. And that's just from Gateshead. Every street lost sons, husbands and fathers. They reckon seven hundred and fifty thousand British soldiers or thereabouts died overall.'

Bill thinks for a while then says, 'Did any good at all come of it?'

'When I joined I thought I was doing good, Bill. But I was caught up in a squabble between rich men. That's what modern wars are, really.'

Da's words echo in his mind. 'Aren't you insulting the men that died by saying it was pointless?'

'The truth isn't insulting. It is just the truth. And don't let anyone tell you different.'

Bill places his hands on the stone. 'Daniels has been making aircraft parts. The War Office places more orders every year.'

'It's the same across Europe. They preach peace at the League of Nations and to the public but prepare for war in private.'

'But the people don't want it, Thomas. There's no appetite for war. Even Da is quiet.'

'That's what we must cling to, Bill. But where there are nations competing for markets and land there will eventually be war.'

*

Purse pushes a pillow into Bradley's hand and growls quietly into his ear, 'Keep it fucking down. I don't want this on me record. Now hold the pillow over his head and do not let go until I'm done. Got that.'

Bill awaits the softness of the pillow then the first blow.

Bradley glances at the door. 'He ain't moving, marra. I think he must have croaked it in the night.'

Purse shoves him aside and rips off the blanket. Bill's near naked body is grey and white from hunger and fever. He jabs him hard in the ribs. 'Wake up, you conchie bastard? Come on, you conchie bastard? Where were you when our Charlie's legs were blown off?'

Purse's voice grows louder and Bradley dashes to the door.

'They're coming. There's no need if he's dead.'

'I said shut up.'

*

The chairman clears his throat and thumps the table. The boys at the back swapping stories and jokes fall silent.

'Comrades, it gives me great pleasure to welcome the Independent Labour Party chairman and the Member of Parliament for Glasgow Bridgeton, James Maxton, to Gateshead. I hope he doesn't mind me saying but he would make a fine Labour prime minister – except for his scruples.'

James Maxton rises from behind a white-draped table and holds his hands up to quell the applause. He is stick thin and looks ever so slightly frail. His generous jacket is draped over his wiry shoulders and his baggy trousers quiver in the warm summer breeze from a window.

'Thank you for those kind words, Chairman. I'm pleased to be back in Gateshead. This is a wonderful city of which you should all be proud. But we meet as the dark clouds of war gather on the horizon. The same nations that drenched this world in blood just over twenty years ago are rearming and quietly mobilising their armies, navies and air forces. Some want to redraw the map created at Versailles because they want more territory and markets, others want to keep is just as it is because it suits them very well. But let me tell you all this evening the Independent Labour Party will not take sides in this ruling-class carve-up and will oppose any move to war.'

Bill scans the hall. There is not a spare seat in sight; men and women are crowded at the edges and along the back wall. Yet they are all concentrating on Maxton. The silence is intense and powerful; it is as if they are all at church or all holding their breath at once.

Maxton flicks his lank hair back as it falls over his gaunt, serious face. 'We make this pledge in the full knowledge that we will be misrepresented and misunderstood by our enemies in the press and the pulpit.'

Florence rushes down the aisle to a flutter of turned heads. She mouths an apology and searches in vain for somewhere to sit. Bill impulsively edges along his own seat to make space for her; she catches his eye and lowers herself beside him.

'We have every sympathy with Czechoslovakia. We have the same sympathy for them as we had for the people of Belgium in 1914, but we did not see that as the issue. We saw that the war in 1914 was fought for four and a half years as a war to end war and it did not do that. It was fought as a war to make this land fit for heroes and it did not do that. It was fought for democracy and it did not do that, because today the big menace with which we are confronted arises from the fact that the aftermath of the last war was not the spread of democracy in Europe but the spread of more dictators.'

Florence's bare knee is resting against Bill's leg. She doesn't flinch or pull away. It is more than an accidental brush – the guilty leg is angled towards him deliberately. He can feel a slight pressure on his shin as if she is pushing herself softly against him. Bill glances at her face to see if she is trying to get his attention but her eyes are fixed on the front table and Maxton. He can feel each slight movement of her body and the warmth of her skin.

Suddenly, Lizzie has her hand up and is asking a question. 'The ILP has lost hundreds of members since leaving the Labour Party. How can we oppose the war if we are losing influence?'

Florence moves her leg away.

Maxton's eyes narrow for a moment; the question appears to have thrown him or annoyed him – but he responds confidently enough, 'There's a fairly unanimous view in establishment circles we committed political suicide in 1932 and it is true, comrade, we lost some members. But if we hadn't taken that course then we would be in a much worse position. We would still be hitched to a party keen to show it can be as bloodthirsty as the Tories.'

Florence's knee returns to the same position. Bill studies her face again: it provides no clues. He feels guilty for letting his mind wander instead of following the meeting so he concentrates as a sickly woman is led to the front by a young man. She has a grey woollen shawl over her head and her skin is deathly white.

Maxton smiles and urges her to speak. 'Take your time, comrade.'

She holds the man's arm for support and says with a quivering voice, 'My husband died in the last war, Mr Maxton, leaving me to bring up his only son. What can be done to stop war breaking out again, Mr Maxton? It is happening all over again. I don't want my boy here to die far from home like his father.'

Maxton climbs down from the stage and holds her hand. He speaks to her with a tender tone more suited to a private conversation between old friends than a political rally – but the hall is so quiet every word can be heard. 'The vast majority of the people of Europe, like you and me, still want peace. We must keep that flame of hope alive and fan it whenever possible.'

Her son thanks Maxton and then leads her back to her seat. There are cheers and some applause before Maxton invites more questions.

A man with dirty skin and a ragged coat asks, 'But what should we do about Herr Hitler? He would kill the lot of us.'

Maxton returns to the stage and projects his voice, 'We are told we need to go to war against Herr Hitler. But if I went to war against Germany, I would not be going to war against Herr Hitler anymore than we went to war against the Kaiser. I would be killing German working folk and I will not do that.'

Thomas stands to applaud. The rest of line follows and within moments everyone in the hall is on their feet cheering and shouting slogans like 'The workers united will never be defeated' and 'Forwards to socialism'.

Maxton strides off the stage with his scrawny arms held aloft.

Bill forgets Florence and joins the standing ovation. The men and women around him seem so determined and united in their cause. It can only be a matter of time before their resolve wins out.

When he turns, she has gone to sell tickets for the red raffle. He queues up behind a line of young men. She smiles at their jokes and laughs off their compliments. By the time she gets to Bill, he has lost his nerve; he stands in front of her, unsure and awkward. He questions his recollection: was she even aware her knee was there? Maybe it was just playful flirtation, no more meaningful than her exchanges with the men in the queue?

'Bill?'

'Any left for me?'

'There are lots.'

Fumbling desperately in his pocket, he produces a few coins.

She squeezes his hand as he lays them in her palm. 'I'll see you at the dance next week, Bill?'

'Aye,' he says with a nervous grin.

'Felling Hall. Saturday. Don't forget. It could be our last chance to dance.'

*

Bradley drops the pillow in a panic as Purse takes aim; he raises the table leg and adjusts his grip, once, twice, three times.

'You bastard,' Purse says through gritted teeth steeling himself for the strike. 'You bastard.'

Just as he is about to bring it down on Bill's skull, Fry arrives on the landing. 'What the hell is going on here?'

Bradley edges along the wall. 'I had nothing to do with it, officer,' he says, nearing the door.

'Be quiet, you little spiv, Bradley.'

Fry is joined by Rogers, who is wheezing after dashing up from the store. 'Shall I contact the medical wing, sir?'

'If you must, Rogers.'

Fry places his hands over Bill's nose and mouth; he can feel the hard tobacco-stained scales of his forefinger against his top lip.

Fry seems satisfied with his slight breath and folds the blanket to cover the fine spirals of blood.

Purse ,who is still standing with the table leg in his hand, suddenly finds his voice, 'Shall I make myself scarce, guv?'

'Aye, the doctor is coming.'

Purse drops the leg; it spins in the air and bounces a few times on the stone stabs. 'I didn't mean to cause any...'

'Go.'

'I don't like his sort...'

'Nor do I, Purse. Now go before our bleeding-heart doc gets wind of this...misunderstanding between you and Rowe.'

Fry kicks the table leg under the bed and returns to Bill's side. 'They'll bury you here, Rowe. And your family, if they can bear the shame, will have to come here to pay their last respects. But I doubt if they would do that for a man like you. For a coward. No. No. No. They will stay away and your grave will—'

'Get away from that man, you bloody idiot.' Doctor Neave strides purposefully into the cell; he is tall with grey hair and thick black glasses.

Fry stands back uncertainly. 'I was just checking his breathing, Doctor. There's—'

'I don't care. What's your name? Oh yes, Mr Fry. I can tell you from here that he has tubercles bacillus.'

'Sorry, Doctor?'

'TB, Tuberculosis, Consumption,Vampirism. He should have been isolated on the medical wing. It's incredibly infectious.'

Fry stumbles over his words as he rushes to get his excuses out. 'The men thought he was putting it on to avoid work. He's in here for refusing to fight. He's a coward.'

Neave removes his glasses and points them at Fry like a sword. 'I don't care a damn about him or any of the other miscreants on this wing. But we are going to have an outbreak in this prison if you do not take more care. And an outbreak of TB will not look good for me or you. Do you understand me, Mr

Fry? Now keep this door shut until the orderly arrives.'

*

Bill watches his fag smoke curl upwards, drifting around the large dangling lamps and edging along the vaulted ceiling towards the skylights. He enjoys pinching the burning fag between his fingers and flamboyantly flicking the ash, more than actually smoking it.

The wooden boards in the hall vibrate pleasantly as couples move back and forth, but he doesn't feel like joining them because he is waiting for Florence. He checks the door again. Could she have had second thoughts? Or perhaps he had misunderstood entirely and she was coming with someone else.

A small woman approaches. He recognises her from the branch meeting; her name is Doris. She is athletic and not bad looking.

She nervously curls her hair in her finger as she speaks, 'I liked your article about that mine in the *New Leader*.'

'Thanks. I hope it's the first of many.'

She turns to admire the red and gold banner behind the band, which says ILP Gateshead Unemployed Workers' Rights Committee. He notices her friends giggling and glancing over from the other side of the hall.

'It's a ladies excuse-me dance isn't it...'

'I'm not in the mood tonight, Doris. I'm feeling a bit out of sorts.'

She smiles weakly, then walks back to her friends.

Bill lights another Woodbine and coughs as he draws the smoke down into his lungs. He watches her friends summon up the courage to approach men. Girls – even socialists – are not used to taking the lead. Sometimes it is hard to imagine the more-equal world of Lizzie's dreams.

A cool hand touches his: it is Florence. She must have come in unnoticed. She pulls him gently into the edge of the hall where only the glowing embers of his fag can be seen and whispers into his ear, 'When did you take up smoking?'

'The lads I work with all smoke. It just appealed to me.'

'It makes you look older.'

She pushes herself against him and kisses him on the lips. Unlike her hands, her lips are warm and pillow soft.

'Let's get out of here, Bill. I fancy a walk. It's lovely out.'

Bill is flustered – he had not expected that kind of a greeting. 'The dancing will pick up in a moment, I'm sure.'

'Come on, it's nothing to be scared of. I've not been with a man either.'

Bill laughs nervously. Sometimes it appears she can see his innermost thoughts and feelings – the ones that are normally safe behind layers of flesh, bone and skin.

'Well, it is getting a bit hot in here,' he says, as if to convince himself.

They tiptoe along the back of the musty curtains that line the hall and leave by a side door. A nearby park draws them into its dank, verdant heart. On a grassy bank surrounded by thick brambles they spread their coats over clenched little white daisies and lolling dandelions.

Undoing her blouse slowly, she says, 'Did your Ma ever talk to you about the facts of life?'

Bill looks away. 'She thought lust was sinful. But I heard them sometimes in the bed opposite. I don't think she liked it much.'

She stokes his forehead and neck. Her other hand works its way falteringly down his body. Too nervous to touch her back, he lets her explore underneath his clothes.

'There was talk of it in the workshop. The unmarried men were always bragging about what they had done with different mill girls.'

She rests a finger on his mouth. 'Just remember to...take it out before.'

Her touch is a fumbling yet determined. When he is ready, she lies on her back, hitches her skirt up and guides him into her. She gasps but he loses control almost immediately; his body straightens and breathing quickens. She pushes gently at his hips but he cannot stop himself. He rolls off her and looks down at his shrivelling manhood. While he does up his shirt, she pulls her underwear up and dusts down her coat.

'I'd better be off, Bill. They'll be wondering where I've been.'

'Sorr—'

'Don't say it, Bill. It was still lovely.'

He watches as she pushes her way past the brambles; one spiky tentacle catches her bare calf leaving a line of red dashes.

She turns and smiles shyly. 'It's a funny business, isn't it?'

'Will I get to see you again?'

'Aye.'

The undergrowth closes behind her and she is lost to the night. He feels relieved; he has done the deed. He no longer needs to stay quiet when they joke about it in the workshop. But he has no desire to talk about her in the same way they talk about other girls; she is different.

*

The light is white and searing. Bill is desperate to block it out or roll over but his arms and legs are unresponsive. Instead he squeezes his eyes shut; dark shapes move across the red insides of his eyelids.

'He's coming to, Doc.'

Fingers roughly pin open his eyes and the light dazzles him again. It is excruciatingly painful – like looking up at the sun.

'Hello, Mr Rowe. Hello, Mr Rowe.'

Bill struggles to form words; the light is disorientating and his tongue feels like the surface of a digestive biscuit: dry and rough.

'Hello, Mr Rowe, this is Doctor Neave. I saw you earlier. In your cell. Do you remember?'

Bill can only breathe in response and even that feels like an effort.

'You have a very serious condition. The guards didn't realise. But you're now in the isolation wing of the infirmary. All your needs will be taken care of by the orderly. If you need anything ring this bell.'

Bill again tries to speak. This time his throat muscles move: a weak, strangled croak escapes from his lips.

The lamp is pushed away. For a moment he fears that he has been blinded as he cannot see a thing, yet eventually his new world comes into focus. The doctor is standing over him; he looks a little like a white-coated giant; his black-rimmed glasses and silver stethoscope glint in the light.

'Mr Rowe, did you say something?'

Another croak.

'Look, don't try to speak, you need to rest. You are severely emaciated and dehydrated. This chap here will help you if you need anything.' He gestures towards an elderly man standing by the door. 'Is that clear? Jolly good. Now get some sleep.'

Bill blinks and sinks into his thin pillow as they leave. As far as he can tell he is the only person on the wing. Moving his head is too much effort so he stares at the ceiling, where electric bulbs burn and fizz in metal lamps.

His eyes open and close; he sleeps; he wakes; he sleeps again. Images of Tyneside – of water the colour of stewed tea and rusting red boats; of wooden cargo boxes, giant cranes and metal foundries; of old men playing dominoes, bare walls and spilt ale – come and go.

*

Bill wipes his forehead and loosens his shirt ready to vault the wall. He stops when he hears a back door in another yard creak open. Florence's neighbours are bound to come out if they see him leaping over. For a moment he considers turning back but he wants to see her again; he can still feel her hips pushing against his and taste the freshness of her mouth. He waits until he hears the door closing then hauls himself up in one go, scraping his legs on the bricks. On the top he lies flat for a second then slides down the other side landing in a warm haze of dry soil. The dirt clings to the fine hairs of his thighs and mixes with the blood of his knees and shins.

A familiar voice greets him. 'Come in before somebody sees you.'

The contrast between the brightness of the yard and the gloom of the house is striking. At first he cannot see a thing. Clammy hand in clammy hand, she leads him, without saying another word, though the scullery, the front room and up the stairs.

As his eyes become accustomed to darkness, he follows the back of her head, the way her hair bounces up and down, on the white stem of her neck. His mouth is dry with anticipation, which is only heightened by the secrecy; an animal-like desire takes hold. He thinks about thrusting her down on the landing, kissing her furiously, pushing himself into her, satisfying her in the way he failed to do on the grassy bank.

Yet, as he glances to his sides, he can see Thomas and Lizzie and Len everywhere: socks drying on the banister, books piled up and mail waiting to be opened. His stomach begins to turn and he feels sick.

He lets go of her hand. 'Flo?'

Her head swings gently, green eyes glinting.

'Can we have a cup of tea first?'

She begins to laugh. 'We haven't got long, Bill. They'll be back from the meeting soon. I thought you wanted to spend time with me?'

'Aye, I do. But...'

'There's some Scotch in the attic. Frank brought it round last

Christmas even though he knows Thomas is a teetotaller.'

'I'm not sure anymore.'

Bill doesn't just mean the drink; he means everything. His desire is draining away with every second; he wishes they hadn't met in her house after all.

'I had some myself when I couldn't sleep. It's burns a little but it warms you up inside.'

Bill sits on the very edge of her bed while she rummages in the attic. He inspects an old photo on the wall: a young-looking Thomas and Lizzie are sitting, quite formally, in a group of people outside a stately home. In the background is a cumbering stone wall and an overgrown pond. Their monochrome eyes glare accusingly at him. They had treated him like one of their own; they had fed him and educated him; they allowed him to take the pick of the books on their shelves. And yet he is about to lay down with their unmarried daughter for the second time.

Florence appears, cheeks pink from the efforts of climbing up the ladder, she is holding a glass and a bottle. He accepts the glass hoping it will banish his sense of impending betrayal. She turns the photo around as she passes.

The Scotch makes him cough and sputter. He doubts if he will ever be man enough to drink in a pub. 'I can't drink this stuff. It makes me think of Da.'

'Give it to me then.'

She throws it down her throat and sits beside him on the bed. A hairline fracture in the curtains is allowing a sliver of light. Her blouse is open exposing a triangle of fine, almost translucent skin at the base of her neck. Tiny veins lead down to the swell of her breasts.

She follows his eyes and lifts his hand from his lap. He trembles as she places his hand on her right breast. He can feel her nipple pushing through her blouse.

She leans forward to kiss but Bill is suddenly overcome with the suspicion that this might be all a cruel joke. She could have had any of those lads at the meeting; why did she choose him?

'Why are you doing this?'

The question startles her and she drops his hand. The pleasant faraway look that had settled on her face fades into something akin to irritation. 'What do you mean?'

He coughs, wishing he had some water to wet his tightening throat. 'I mean you're older than me and bonny. Why me and like this? You could wait and get married to a handsome university lad or something?'

She smiles sweetly, instantly regaining her calmness. 'You're kind, Bill, and I'm ready. Don't believe everything you hear in church.'

'I don't.'

'Life is about living, not fretting about *Das Capital* or the Bible.'

'We can't just ignore the world...'

'War is coming, Bill. So let's enjoy each other while we can.'

'But Flo...'

She places her finger on his lips like she did in the park. Her touch tickles and this time empties his brain of troublesome thoughts.

'Come a bit closer.'

He leans towards her and they start kissing. The curtains ripple as the air between them is displaced.

*

The darkness is thick like the moments between reels at the Picture Palace. Bill puts his hands out in front of him, expecting to find something solid, but they plunge into a black void. He moves his arms to his sides where they also meet no resistance. Without bricks to reassure him, or mortar lines to follow, he is lost. Has he been moved in his sleep?

Instinctively, he brings his hands back to his body. At least he can be sure of his own face; his features are familiar but his skin feels waxy, pitted and unreal. Like the orange he was given as a boy when he fell ill. His thinning hair is fused in long rough strands, made brittle with crystallised sweat.

He picks up on movements out there in the darkness; the air shifts as unknown things make their way past him and around him. A screw? A prisoner? Surely not in his cell at night?

Then he hears it: heavy breathing. It is animal and gruff, like an injured, aging bull, or a broken-down, hobbling mare. The beast, or whatever it is, comes to rest in front of him.

*

Bill produces a small package from his coat as fish-and-chip paper and tin cans clatter down the street in the wind. He has spent an age choosing Florence a present; it is special but not so special as to arouse suspicion. He runs his fingers over a folded-up sheet of paper in his pocket and knocks.

Len fills the doorway, blocking his path. Bill can immediately tell something is wrong but he decides to bluff.

'Len, pal,' he says over the din of the wind. 'What did you think of Chamberlain's peace mission? He's due back today.'

'What do you want?'

He offers up the package. 'It's for Flo's birthday.'

Len grabs him, digging his fingers into the fleshy part of his upper arm. He yanks him around the corner of the street like an errant child.

'Come with me.'

'What's got into you, Len?'

Len pushes him up against the wall he has been clambering over every Sunday afternoon. Bill goes limp – as a boy he used to go droopy when his father thrashed him because it seemed to put him off his stroke. Len just grips him tighter still.

'I know about your little fling.'

Bill's gaze falls with guilt; he had dreaded this moment. Florence must have spoken to him or perhaps they had seen them together. 'What're you talking about?'

Len shakes him roughly, banging the back of his head. 'Don't treat me like a fool, Bill. Isn't our friendship worth anything? Doris let it slip months ago. She saw you in the park...like rabbits you were.'

Bill begins to feel a little indignant. What gives Len the right to rant at him and to manhandle him in the street? He has done nothing wrong. He has not killed anyone or stolen anything. 'It's none of your business, Len.'

'It is when you lie and cheat. How could you carry on like that behind our backs? How could you pretend you were interested in the ILP when all you were after was my sister?'

Bill's eyes water from the pain. He can feel the Weaver family is slipping away from him. 'I didn't pretend. I meant it all, Len. I've never been more serious about anything in my life. Have you told Thomas and Lizzie?'

Len releases him; his rage seems to have run its course for now. 'No, they still think the world of you.'

'When the time is right we will tell them. I really care for her, Len. I'd like to marry her one day.'

Len steps away. 'I know you...like her. I've seen the letters you've sent. She hides them in her poetry books.'

The drag of heavy footsteps makes them both pause; Thomas rounds the corner. He is sporting a large grin and his cheeks are red from laughing. He doesn't appear to notice Bill's ruffled shirt or the cloudy dribbles making their way down the sides of his nose.

'There you are? Hiding from the gale? Come in, we are about to cut the cake? Glad you could join us, Bill.'

All the chairs are at the edge of the room. There is a large sponge cake filled with cream and strawberry jam on a table. Brightly coloured streamers hang from the ceiling, and light filters in through the faded lace curtains.

Florence glances his way briefly then continues talking to her friend, Sarah, who works in the chemist on Bensham Road. He considers joining them but they are deep in a whispered conversation. Thomas is positioned next to Frank on the other side of the room. Bill weighs up his options before sitting down next to the two men. He doesn't want to upset Len after they came so close to blows.

At Lizzie's request, Thomas goes to the piano; he complains that it reminds him of work before leading them through a verse of "Happy Birthday to You" and "For She's a Jolly Good Fellow".

Once the cake is shared out, Florence gets up abruptly. 'We need some more coal for the fire. Bill, can you help me?'

Bill can see Len scowling but follows her out into the garden. Her friend smiles supportively at him as he passes as if to say she knows everything but doesn't mind. Indeed he feels like everybody in room is studying him and judging him. Although Thomas and Lizzie can't suspect anything.

Outside, the wind is stronger than ever. Florence flicks her hair out of her face just like the first time they met but on this occasion she pulls him behind the coal shed.

'I've missed you.'

'Me too but—'

Before he can finish his sentence, she kisses him fiercely and presses herself against him. He hardens as she slips her right leg between his legs. He lets her linger a while; her scent and heat are hard to shun. But he knows he must tell her about her brother.

'Len knows.'

For the first time he sees a suggestion of doubt he her eyes. It is a rare sight because she is so normally so sure of herself.

'How?'

'We were seen going into the park.'

She steps back and checks they are alone. 'He won't tell them.'

Bill strokes her arm. 'Would they even mind?'

She looks past him, deep in thought or looking for an excuse. 'I'd like to keep it a secret for now. I don't want to explain myself to anyone.'

'We've done nothing wrong.'

'I know,' she says, holding his hand. 'But what Thomas says about marriage and what he actually thinks is best for his only daughter are two very different things.'

Len's ghostly face drifts across the back window. She releases him and turns to face the house.

'Hold up, Flo. I wanted to give you something,' says Bill rummaging in his pocket.

'Not now. Let's get back before they suspect something.'

Later, as the wind rattles the window frame, Frank turns to Thomas and Bill. 'Can we listen to the wireless? The PM should be landing now.'

Thomas gets up and turns the dial on the Phillips wireless in the centre of the room. Lizzie and Florence pull their chairs closer as if they were children listening to an elderly relative at Christmas.

'Circling round up above now in very dirty and murky skies is the machine bringing the prime minister back to Heston. And we're going to wait a minute or so before it comes down. We were all waiting very happily about twenty minutes ago under a rather threatening sky but not a particularly bad one. Suddenly rain began to fall and it got harder...'

Florence rubs her eyes with a theatrical exacerbation. 'I'd rather dance to a waltz or something than listen to this drivel about the rain.'

'Quieten down,' Lizzie says.

'What does it matter anyway? Politicians wage war if they want to. We can't do a damn thing to stop them.'

Frank frowns in irritation. 'He's landed now and is going to speak soon. I'd rather listen to him than your slogans.'

Under her breath, she mutters, 'We all know what he's going to say anyway.'

'They are beginning to wave now. Off come the hats. Just in the nick of time, Lord Halifax has arrived in a small American car. Mr Chamberlin is smiling and beaming. The crowd has got through the police as we knew they would and they are all streaming around the plane...'

'This is so tiresome,' interrupts Florence. 'What a marvellous man.'

'Quiet,' snaps Thomas. 'I can't hear.'

Bill finds himself agreeing with Thomas; Florence is clever and feisty but can be quite petulant if she doesn't get her way.

'I want to say that the settlement of the Czechoslovakian problem, which has now been achieved is, in my view, only the prelude to a larger settlement in which all Europe may find peace.'

Once Chamberlin has finished speaking, Thomas turns down the volume a bit. 'This agreement. Do you think it will hold?'

Frank sighs. 'Hitler will have to be confronted one way or another, Thomas.'

'So there's no chance of peace?'

'I'm sorry to say I can't see it lasting.'

Bill shakes his head irritably; Frank is talking about war as if it is a regrettable yet inevitable natural disaster. But giving orders to build aircraft and bombs and to recruit and arm young men are not like storms and floods – they are choices by generals, industrialists and governments. 'By confronted, do you mean Germans will have to be killed?'

Thomas gets in first. 'That's precisely what he means.'

Frank, however, is not impressed. 'Why are you filling these boys' heads with such poppycock, Thomas?'

'I'm no boy,' says Bill curtly. 'I work for a living.'

Frank rests the bottom of his nose on his hands as if he is deep in thought or praying. He seems to be relishing the attention his pause has brought. In time, he says to Bill, 'What do you know of war?'

Bill, however, has seen him pull the same trick on others and doesn't let it get to him. 'It destroys people. Look at his leg, and my Da's lungs. Look at the war memorial. That's all I need to know.'

Frank smiles with the kindly condescension of an elderly man indulging his grandchildren.

Thomas eyes him with annoyance. 'Bill here has got principles. Remember them?'

The two old adversaries fall silent for a while although Frank cannot allow him to have the last word. 'Why are the ILP indulging Chamberlain? The man is a bloody fool. He's giving Hitler everything he wants.'

'The ILP won't vote for this agreement.'

'But will it vote for Attlee's motion opposing it?'

Len joins in. 'Chamberlain deserves some praise for trying to stop the war but he shouldn't have let it get to this point.'

'You're dancing on the head of a pin.'

Thomas puts his hand up, perhaps aware that the argument is growing louder and taking over his daughter's party. 'We just don't want another war. Do you remember what the last one was like? Ten million died and it laid the foundations for this mess.'

'Look, Thomas, it's a relief we aren't fighting yet. Of course it is. Only an idiot would say otherwise. But this isn't peace in our time. This is a victory for brute force. Hitler cannot be allowed to invade other nations and crush democracy.'

Florence spins the dial on the wireless. There is a blast of static, which sounds as if a large sheet of paper is being crumpled into a ball. Then she flicks the off switch and the room is quiet again.

'That's enough, please. You're all shouting. There's plenty of time for worrying about Munich. Can we forget for one day at least?'

Bill makes his excuses shortly afterwards. There isn't going to be another opportunity to talk to Florence and he doesn't want to undermine his apparent truce with Len. He places her gift on the table beside the half-eaten cake. It is a leatherbound journal. He glances at her longingly as he closes the door.

Alone in the hall he suddenly remembers the paper in his pocket and finds himself going upstairs. It is a silly and risky thing to do but he wants her to read his poem tonight. Her bedroom is untidy; there are socks and woollen tights on the floor. As usual, the photo of Thomas and Lizzie at the stately home follows him as he steps over her clothes. Impulsively he picks up one of her dresses on the bed and brings it to his face. It smells of soap and the oil she puts in her hair; he recalls her naked body against his on the mattress.

A squeak on the stairs makes him drop the dress; he takes one last look at the poem and places it below the sheet so she will discover it when she beds down for the night.

In the corridor he comes face to face with Lizzie.

'I thought you were leaving.'

He hopes she can't tell how flustered he is but he can feel the sweat on his back and under his arms. 'Thomas told me there was a book up here I could borrow.'

She looks at his empty hands.

'It wasn't there.' He squeezes past, anxious to escape.

*

The movements start again. Bill feels air rush over him as if the beast is charging around and around in a frenzy.

It pauses to gather breath. The fear he felt at first ebbs away: it is replaced with compassion and strange sense of closeness. The beast sounds like his father because each breath it takes does not replenish its powers and strength but appears to diminish it and bring it closer to death.

'Da.' His weak, childish voice bounces off clean, hard-scrubbed walls.

The beast does not respond.

'Da? Da? Talk to me. It's your son Bill. I know talking isn't easy for you. What's the matter?'

*

At the top of the stairs, Bill pauses as his door to his lodgings is ajar. He lingers apprehensively; he definitely closed it when he left in the morning. Could one of the other lodgers have gone in to fetch something? He has little worth stealing – just books, pamphlets and clothes – but some of them are desperate creatures.

He pushes the door with his right boot; it creaks and swings on its single hinge. There is a woman's outline against the shimmering blue of the window; she is looking out over the city.

'This is my room.'

'Bill, I was wondering when you would get home.'

'Florence,' he says with some relief. 'I thought you were a...robber.'

'Your landlady let me in. I wanted to say thank you for the poem,' she says flatly.

Bill is embarrassed but also pleased; he hopes she is not just being polite. 'It's about the dawn on Tyne Bridge.'

She takes out the paper and starts reading. 'Have you ever seen, the first glints of dawn, in the darkened sky, have you ever stopped to wonder why, natures gift to man, to see to feel to breathe, the freshness of another day—'

'Enough,' he says with a nervous laugh.

They come together and kiss passionately. Bill fumbles impatiently with her blouse buttons but she takes hold of his hand before he reaches her breasts.

'Can we just cuddle tonight? I've got to be back later.'

Bill feels a touch foolish and regrets his impatient manor. 'Aye.'

They lie on his bed; she rests her head on his chest and draws her legs up to keep warm. They watch the moonlight play on window frame and listen to the sounds of men returning home from work; the clip-clop of horse hoofs, the rasp of wheels and the squeals of children greeting their fathers.

Florence pushes her nose and mouth into his neck. 'I shouldn't fall asleep. They will be expecting me. But I can't stand being there at the moment. Thomas has built himself up into frenzy about war.'

Tenderly, to make up for his earlier haste, Bill runs his fingers through her hair. 'Stay a little longer.'

When he wakes, Florence is still half dressed and pressed into his neck. He can hear Mrs Bradshaw clumping around. She normally gets up much later. He dreads her rows with her husband because the screeching echoes through the house.

There is a muffled shout from her husband. 'I'm trying to listen to the wireless...you old bat...the German's are bombing Warsaw...'

Did he hear him right? It shocks him out of the blur of his sleep. 'Could you make that out, Florence?'

'No...'

'Sounds like Hitler's invaded Poland.' Bill untangles himself from her embrace and sits on the edge of the bed. 'I'll try and find out more.'

Florence opens one eye. Her expression is drowsy and strangely sad. 'There's nothing we can do. Stay a little longer. Please. I need to talk to you.'

Bill's head is racing. 'I'm sorry. This is important, Flo. We'll be drawn in soon. We can't rest if we want to stop another war happening.'

Hurriedly he kisses her on the forehead and rushes down the stairs.

The wireless is blaring out of their room. He knocks twice on the door. 'Can I come in and listen, Mrs Bradshaw? It's Bill from upstairs.'

It takes an age for his landlady to come to the door. Instead of opening up to him, she calls though the keyhole. 'Nah, we don't have lodgers in with us. Where would we be then? This is our private area.'

'But this is important.'

'Rules are rules, laddie.'

Bill is eager to know more, and fed up with her petty-mindedness he hammers violently on the door. 'We are going to bloody war. Let me in.'

The whole frame vibrates and Mrs Bradshaw shrieks at her husband to do something. 'He's destroying the house.'

At that moment Florence squeezes past him. Her coat hangs open and her woollen tights are saggy and bunched up; she has thrown her clothes on in a rush.

'Shall we go to yours? Thomas and Lizzie will know what's going on. We can arrive there separately.'

He notices her eyes are red and the skin underneath shiny. She wipes her nose with the back of her hand and skips down the last flight of steps. Her hair is flattened at the back from lying in the same position for so long.

'No, that won't work, Bill. I'll see you when all this has calmed down,' she says, fighting back tears from the entrance hall.

'Florence, I'm sorry—'

She doesn't stay to listen and escapes into the early morning. Bill waits for the door to close before trying again; he can patch things up with her later.

'Please, Mrs Bradshaw. I'm sorry about pestering. I don't know anyone else with a wireless here.'

'Eric, come and see off this boy. He won't go away.'

Bill doesn't hang around to find out what he is capable of – she liked to brag he had been a fireman and a champion boxer in his day.

The street is empty apart from a few vagrants, probably between spikes, sifting through a bin. A police constable watches them from a safe distance. Florence is long gone. Bill runs off in the other direction.

Peggy hugs and kisses him as soon as she gets sight of him and then in the same breath complains he has not been to visit enough.

'I'm sorry.'

She turns and covers her mouth when she coughs as if her illness was a terrible secret. 'I missed you, that's all.'

For a second Bill forgets the news from Poland. 'Did you see a doctor? I've been giving Ma money to put aside.'

'Aye…'

'Are you feeling better?'

'A little.'

'Then you must go back.'

The range is spitting and smoking with a large fire. Ma is at the table folding up clothes

'It's warm in here,' he says.

'Got to get these clothes dry somehow,' Ma says.

'Where's Da?'

'Out and about.'

'Drinking his life away?'

'Don't badmouth your father, Bill. He's out looking for scrap.'

There is only one chair so Bill leans against the table; they must, he realises, be burning the others.

'Have you heard about Poland, Ma? I picked up a special edition of the *Chronicle* on the way.'

She shrugs as if to say there is little point in her taking an interest in things she doesn't have any control over.

Peggy plays with her hair. 'Will I have to be evacuated?'

Before anyone can answer, Da appears in back yard. He must have come from the alley. They watch him inch towards them like a man who has forgotten how to walk. Opening the door, Ma turns away from his stinking breath.

He plants himself on the chair and starts reading Bill's paper. Once settled he decides to acknowledge his son with a nod. 'There'll be a-a-a call up soon, son. Now this phoney war is over.'

Bill readies himself for an argument. 'I'll be staying put, like.'

Ma gestures for him to keep his voice down. She closes the swinging back door as if the neighbours care what he plans to do. 'This is no time to think of yourself; those Krauts have got to be stopped. We fought them once and we will fight them again.'

Da throws down the paper. His voice crackles with irritation. 'Let him have his say. Why, son?'

Bill swallows. 'You of all people should know? Look at you, man? The last war turned you into this...'

Da stands and rolls his shirt sleeves up. He crouches and raises his fists like a prizefighter or circus strong man. 'What y-y-you mean?'

Bill starts laughing. 'You ridiculous old man.'

Ma stands between them; she is tearful. 'I think you had better go, Bill. Why come here and make trouble? We get along just fine without you.'

*

The beast is long gone. Instead of breathing he can hear creaking and something flapping in a strong wind. Is he on a ship? It is still too dark to know for sure. A frosty leaf lands on his forehead.

'Trees. It is trees.' Even though he is alone, he proclaims his discovery out loud. 'I'm in a forest.'

Beneath him the earth is hard and cold. He inhales deeply,

letting the chill in the air fill his body. It feels familiar. It must be Crow Wood. But where are his pals? Are they playing somewhere else? Better get going otherwise he will be late for church. He attempts to lift himself but his arms are rigid and stiff. What has happened? Have his limbs frozen to the ground?

More leaves flutter down and land on his face. They cover his eyes and fill his mouth. Their ragged icy edges prick and scrape in his throat. He starts retching and choking.

*

Thomas is coming to the end of his talk. He limps across the floor and throws his arms about with as much energy as he can muster. He appears even more possessed than usual. It is as if he thinks that through sheer willpower and rage he can prevent Europe's different peoples from slaughtering each other again.

'British capitalists talk a great deal about patriotism but it is always instructive to look at what they have been doing rather than what they have been saying.' Thomas unfurls a newspaper. 'And there's no better way to do that than to read their newspapers. So this edition of the *Financial Times* from five years ago reveals that Britain, France and Poland have been supplying Germany with the raw material essential to her rearmament programme: iron, nickel, copper, tin, aluminium and rubber. In our case, the materials were supplied on credit with the backing of the Bank of England. So take what they say with a pinch of salt.'

After the applause dies down, Bill goes up to him. Thomas hugs him tightly. His normal greeting is a handshake but the declaration of war has upended social customs and rules. He holds him for a long time without saying a word. The smell of sweat, worry and strong tea is inescapable; he pongs like a man who has been awake for days on end.

At last he releases him and says breathlessly, 'Bill, I'm glad you could make it. Have you brought your mask?'

Bill pats the khaki gas-mask hanging on his hip. 'Aye.'

'Take it everywhere, Bill. They put lung irritants, tear gases, sneezing gases and blister gases in these modern shells. Our rulers are good at coming up with new ways to destroy people.'

Close friends and comrades hug Thomas as they leave. They are behaving as if it is the last time they will see each other. Bill notices Florence hovering by the door; they have not spoken since she left his digs in a huff. He has been too busy fretting about his options and reading reports from Poland to make amends. He tries to get her attention but she is in conversation with Len.

Thomas takes the hall keys from the chairman and turns back to Bill. 'Have you heard the call-up proclamation? They are calling men up by the year of their birthday. You need to think about what you are going to do?'

Bill nods in agreement; he is determined not to fight but knows little about the law. 'What happens if you refuse?'

'Conscientious objectors have to go to a tribunal, which can either exempt them from service or send them off to fight,' he says.

'And if you still refuse to go?'

Thomas hesitates as an old comrade seizes his shoulders on her way out. 'Then it's prison I'm afraid, Bill.'

Now Bill understands the hug; the stakes are very high. He looks Thomas in the eye. 'I'm not going to kill young men like me just because they were born under different flags.'

Thomas exhales roughly and holds Bill's shoulders. 'I'll do what I can to help, Bill. We all will. But it won't be easy.'

They embrace again and Bill leaves him to lock up. Outside, Florence is waiting in a doorway. Her breath forms little clouds of moisture in the night air.

'Bill? Do you want walk back with me.'

He is grateful there is no bitterness in her voice. But he can tell something is weighing on her; he is not sure what though; it could be the war or their argument.

'Has Thomas persuaded you to object to the war?'

'It's my choice.'

Her voice trembles with emotion. 'That's what he said to Len and he's going to register as an objector. But they won't show him any mercy. Nor you if you follow him like...like some naive idiot. You're too political, too dangerous. They'll lock you up forever.'

Bill ignores the insult; he can see she is upset. 'I can't run away. They'll find me and it will be much worse. I'll be a coward and a criminal. I'll be all the things they say we are and I'll still end up behind bars.'

'I can't lose both of you,' she says pulling her hand away from Bill.

She does not seem herself. When he had first met her she was so at ease with herself and the world, but in these last few months that calm confidence has all but disappeared. 'Are you worried about something, Flo?'

'Not really. But there is—'

Bill steps in front of her and plants a kiss on her lips. 'I love you, Flo. I'm sorry about the other night.'

She pulls her head away to avoid any more kisses. 'Can we go to your room to talk?'

He frowns and says with some trepidation, 'Mrs Bradshaw still hasn't forgiven me but I keep paying the rent so...'

They make their way to his digs without speaking further. Florence is slower than normal and sounds slightly out of breath. On the stairs she suddenly doubles over and wretches into her handkerchief.

Bill worries Mrs Bradshaw might emerge at any moment. 'Are you sick?'

'I've eaten something disagreeable,' she says, swiftly folding up her wet handkerchief and depositing it in her coat pocket. 'I'll be fine once I sit down.'

He makes a pot of tea in the lodger kitchen as quietly as he can whilst she undoes her coat and leans exhausted on the doorframe.

In his room she sits beside him on the bed, making sure her legs, which were so recently intertwined with his, do not touch.

He sips his tea and pulls out a packet of Woodbines. 'Do you mind?'

She looks straight ahead. 'Go ahead, you always do what you like, don't you, Bill?'

Bill frowns with irritation but continues smoking. 'You can tell me, Flo, if something is bothering you?'

She pulls her coat together suddenly as if changing her mind about staying. 'I want this to stop.'

'What?'

'Us. I don't want it anymore. We are at war and you're going to end up in some army camp or cell… And I don't want to be tied down, Bill. I don't want to get married. I don't want any of it. I'm not even certain I want to see you again.'

Bill feels his chest tighten. Is it the fag or her words? 'Are you going? Is that it?'

She does the last button up. 'Aye.'

'I thought you loved me?'

'I tried.'

Panic and anger rise in him. He is scared how he will feel once she has gone through the door. At the same time he feels incensed that she has this power over him, this hold over his feelings.

'This is your bloody fault, Florence. You led me to that park and up those stairs to your bedroom.'

She stops at the door and retches again as if bitter liquid had been poured down her throat. 'Go to hell, Bill.'

He throws the cup down: the cheap china he stole from the workshop shatters instantly on the black floorboards.

'You can't understand why I would put myself in harm's way because all you care about is yourself.' He goes to the door and hollers at the back of her head as it bobs down the stairs. 'The war is coming and it's up to us to stop it. If not us, Florence, then who will?'

*

Bill can hear birds singing. He is confused and scared. Is he still buried under the leaves in the forest?

'Please help.' His words are breathed rather than spoken.

'Mr Rowe?'

'Where am I?'

'I still can't hear a word you are saying. You are on the medical wing, Mr Rowe. We spoke about this when you arrived. Do you remember? I'm Doctor Neave.'

'What?'

'You are hallucinating. I'll come back in a moment with my colleague. He might learn something from seeing a case like yours.'

Bill tries to calm himself. He surveys his surroundings: the walls are white and the floor is polished. There is a small well-kept kitchen garden, with a large apple tree, beyond large open windows and flapping blinds.

Doctor Neave marches back to his bedside with a companion in a white coat. 'You like our little Garden of Eden?'

Bill is unsure how to respond. He notices an old man filling a large tin can from a bandaged standpipe in the garden. Birds flap and squawk when he starts watering, before settling on the branches of the tree.

'Not what you would expect to find in the middle of a prison I'd wager?'

Bill moves his head from side to side with difficulty.

'Are you feeling better, Mr Rowe.' It is as if he is speaking to an imbecile; each word is emphasized. 'You mentioned all kinds of strange things in your delirium?'

'I don't remember much...'

'Good. I can see you have recovered a little since last week,' Neave says, turning to his companion. 'That's only the third or fourth sentence he has uttered since he arrived. He was in quite a state.'

The other doctor, young with thick curly blond hair, nods. 'Indeed. I can see that from the notes. Now, what is it you need from me, Hugh?'

'Well, I think you'll agree with me this is case of pulmonary tuberculosis. A sanatorium is not possible of course.'

'And the sputum test? Any results?'

'Still waiting – the lab is taking forever.'

'May I inspect him?'

'By all means, but I'm not sure it'll be necessary.'

Bill realises he is not party to this discussion. He is just an interesting specimen. He wants to ask if he has really been here for a week – he has no memory of waking or sleeping or eating. But he hasn't the strength to step out of his role of the helpless invalid.

The young doctor rolls up his sleeves and asks Bill to relax. His arms are muscular and hairless. He pulls Bill's gown apart and listens to his chest with a stethoscope.

'I think, Hugh, the best course of action maybe a pneumothorax. His lungs need a rest to allow the lesions to heal. We will have to move him if you don't have surgical apparatus here.'

'Of course we do. This is not some two-bit operation.'

The two doctors fall silent.

Doctor Neave circles the bed. 'I'll be in touch if we need any more advice.'

'Hugh?'

'Thank you, Doctor Pickett. Shouldn't you be getting back?'

The door swings shut as the younger man leaves. Doctor Neave grips the metal rung at the end of Bill's bed.

'The arrogance of the young,' he grumbles to himself.

Bill swallows and wets his dry lips. 'Doctor?'

Neave seems startled by Bill's voice – as if he had forgotten he was even there. He takes a few moments to reply. 'Yes, Mr Rowe?'

'Am I dying, Doctor?'

Neave's face softens. 'No, Mr Rowe. Not anymore. We will get you through this with a little bit of luck.'

'You don't understand. I don't care.'

The doctor's black brogues squeak uncomfortably on the highly polished floor. 'Don't care about what, Mr Rowe?'

Bill coughs violently and his lungs explode with pain – but he gets his words out all the same. 'Dying or living.'

Bill detects a slight reddening in Neave's clean-shaven cheeks and a twitch in his moustache; perhaps it is not polite to talk about such things in educated circles.

'Pull yourself together, Mr Rowe,' he says with an uneasy chuckle. 'You just need more rest. Would you like something to help you sleep?'

*

Gateshead Labour Exchange is old and shabby. The waiting hall carries the musty whiff of piles of dank, decaying paperwork. Young men crowd around the long wooden counter, worn to a pleasant smooth sheen by thousands of impatient elbows and hands and drumming fingers.

There is a hum of nervous, exited conversation as friends shake hands and slap backs. They ask each other what service they hope to get, where they plan to take their sweethearts and what dance is good this weekend.

Bill checks the doors before making his move; he fears what they will do if they discover his reason for attending is very different to theirs. Pulling his cap down and dropping below his turned-up coat collar, he squeezes through the mass of bodies.

On the other side he approaches a clerk sitting behind a sign, which states: Register of Conscientious Objector. 'I heard the announcement on the wireless this morning. I'd like to register. My name is Bill Rowe.'

The clerk spits his response out as if he chewing on an indigestible gristle of fat. 'Register? Register as what, Mr Rowe?'

'Conscientious objector.'

The clerk raises his voice. 'You cannot declare yourself one, Mr Rowe. Those who wish to apply to join the register can do so here. But you'll have to go before a tribunal, who are charged with rooting out vexatious and disingenuous claims.'

The chatter in the queue dies down. Some of the men nearby take an interest in their conversation.

Bill is trembling slightly, but he keeps his head and rests his elbow on the counter to hide his face. 'I know all this. Do you want my particulars?'

The clerk sniffs and reaches below the counter for a sheet. He fills it out slowly, taking considerable pleasure in explaining every last detail of the registration and tribunal process. 'There are a number of possible decisions the tribunal may reach, Mr Rowe: full exemption; dismissal; exemption conditional on alternative service; exemption only from combatant duties.'

Once the form is completed, Bill tries to get out. The crowd has grown so he has to push with his shoulder, he twists around a few torsos but becomes stuck.

'Excuse, pal, I need to get to the door.'

'Bugger off. I can't move a sodding inch.'

'Can you step out so I can get past?'

'No, you traitor bastard.'

Some lads around him start jostling. A narrow-faced lad shoves him; he stumbles forward. Another one trips him, but there is nowhere to fall, so he crashes into the stomach of a bystander.

'Watch out, you clumsy clot.'

Bill scrambles on his hands and knees to the door. Boots fly in from all directions, striking his sides and head. But he keeps pushing towards the narrow strip of daylight between their legs. The pain in his ribs is intense and more than once he almost collapses. The last men in the queue, however, part, letting him clamber to his feet in the morning sun; they haven't a clue why the others are attacking him and make no attempt to grab him. He half runs and half falls around the corner. To his relief, no one follows. He takes a second to wipe the blood and spit and shoe polish from his face and then sets off again; he has no desire to hang around.

The alley he takes is home to an old sailor's tavern, the Shipwreck Arms. He curses his luck when he sees Walter Kelly and Harry Bags standing outside. It is far too narrow to slip past them unnoticed, and turning on his heels would just arouse more suspicions and lead him back to the Labour Exchange anyway.

Walter pipes up straight away. 'Bill Rowe? Is that you?'

'Aye,' he says, heart sinking.

They both stink of ale and tobacco.

Harry steps forward so their noses are just about touching. 'You look a right fucking mess, man. You been in a fight?'

Bill decides to lie; he is in no state to defend himself. 'I think some bugger shoved a man to the ground in the Exchange. There was a bit of pushing, like. That's all.'

'Have you signed up?'

Bill looks away and coughs up a little blood. 'Nah, the queue was too long.'

Harry puts his hands on his shoulders and grins drunkenly at him. 'I'm going to get in early. Get an easy posting with the Navy, like. I don't fancy living in no trench. Da told us it was hell.'

Bill shrugs himself free. The longer he stays talking to them the more likely it is they will discover his real reason for coming. 'I've got to go. It's too cold to stand around.'

Harry's demeanour changes suddenly again. 'Fuck off then.'

Bill limps down the alley with their laughter ringing in his ears.

*

Doctor Neave retrieves a blue glass bottle from a deep pocket and carelessly scoops out some pills; a couple fall on the floor and roll under Bill's bed.

'Bloody little devils. We are running low on these as it is. Now, Mr Rowe, take these with some water and lay back.'

Bill holds them in his mouth then he transfers them to the back of his throat. What right has this doctor to tell him his own mind? He knows what he wants and it is not sleep. He desires nothingness: no feeling, no pain, no longing.

'For God's sake, Mr Rowe, swallow them down. Or I shall get the orderly in to hold your nose.'

Bill relents as he cannot keep them in his mouth any longer, and after five minutes or so a pleasant heaviness spreads across his limbs.

*

It is late afternoon and sleet is falling. Bill turns away from the cold wetness and rocks back and forth on his heels to keep warm. The sludge covering the pavement is seeping slowly into his boots and woollen socks. He wriggles his toes to keep them warm. Every now and then he shakes his head to dislodge the ice building up on the top of his scarf and the soggy peak of his flat cap.

A woman in a long woollen coat appears at the other end of the street; he strains to make out her face. She is carrying a broken, elegant umbrella. Might it be Florence? She keeps close to the wall where there is less snow on the ground. Metal spokes scrape along the bricks. When she passes him, she lifts the umbrella; great creases and folds cover her face like slept-in bed sheets.

'You don't want to stand around in this weather, bonny lad. Get yourself home before you are frozen to the spot,' she says.

Bill swears to himself before returning his gaze to the Weaver's house opposite. There is a dim glow behind the blackout drapes on the upstairs bedroom. Thomas probably, working on an article for the *New Leader*.

He shakes his hat again and considers going back to his digs. He has to be up early to start work and his body is sore and sleepy. Still, he needs to see her; he is worried about her and wants to make amends whilst he still has a chance.

A couple emerge from the sleet; they are arm in arm. The woman is tall and has wavy hair; the man is shorter and wrapped in a brown coat. Bill is sure it is Florence this time. He retreats into his doorway hideaway and watches them come down the street.

As they near the wind changes direction and blows sleet into his face. They pause outside the door while the man looks for something in his pocket.

Bill pulls his scarf right up around his nose and comes across the street. He moves falteringly – his knees feel stiff and his ribs still ache after the beating at the Labour Exchange. He is not sure what he is going to do but his fists are gripped in his pockets.

'Florence,' he shouts.

Florence and the man look up; it is Len. All three exchange glances while they weigh up what to do next. Florence takes the lead and ushers Len inside, where he goes without a word of protest.

'What do you want, Bill?'

'Florence, please hear me out? I'm sorry about what I said. I know it wasn't all your fault. I wish I could change what has happened. But war is coming. There's nothing I can do to change that.'

'Bill, leave us alone.'

Thomas's voice travels from the bedroom down to the front door, which is slightly ajar. 'Who are you talking to?'

She tells him it is his imagination then murmurs softly to Bill, 'If this family means anything to you then you should stay away.'

'Is that what you want?'

'It is.'

Bill's voice trembles with fury. 'I don't think you ever loved me. You just wanted adventure.'

While holding Bill's gaze, she carefully steps backwards and closes the door on him and the blizzard.

*

He comes round to the sounds of the night: the rush of the trees in the garden and the faint slap of moth wings against the dark glass. It is an odd state to be in – somewhere between wakefulness and sleep. He lets his mind relax and memories return.

*

Bill can hear the union meeting in the workshop but stays put in the yard. The union man's booming voice quivers with emotion as he praises the newfound solidarity between owners and workers. He talks about the better, fairer world which will come to fruition after the fighting has finished.

Bill concentrates on unloading and tries to ignore the cheering. How have they gone from militant strikers to flag-waving idiots? He hauls the boxes to the edge of the lorry, climbs down and then lifts them to the ground. His shoulders ache with each movement.

Ted's voice carries on the breeze once more: he urges the men to contribute to the war effort and make sacrifices. Bill stops and for a moment considers bursting in and pointing out that it is working men of all nations who will be doing all the sacrificing – while Ted Pope and Bob Daniels are safe in their offices. But something, perhaps fear of his workmates' reaction, stops him.

As he climbs back on the lorry, he hears his name being shouted. Puzzled, he looks around; he thought he was alone in the yard. Len is standing near the gate. He approaches him apprehensively as he has not seen him since his doorstep encounter with Florence.

'You've come out of your way?'

Len glances towards the river. 'Can we talk?'

'I don't want any trouble, Len.'

Len shakes his head. 'It's not about that.'

Bill scans his erstwhile friend's face for clues about why he has come to see him or what he might want; his eyes are bloodshot and his skin is a shade whiter than normal. He doesn't look like he has been sleeping well either.

'What's this about, Len? I thought you didn't want to see me?'

Len rubs his hands together to keep warm. 'That's between you and Florence. I just need to speak to you.'

Bill is tempted to tell him to go to hell. Len hasn't sought him out for months and yet here he is demanding attention. But he does the decent thing. 'They won't miss me for a half an hour.'

They find a quiet spot beside some wasteland and sit on a broken-down wall watching trawlers and the occasional tug ship splutter past in clouds of oil and smoke.

Len picks up a fragment of brick and tosses it in the ice-flecked water. 'How's work? You looked busy in that yard.'

Bill lets his question hang, unanswered, in the cool air. He thinks of all the lonely nights in his digs.

'Bill?'

'I was beaten when I went to register at the Labour Exchange. I needed my pals but I had no one.'

'I'm sorry, Bill, but...you lied to us about Florence.'

'I loved her.'

Len follows the frothy waves from the bow of a red cargo ship run to the shore. 'I think I understand now.'

'What's changed?'

'You can't choose who you love.'

'It's taken you a while to realise that.'

'I've met someone.'

Bill's tone softens. 'What's her name?'

Len kicks his heels against the wall. 'It's not easy for me to say —' he checks Bill's expression and then continues '—but we do everything together, youth hostelling, biking, walking. She's a great person.'

Bill is confused. Did he mean this girl was his lover? Why wouldn't he mention her name? Was she married? Len should know he couldn't care less; he instinctively felt that people should be free to love in almost every way, especially after his affair with Florence. And there were plenty of adulterers in the ILP.

'Has she met Thomas and Lizzie?'

'She's quite shy and not at all political.'

'I'm sure they'd like to meet her anyway.'

Len blinks nervously. 'She can't understand why I'd put myself in harm's way and oppose the war. She thinks we should go to Ireland or something. She's got relatives over there.'

'And are you going to?'

Len looks him in the eye for the first time since he called him over. 'I'm not a coward, Bill. This war will kill thousands unless people like us refuse to fight. But I don't want to lose her.'

'Have you got a date for your hearing yet? I'm still waiting.'

'Aye, next month.'

They make their way along the river back to the yard as

seagulls swoop and squabble above them.

Bill cannot resist asking him about Florence before they part at the gate. 'Is Florence happy?'

He shrugs his shoulders. 'She's always got her head in a book or arguing with Thomas.'

'She'll never be happy.'

Len pauses, apparently unsure if he should defend his sister. 'Thomas misses you, though. He'll be at the branch meeting tonight.'

Len backs away and waves. Then he is off into the evening, coat tightly buckled around his waist. Bill hopes he hasn't upset him because, despite everything, he pines for his company. He should have told him he doesn't mind who he shares his life with, but these matters are difficult to discuss.

Bill catches Thomas as he locks up the church hall. He missed the meeting because the foreman made him stay until the lorry was unloaded.

Thomas smiles warmly. 'Good to see you, Bill. I've not set on eyes on you for months.'

He decides not to mention the Labour Exchange. 'I've been busy working my way through the library.'

Thomas fiddles with the key in the lock. 'We have to finish early otherwise the warden gives us a hard time.'

'I saw Len today.'

Thomas's face changes; he looks fretful. 'What did he say? Something has changed in him. I fought for him to go to night school but he's mixing with some odd sorts. He mentioned an Irish lass a couple of times. Do you know anything about her?'

'You just need to give him time, Thomas.' It is for Len to tell his father about her but Bill can't help wondering how he will take it if she is married.

'We haven't got time. Soon we will be back to the mud and blood I saw as a young man. I swore I'd never let it happen, but here we are again and I can't even convince my own son.'

*

Rusty metal wheels scream in protest as they are hauled over concrete. What time is it? From his prone position, he can see the tops of the trees in the garden and the wall beyond. There is a faint glow behind the barbed-wire coils that run along the wall. Breakfast?

*

Len stares out of the window. The winter sun is beginning to dip below the rooftops, leaving behind a watery red and purple stain on the blue sky.

'She's going to Ireland to stay with her family in County Kerry. She reckons she could bring me if I changed my mind.'

Bill hugs his knees and pushes his bare toes under his bed sheets. 'And will you?'

Len breathes out slowly and runs his hands through his hair. 'I thought about it but I can't.'

'If you are exempted by the tribunal then you might be able to find a way to see her?'

The sunset in the window behind casts Len's face in shadow. Bill can't see if his expression is sad or angry or both.

'There are travel restrictions coming in. I won't be able to travel even if I'm a free man on Thursday morning.'

'Is it that soon?'

'Thomas is coming and Florence—' Len pauses as if he is unsure if he should go on '—but I'd like you to be there and all.'

Bill plays with the strap of his gasmask; he could skive off but there would be trouble if he was caught. 'Old Bob is on the attack now the union has caved in to help the war effort. He's been after me ever since the strike. He would love to catch me at a tribunal or something like that. And the union would not stick up for me. Then there's Florence, you know how she feels about me.'

Len's voice sags with defeat, 'I understand.' He collects his coat from the floor and slowly buttons himself up. Before he leaves he presses Bill's shoulder. 'I'm sorry about shunning you. I was jealous, I think. I didn't know what it was like to be in love.'

'It's in the past, Len.'

Dusk falls over the city as Bill stretches out on his bed. Yet again he thinks of the mob in the Labour Exchange; what awaits him if he continues to resist the war? Patience and tolerance are already wearing thin; sooner or later they will turn on him. Eventually he tires of thinking and pulls on his overcoat.

The air in the street is so cold each intake of breath stings the back of his throat. He heads in no particular direction until he reaches a shopping parade. Many of the women and men have not bothered to bring their gas masks. At first, people took them everywhere but when the poisons they feared did not fall from the sky they grew weary of lugging them around.

He stops by a butcher's shop and watches the owner bag up grey trimmings to a line of eager women. Feeling a tug on his sleeve, he turns. It is Peggy; a small basket of swedes and potatoes dangles from her bird-bone-thin wrist.

'I didn't see you there.'

'Aye, well, I'm only your sister.'

He smiles, forgetting his troubles for a moment.

'How come you don't drop by anymore?'

'I've been working dawn till dusk.'

'Aye, you look it.'

Bill chuckles, pleased they can still share a joke. 'Why haven't you been evacuated?'

She coughs violently and Bill frowns with concern.

'Da wanted me gone. He got me to pack my belongings the night before, but Ma couldn't bear to be parted. She said I should stay and help at home.'

'How's Da?'

'Believe it or not he did a bit of labouring on the new trading estate they are building in the valley. They are covering over that stinking river and pulling up the woods where we used to play, like.'

'Bloody hell, that's a miracle.'

'He keeps talking about getting work in a munitions factory now.'

'And Ma?'

'Ask her yourself.'

Ma emerges with a paper package; she slings it into Peggy's basket before she spots Bill. She squeezes her lips in disgust; it is as if she has just bitten into a bitter fruit. She can barely bring herself to look at him.

'Da has been asking after you. The lads in The George say you're a conscientious objector,' she says hesitatingly. 'It's not true is it, son? It's not true that you've gone and brought more shame on your family?'

Bill doesn't answer but his silence is enough for Ma.

'We should get going before blackout. Don't bother sending any more money over.'

Ma breaks eye contact and turns to go. Peggy's head drops and she follows behind.

Bill watches their familiar shapes grow smaller and smaller until his temper gets the better of him; Ma has no right to cut him adrift from his own family. He catches them before their reach the corner. Ma increases her pace so he rounds them blocking their way.

'It's not shameful. Look what the last war did to Da. You've told me all those stories about what he was like before. How you got him to talk and went for strolls in the park together. You loved him. And that war killed your love. There's nothing left now. It would have been better if he hadn't come back at all.

That's what you said to him.'

Ma thrusts him aside – she is surprisingly strong. 'You don't know a thing about what he's been through. Nobody knows. But you want to use it for your own ends and upset Peggy here. Stay away from us.'

*

Doctor Neave rears up in front of the bed. He inspects his papers and mutters something incomprehensible under his breath. Bill strains to get a look at his notes.

'How many times, Mr Rowe? Please do not attempt to move. You are still in a very bad way.'

Bill inhales and prepares to speak but Neave holds his hand up until he has finished writing.

'Your operation has been delayed slightly. As I'm sure you can imagine, medical supplies are rather scarce at the moment. It is a time of national emergency after all. But you can rest assured we plan to do it as soon as we can.'

'Please...'

'How are you sleeping, Mr Rowe? Have you recovered from your funny turn?'

Bill slurs his words like Da after a night at The George. 'I'm too drugged...to think of death... if that's what you mean.'

Neave scribbles something. 'That's just the attitude you need.'

Bill cannot take much more of this; Neave is wilfully misunderstanding him. 'Did you even hear me? I'm too...drugged to think.'

Neave adjusts his black glasses and tugs at the wiry hair on his top lip. 'Mr Rowe, believe it or not I'm here to help you. And I'm not in the business of letting my patients roll over and give up.'

'This is all about your pride...isn't it? I wish you had left me...'

Neave pulls out the bottle from his pocket. His demeanour

slips for a second. 'You do not know me, Mr Rowe.'

Bill is furious but he accepts the pills as they promise escape.

*

The moustached motorman pulls his weatherbeaten cap down to shield his eyes from the bright sunshine as Bill and Len climb into the car. They sit near the back well away from a tall woman.

'I've got to report to Alexandra Barracks in Liverpool next week,' Len says, cleaning a hole in the filthy window. 'But when I'm done, I swear, Bill, I'm going to get the first ship to Ireland, whatever you or anyone else thinks.'

'What about her husband?'

Len laughs. 'Is that what you think?'

Bill regrets his carelessness. 'It's just I've never met her, and nor has Thomas or Lizzie.'

Len checks the car; the tall woman is chatting to the conductress. 'I've got nothing to lose anymore so I may as well tell you...his name his Aidan.'

The tram wheels scrape in the grooves and the electricity line crackles above their heads.

'Aidan?'

'Aye.'

Bill doesn't know what to think or where to look; he studies his ticket. He had heard gossip about men who went with other men. They called them pansies, fairies and brown-noses in the workshop. He had never suspected Len was that way inclined.

After a long pause, he says, 'I thought you said you were courting a lass?'

'There are people who blackmail men like me and if the police find out they'll lock me up. But it's all over now. He's in Ireland and I'm here.'

'I had no idea you were like that.'

Bill goes quiet again as he attempts to make sense of Len's

secret. He feels silly for thinking Aidan was a married woman. But why had he lied to him? Did he even know Len?

Len gets up abruptly. 'This is my stop.'

'You're miles from anywhere.'

'I know,' he says, swaying in the aisle.

'Why didn't you just say?'

The tall woman twists her neck to listen over the din of the tram breaks.

Len clasps the rail running round next seat as the car comes to a halt. 'Because it shouldn't matter who people love, Bill. Haven't we got more important things to worry about?'

*

The old orderly Bill saw when he arrived on the ward is watering the garden. He soaks pots full of bright green parsley, spiky chives and gnarled rosemary as the sky bruises with purples, blues and blacks. The colours swim and Bill drops back into the pillow.

*

The water on the boating pond ripples in the wind. Tiny frothy waves lap at the feet of scrawny ducks huddled on the muddy, rubbish-strewn shore line. It is late afternoon and Saltwell Park is empty apart from a couple of bored boys throwing stones into a partially built air-raid trench.

Florence is waiting on a bench; her arms are wrapped around her body to lock in what little warmth there is beneath her thin blue coat. She moves her legs and wiggles her feet to stave off the cold.

Bill lifts his forearm and opens his fist from the other side of the pond. But his fingers never fully extend and recoil almost immediately. It is the greeting to some half-remembered acquaintance, not a former lover. There is no accident in that, he means to offend her, just as she has offended him. The walk to the bench is awkward; too far to talk and too short to look away. She doesn't offer her hand and nor does he want her too; instead he sits down with a casual nod, almost at the other end of the bench.

She inspects the granite-coloured water, which mirrors the sky. 'Do you want a smoke?'

'I stopped that a while back. It was making me feel sick.'

She lights up herself. When had she taken up smoking?

'You look tired,' she says, giving him the once over.

'We're doing extra hours. Bob has got a big order for transmissions. He won't say what they're for but looks like tanks to me.'

'I'm sure you're right. The German's are making them, so Churchill must do the same,' she says.

Is she trying to provoke him? Churchill had a choice, everybody had a choice. But he doesn't rise to it – instead he pulls his holey jumper sleeve down to cover his cold palms.

'How's Len?'

She catches his eye as if to judge how much he knows of Len's secret life. 'He leaves in a week or two,' she says.

'We'll all miss him.'

Florence smokes the end of her cigarette while Bill grows impatient. He should go, as he needs to prepare for his hearing.

'Why did you invite me here, Florence?'

'I'm leaving soon as well,' she says.

'Where?'

She drives her glowing fag butt into the bench; it burns through the peeling blue paint and into the grey wood.

Bill cannot take anymore of her games. 'Where?'

'I've joined the Women's Land Army,' she says with a defiant smile. 'I leave for Hexham next week.'

Bill is stunned that she would do such a thing but he doesn't want to show it; instead he lets out a strained laugh. 'Your brother is going to be imprisoned in an army camp and you've volunteered to help the war effort. Do you know what the land girls do? They dig fields and milk cows so the government can make labourers and herders go off and kill other farm labourers and herders.'

Florence leaps up, dropping her Woodbines. As she reaches down to pick them up, Bill grabs her hand.

'Is that it?'

'Let me go,' she says through clenched teeth. 'I want to work – that's what the women in my family have fought for and that what I'm going to do.'

Bill pushes her hand away in disgust: her grandma didn't go to prison to support rich men's wars.

'I knew this was a mistake,' she says, looking down at him. 'I wanted to talk to you about what happened but you're as blinkered as Thomas. You say you want to save humanity but you can't cope with flesh-and-blood people, with all their flaws and compromises, with life, in all its complicated, messed-up glory.'

Bill doesn't move as she makes her way round the darkening pond and out of the gates. He watches the night fall over the alien city of cardboard, tape and blackout paint beyond the walls.

*

The orderly is propping up an apple tree towards the back of the garden. The branches are buckled and bent with large brown Russets.

Bill watches him work from his bed. He cannot move his limbs more than a couple of inches but at the same time he feels a strange sort of feathery lightness and freedom. It is as if he could drift off at any moment. In his heart he knows it is the pills, but it is still quite pleasant.

The orderly curses and grunts as he thumps in a pole with a

mallet. He is too frail for this kind of manual labour; his thin, suntanned arms shudder with each strike and his leathery forehead glistens with sweat. It takes him a couple of hours as he has to pause for breath every five or ten minutes. When he is finished, he collapses against the trunk and takes a bite from a pile of fallen apples.

*

The reading room is as cold as ever. Bill strains his eyes and spots Len at the far end; his head is resting on his outstretched arms and his coat is draped around his shoulders like a blanket.

Bill touches his shoulder.

Len says woozily, 'I'm not finished with the paper, pal.'

'It's me, Len,' says Bill, with the best friendly smile he can muster. 'And I've got my own paper.'

He blinks at him; he must have been asleep.

'What do you want?'

'I've had a think about what you said. You're right. It doesn't matter. I wanted to say goodbye.'

Len is not in a forgiving mood. 'It matters to me.'

A passing librarian gestures with his hands to keep the noise down. 'You both know the rules. This is a reading room.'

Bill pulls up a chair. 'Did you hear about that Royal Navy ship? It was sunk off the coast.'

'Aye,' Len says wearily.

'But have you seen who was onboard?'

Len takes Bill's paper turns the page so he can read.

Local pals, cadet Harry Bags and cadet Walter Kelly, were lost at sea when the HMS Exmouth was sunk by German U-boats whilst escorting a merchant boat off the Scottish coast last week.

'My God.' Len rubs the sleep from his eyes. 'Harry and Walter.'

'I saw them when they signed up. They were as dunk as lords.'

'No bodies recovered.'

'Aye,' he says tenderly.

After a while Len folds the paper. 'When are you up for the tribunal?'

'Next week. I've been working on my statement every night after work.'

Bill lays four pages of neat handwriting on top of the newsprint. Len reads while he fiddles with his bag strap.

'It's good. There's a hell of lot of learning in this.'

They stop talking as the same librarian, who told them to be quiet earlier, returns to the table and indicates the library will be closing early.

They stand together and Len says, 'Aiden's gone. He left for Ireland last night. He didn't even say farewell. And I'm...'

They both know he leaves for the army camp tomorrow but Len leaves it unsaid.

Bill gently rests his hand on his friend's elbow. 'It can't have been easy, Len, but you wouldn't be the man he fell for, and you wouldn't be my dear friend, if you give up your principles for convenience.'

Len coughs and glances at the golden hands of the ornate clock hanging on the far wall. 'He said "you would come if you loved me". He said "you don't know what love is". But I am doing this for love. That's what he doesn't understand. It's just not for one person.'

*

There is a hard tap on Bill's shoulder; he shrugs angrily and turns over to sleep. There is another tap on his shoulder.

'Mr Rowe, I need to speak with you?'

Bill sighs groggily.

'Hello, Mr Rowe? It is Doctor Neave here.'

'Aye,' he says blinking.

Neave is leaning over him; there is a thoughtful look in his eye. 'How are you?'

'Let me sleep.'

'Well, this is going to be your last dose. I can't use anymore on you – supplies are very low. But don't worry I'm going to keep a...'

*

The pale yellow stone of the town hall appears to glow despite a thick blanket of white and grey clouds. Bill helps Thomas, who is carrying a file of papers, up the steps. They pass heaps of sandbags and anxious-looking Local Defence Volunteers, who inform them they are on lookout for fifth columnists and parachuted German spies. They decide not to mention the reason for their visit and instead mutter something about dog-breeding licences.

'Ask at reception, pal.'

Inside they are directed to a mahogany-panelled corridor behind the main council chamber. There are some faded red-felt chairs but they decide to stand. A young man in a smart suit introduces himself as the clerk and tells them the tribunal will be ready for them in five minutes.

Thomas mops his head with a handkerchief while Bill watches light play on the stained-glass windows. He wonders how much longer he will be able to wander the streets of Gateshead.

Thomas rubs his arm affectionately, apparently sensing his thoughts. 'What you are doing is very brave, Bill lad. You are setting yourself against some very powerful people in this city and this country.'

'I just hope I can hold my nerve.'

The clerk pops his head out of the room. 'I'm sorry, Judge

Watson Brown is late back from his lunch engagement, so we shall have to wait a further five minutes. I trust that's acceptable.'

As it is more of an assertion than a question, they both nod obediently.

'Any word from Len yet?'

Thomas's eyes shift to the door. 'He's fine.'

'And what about Florence?'

'She's fine too.'

Bill knows he is lying but doesn't protest because he can see the turmoil in his eyes. It must be hard to have your daughter betray your beliefs so soon after waving goodbye to your terrified son.

The room is small and cramped. There are boxes of mildewed files stacked up against the far wall. The three members of the tribunal are sat behind a plain wooden desk. A man, probably from the *Chronicle*, stands at the back fiddling with a pen and pad.

There is no table, so Thomas rests the documents he has brought on his lap. Bill is aware of being studied by the panel; he notices his hands and knees are trembling.

The clerk hands the plump man in the middle a document. He peers at it through his dainty brass glasses and clears his throat loudly. His words are ever so slightly slurred. 'Now, Mr Rowe. I should like to apologise for the late running of Northumberland and Durham Tribunal. Our luncheon rather overran. But that's of little importance compared to our task today. We are here to establish if your name should be added to the register of conscientious objectors. We will ask you in a moment to talk us through your written statement and then we shall ask you some questions to ascertain your motives.'

His glasses slip down his nose. 'Are you comfortable, Mr Rowe?'

'Aye, sir.'

'Before we go on I must introduce myself and the other

members of this tribunal. My name is Winifred Watson-Brown. My day job, as it were, is a county court judge over the river in Newcastle. As you'll be aware there are no military representatives on this panel. This was because it was felt that such arrangements were not conducive to reasoned argument and the proper administration of justice in the last war. To be frank with you, Mr Rowe, there were some cases where young Christian men were frightfully mistreated. I for one intend for that not to happen here. Now to the other members. On my left, appropriately enough, is Mr Gardner. Mr Gardner is an official of the Transport and General Workers Union. I'm sure you won't mind me saying, George, that it is of course the very same union that beget us our new and very industrious Minister for Labour, Ernest Bevin.'

Gardner fiddles with his expensive-looking watch. He looks a little embarrassed by Watson-Brown's rambling introduction. His shirt sleeves are stained with the same purple sauce that decorates Watson-Brown's jacket.

'On my right is Mr Albert Appleby. Albert is a very active member of Newcastle's Chamber of Commerce and an extraordinarily generous man who devotes much of his time to raising money for the poor and needy children of this city, of which I'm sad to say there are far too many.'

Bill blinks; it is Mrs Appleby's husband. He recognises him from the doorstep and the picture on the mantelpiece. His fashionable baggy oxford suit also looks familiar. Memories of lugging the Appleby's clothes down sodden streets and through deserted parks come back to him.

'Well, that's the introductions almost over with. Out of interest could you tell us who is with you, Mr Rowe?'

'This is my representative, Thomas Weaver.'

Watson-Brown addresses Thomas. 'What's your relationship to Mr Rowe?'

Thomas clears his throat. 'We are members of the same party, sir.'

'And what party is that?'

There is defiance in his voice. 'The Independent Labour Party.'

'Thank you, Mr Weaver. Would you like to explain yourself, Mr Rowe?'

Bill climbs to his feet. In his hand is his statement. He starts to read but his hands are trembling too much. The letters and sentences and paragraphs slide across the page. He attempts to compose himself but he cannot; his whole arm is shaking. His vision blurs, the room turns fuzzy and indistinct. It is as if he has been struck around the head.

Brown says, 'Mr Rowe? Mr Rowe? Would the clerk fetch Mr Rowe a glass of water please?'

This is humiliating – he is as inarticulate in the face of authority as his father. He thinks of his pathetic silence during the means-test inspection.

Thomas rises beside him and they hold the paper together. He starts reading again: his breathing is too fast and he stumbles over some of the longer words – but he persists, his voice growing clearer with each completed sentence.

'We are told again and again we must defend our country. But what are we defending? I was born in this city in 1918. I grew up in a basement, sleeping in the same room as my mother and father and my little sister. I went to bed hungry almost every night. My father, who fought in the last war, a war which was supposed to end all wars, lost his job after the stock-market crash and has been unemployed for most of the decade. I left school before I was ready and worked before I was ready. And all I have to look forward to is an endless struggle to make ends meet.'

Bill takes a swig of water and Thomas turns the page.

'I believe that this war, like the previous one, is a war between competing imperial powers. On the one side are the British who are keen to hang on to their empire and where possible extend their influence over new countries. And on the other are the

Germans who want to build their own empire to make up for their losses after the last war. Neither side can deliver a lasting peace.'

Gardner shakes his head with what looks like utter exacerbation.

'Let's suppose that the Allied armies were standing victorious in Berlin, the German army broken and demoralised. The result would not be a true and lasting peace. War would break out elsewhere soon enough because the economic system that drives countries to compete over territory, markets and natural resources would still exist. Only a co-operative socialist commonwealth, which directed the world's productive, might go towards meeting people's needs rather than lining...'

This time Gardner raises his hand; Bill stops and looks at Watson-Brown.

'Your honour, could I ask the applicant something?'

The way he says honour has a condescending ring to it. Oblivious, Watson-Brown agrees.

'Mr Rowe, I've heard this line of reasoning before but its proponents, who have no doubt influenced your young mind, always leave out the difficult questions. I think it may help this tribunal if you could consider this point: what would you do now as bombs rain down on our great capital city? Would you let us be overrun by Herr Hitler and democracy crushed? Do you think that will help the working man?'

The corners of Gardner's smooth mouth begin slowly and helplessly to curve upwards. It is the smile of a schoolboy who has caught a daddy longlegs and is about to tear its legs and wings off to impress his pals.

Bill sweeps the room anxiously. Thomas nods as if to say "give him all you have got". Bill breathes out and thinks of Bob Pope's warmongering.

'This war you are so keen to fight from your comfortable trade-union offices isn't about democracy or opposing dictatorship. If it were then the prime minister would not be so keen on his beloved empire. He would have long ago demanded democracy and freedom for the Indians and Africans. But he doesn't. Because for him and the generals and financiers and industrialists, who stand behind him, it is about protecting the interests of British capitalism.'

Gardner's mouth drops back to its former position. He leans forward and says, 'What has this got to do with anything? London is being burnt to the ground by the Luftwaffe as we speak and this little pipsqueak has the cheek...'

Bill feels himself growing in confidence. 'We sold those armaments to the Germans. We sold them everything they needed: iron, nickel, copper, tin, aluminium and rubber. And the Bank of England lent them the money to buy it. And you complain when it is thrown back at us.'

'As you can see he has no answer to my question.'

Appleby coughs loudly, indicating he wishes to speak. His voice is calm and slow. 'Can I ask if you oppose all war? You say this society isn't worth defending. If you thought it was, would you fight?'

Thomas decides to intervene. 'This is a hypothetical question. He cannot answer this.'

Watson-Brown shakes his considerable head. 'Answer the question. It is relevant.'

Bill has thought about how to answer this already. 'I'd defend a state that looked after people and didn't throw them on the scrap heap when the money markets collapsed and didn't oppress other nations in the name of freedom.'

Appleby is not sidetracked. 'Interesting. So you aren't against the use of force in all circumstances?'

'Aye.'

'So your conscientious objection only covers some wars. Wars waged by those you happen to disagree with. How convenient, Mr Rowe?'

Appleby and Gardener exchange knowing glances.

Watson-Brown fills the silence. 'Thank you very much, Mr Rowe. There's no need for you to say any more unless any of my colleagues has further questions.'

The clerk directs Bill and Thomas to the hallway. Thomas nudges him: there is an elderly constable sitting on one of the chairs. He looks them up and down but makes no attempt to introduce himself or tell them his business.

Thomas takes Bill to one side. 'You did well, bonny lad.'

Bill is still fired up. 'What're they talking about in there? How can they weigh up a man's conscience? It is ridiculous.'

Thomas gestured towards the constable. 'I know, son.'

'Who the hell are they to judge my beliefs?'

Thomas places his finger on his lips, while the constable writes slowly in his notebook. The discussions do not go on for long and the clerk ushers them back to their seats.

Watson-Brown addresses them. 'Mr Rowe and Mr Weaver, your patience is appreciated. The tribunal has considered your case, Mr Rowe. It has been very difficult.'

Bill notices that Gardner's mouth is curling upwards again.

'We have had a few applicants like you. But we have never been able to reach a satisfactory way of deciding if your type of objection falls under the Act. Some we have given conditional exemption, others we have rejected. It is a most vexing matter. So although we have decided to reject your application to be added to the register of conscientious objectors, I strongly advise you to you appeal this decision so we can have some firm guidance on this very thorny issue.

'In the normal run of things you'll be sent your call-up papers telling you to turn up at a particular barracks at a particular time. This will happen soon. But if you put in an application to appeal I'll make sure it goes through quickly. I trust you have somewhere to stay in London, so you can attend the appellate tribunal?'

*

The soreness in his lungs makes him want to yell. He rolls his head from side to side and claws at his mattress. The last pill must be wearing off.

There is a voice on his left. It has a strange tone – not English. He wonders if he might be hallucinating again.

'Lay back if you can.'

'I can't.'

An earth-encrusted hand lifts a cup of water to his lips. 'Would you like some?'

Bill drinks, letting the water soothe his throat and chest. It is the orderly from the garden. Below a shock of white hair are two kindly brown eyes. His skin is dark from the sun.

'I know you,' Bill mouths.

'Me?'

'What's your name?'

'Basso.'

'Basso?'

'It is Italian.'

Basso glances away and shuffles backwards on the chair. Faced with a bedridden man, his manner seems unduly nervous. Although it cannot be easy to have a name belonging to an enemy.

'I've seen you working in the garden.'

Basso gestures to the ward walls. 'It's my escape from this.'

Bill feels himself slipping away again.

*

Mrs Bradshaw's shape appears behind the door's frosted glass as Bill places his key in the lock. Before he can turn it, the door swings open. She stands aside and gestures dramatically behind: on the stairs are his belongings. His books are tied together with some string and his clothes are roughly stuffed into his canvas knapsack.

'What's all this about?'

'I think we both know,' she says jabbing a copy of the *Chronicle* towards him as if it were a weapon.

Bill loses his temper; it has been a long day at the workshop followed by a long evening at the library. 'Just tell me what it buggering says?'

'You're embarrassing us, laddie. It says here "Bill Rowe of 34 Sidney Grove is taking his case of conscientious objection to London".'

Bill decides to bluff, yet in his heart he knows it is useless. 'That's correct. Now can I go to bed please?'

She squints at him. 'Not so fast, bonny lad. I'm not having a German lover living under my roof. I'd be helping the enemy.'

He tries another approach. 'I've done nothing wrong. I'm doing it by the book. I'll do whatever the tribunal says.'

'I don't care if you are doing it by the book. You lot have too many rights,' she says. 'In my day they shot traitors.'

There seems little point arguing further. He gathers up his belongings while she stands guard over him.

Bill hugs his books to his chest on the steps. He won't miss Mrs Bradshaw but he will miss his room. It may not have been comfortable or clean but it was his home. Over the years he has been become quite attached to the worn boards, musty smell and cracked plaster.

Her shadow ghosts across the glass again; she is waiting for him to go. Pulling his knapsack tight, he strides away. He wants to look like there are many places he could go for the night. He is determined not to give her any satisfaction. Yet in truth he knows only one family that would take him in; the Weavers.

The streets are quiet and empty as it is past the blackout. He manages to find his way with the help the moon, all the time praying he doesn't run into any constables; he doesn't want to be stopped without a place to stay.

The Weavers are out, so he stashes his belongings behind a tree in the park and wanders to St Chads. Under the porch, he sits on the bench. The stone is too cold and rough for resting. Instead he finds himself worrying about the journey to London and prospect of facing another tribunal. He has never travelled much out of Northumberland and doesn't have anywhere stay yet. Nor does he know how to convince the great and the good in a strange city – or his own for that matter.

The scrape of footsteps on the gravel path makes him stand. It must, he reasons, be the vicar or the warder. If they take exception to him they could hand him over to the police. He dashes into the graveyard and vaults the wall; there are a few shouts but no one gives chase. Alone on the street, he decides it is best to keep moving and heads towards the Tyne.

A young-looking air-raid warden peers at him from under his heavy helmet as he nears the steps up to Tyne Bridge, but thankfully he doesn't try to question him. The river and the city are illuminated by the full moon. He stops in the middle of the bridge to take in the view: the water gleams and the edges of cranes, ships and warehouses are lined with faint blue light

Leaning on the thick iron, he wonders how much longer he will be able to enjoy these sights. If the London tribunal finds against him, he will have to choose between war and prison.

As he turns towards the Gateshead side, he sees something move against the moon. A plane? Or a trick of the eye? He watches as it grows bigger; it is long and thin with a bulbous middle – like a spinning top in profile. At first he is unconcerned because there is no siren. He cannot establish for certain what it is and he figures he has plenty of time to run; but in the blink of an eye it is over the river and there is no mistaking its form; it has an ugly fat belly, wings and chopping propellers. The noise is incredible; the vibrating and clanking of a vast killing machine.

There is a cry somewhere below the bridge and the air-raid siren begins its low-then-high-then-low-again howl. He knows he should dive for cover or run but he cannot move. It is like one of his childhood nightmares; he is seized by terror. Time appears to slow; he sees the plane tilt one way and the other trying to locate its target. Behind it other dots appear and grow – like a flock of migrating giant birds. He can almost feel the warm breath of its engines as it nears the bridge.

This is the end, he thinks. He hears Ma telling him stories and feels the tingle of Peggy's breath on the hairs on his neck. He smells Flo's body, and experiences perhaps for the last time the softness of her touch. Yet before it reaches him, it turns abruptly and opens its hatches over the warehouses and cargo ships.

They drop into the blackness and explode in yellow-and-orange ribbons and streamers. Bill is transfixed; it is almost beautiful. A figure runs from a burning building, altering his perception; his body is on fire. For one horrifying second Bill imagines he can hear the low hiss and splutter of his blackened skin – like the protest of damp log burning. But surely he is too far away? He weaves first one way then the other as there are crates of cargo in his path. Finally, more stumbling than running, he arrives at the fence – the only remaining obstacle between him and the brown water below. He gets his hands and then his feet on the chainmail. There he clings until the pain forces him back to the ground.

More bombers bear down on him. Bill feels the strength in his legs coming back. He starts breathing again and he sprints towards the Gateshead side of the bridge. Time speeds up: all round him bombs explode with great crashes. Flames shoot from roofs, and ships crumple into the river.

He runs until his muscles are wobbling with exhaustion. Then he walks and limps. He is not sure if hours or minutes have passed. He only stops when he sees people filing out of a shelter. A warden speaks to him; he follows his lips but he can't hear a word. Bill turns back to the river; the whole of the far bank of the Tyne is burning. The warden taps him on the shoulder and points to his ear and then to a nearby ambulance. Bill can barely hear a thing; the whole world is muffled. Is he injured? Is he in shock? The warden tries to call over a doctor but he shuffles off.

Bill keeps going until his hearing starts to come back; he listens with relief to his footsteps and the rustle of his slacks. He must have been deafened by the bombs and the planes. Turning the corner, he finds himself on a street not far from his old school.

A strange desire to climb into the playground takes hold of him. He hauls himself over the wall and drops down onto the macadam. The classroom where he used to sit and corridors where he used to wait in line are deserted and ghostly; he tries to imagine how his younger self would feel about how his life has turned out: disappointed? Proud? Indifferent?

He finds a sheltered spot to sit down and listens to the bells of fire engines heading to the river. There is no escape from the war. It is coming to these shores and only the very rich or lucky can run away to safer lands. Everyone else has a decision to make: either be part of the destruction and killing or take a stand against it. There is no other way, whatever Florence might think. It is a total war.

*

The orderly is in the same place when the pain wakes Bill again. He is eating some bread and a thin slice of cheese.

Is this is what Neave meant? 'Did the doctor tell you to watch me?'

Basso runs his tongue along his teeth as if he has not heard the question.

'Did Neave tell you to stay here with me?'

Basso swallows then says, 'He thinks you aren't well upstairs.

He doesn't want any mishaps on the ward.'

Bill laughs without joy or pleasure. 'First they try to kill me, and now keep me alive. I wish they would make their minds up.'

Basso offers him food.

'No.'

'Do you want to talk?'

'No.'

*

Thomas answers the door in his dressing gown, holding a cup of tea. He ushers Bill in quickly when he sees his knapsack and books under his arm. He doesn't appear to need an explanation.

'I feared something like this might happen.'

Bill realises how hungry and cold he is when Thomas offers him some bread and jam. He devours five or six slices and gulps down two cups of sugary tea whilst Thomas sits beside the blinds checking for wardens.

'How come you're up so late?'

'I couldn't sleep after the raid,' he says, rubbing his eyes.

Bill prepares to tell of his near escape on the bridge but decides the old man has enough on his mind. Nor is he sure if he has the words or the desire to recall the man on the docks.

'My name is in the paper,' he says, wiping crumbs from his chin. 'That's how my landlady found out.'

'I'm sorry, Bill.'

'You've done your bit, Thomas. It's up to us now.'

Thomas passes him two scribbled letters from under his chair. Bill recognises Len's handwriting and rests them on his lap.

Dear Thomas, Lizzie and Florence
I am writing this short note to let you know I am well. The last few months have been very dull. There has been nothing to do. Nearly every day we sit around playing card games and drinking tea. The

others are a nice but eccentric bunch of Christian types and university men. One other thing, how did Bill get on at the tribunal?
Love always, Len.

Dear Thomas, Lizzie and Florence
Sorry it has been so long. A new officer has taken over – it has all changed and not for the better. He wakes us at the crack of dawn and makes us load large crates on to lorries. My back is sore and my arms ache like hell. I don't know what's in the crates; I fear it might be bombs. I want you to know I will take no part in any bombing of cities.
Love always, Len.

Thomas folds the letters carefully when Bill has finished.

'He is a brave man.'

'Aye.'

'I just wish...'

Thomas takes another sip of tea but he cannot go on; he thumps the armrest of the chair in frustration.

Bill changes the course of the conversation; the plight of his son is too painful. 'Have you heard anything about the appellant tribunal?'

Firelight plays on Thomas's weary face. 'Party HQ have arranged travel and accommodation. They've got you a top-notch barrister.'

'Good.'

'That judge urged you to go to make your case there, so you must have a reasonable chance. The panel might be less small-minded in London.'

Although it is nearly midnight, they stay up for another hour. When the last embers of the fire die, Thomas takes his belongings upstairs.

'You are always welcome here, Bill,' he says. 'We have plenty of space now...'

Bill feels sorry for Thomas. 'Has Florence gone too?

Thomas face goes into shadow. 'So you know? She's been posted to a farm up near Hexham.'

Bill leaves it at that and Thomas heads to his bed where Lizzie snores softly. Alone he sits on edge of Florence's old mattress. He feels uncomfortable and nervous in her room as if he should not be there, like a burglar or thief. She has taken most of her poetry books, but the arms of jumpers and blouses hang out of her chest of drawers. It doesn't look like it has been cleaned since she left – perhaps they are expecting her back.

His mind shifts again to the tribunal. He wonders if it will have the same running order as the local one and if he will get a chance to put forward more of his points. He has done his research and is confident he can do a better job of explaining his opposition.

Before dawn comes, he strips off and slips between her slept-in sheets. He struggles to put the bombers and the burning man out of his mind though. His ears still ring with the explosions and his muscles still ache from his getaway. He pushes his face down into her pillow. It smells strongly of her hair and body. He finds himself excited but is too exhausted to act upon his desires.

*

Basso finishes off his meal whilst Bill fixes on the walls. What would his life have been like if the war hadn't broken out? What if he hadn't met Len and Thomas? Like generations of his family, he would have worked, married, fathered children and died. This prospect had once driven him to despair but it now appealed.

He slams the back of his head into the mattress with what little force remains in his neck muscles and grunts in frustration.

'Can't you just leave me to it?'

Basso looks at him and then to the window. 'The doctor is a

good man. You must understand that. He didn't have to bring you here. He could have left you to those...animals on the wing.'

An hour passes before Bill speaks again. His lips are sore and his throat is itchy. 'Water. I need water.'

Basso pours him a cup from a tin jug and holds it to Bill's scabby mouth. 'There you go.'

Bill slurps even though most of it spills down his front.

*

There is only one man left on the platform at Kings Cross. He is leaning languidly against a newspaper kiosk; his long coat and trousers are dark and shiny from the rain. He looks a little like a seal on a rock. He lifts his grey fedora when he notices Bill standing with his bag.

'Mr Rowe? My name is Percy Williams and I'll be representing you at the tribunal.'

'Thanks for coming to meet me. This is my first time in...'

Mr Williams picks up his black umbrella with a polished wooden handle. 'Well, I hope it is living up to your expectations.'

In the calm of the evening blackout, Mr Williams hails a cab on the Euston Road. Bill sinks into the seat and watches the rain streak down the glimmering windows. As the cab rumbles through the streets, the driver moans about the lack of trade and lambasts the authorities for requisitioning the bulk of the taxi fleet.

'Most of my mates are working for the fire service now – towing trailer pumps and the like. It's a bloody joke though. The motors aren't powerful enough.'

Mr Williams taps his brown brogues impatiently until the driver gets the message, and then presses Bill for information about the case. 'I do so dislike stuffy formalities. Good. I believe the judge recommended an appeal. Is that correct?'

Bill puts his hand up to indicate this is not the time or place.

'We can talk more tomorrow. I'm knackered.'

Instead, Percy, who seems to love the sound of his own voice, tells him about his hosts for night: George and Sally Greenwood.

'George is the son of an infamous high-court judge with a love of hanging. After he joined the ILP his pater gave him a considerable sum of money in exchange for never contacting him again,' he says with a chuckle.

About half an hour later, the taxi pulls up outside a three-storey house in Victoria Park. A man, he presumes to be George, greets him with a gummy grin and a blast of bad breath.

'Come in quick before you catch your death.'

As he walks up the path, Bill notices that the neighbouring house has been bombed; there isn't much left apart from a plaster-and-brick facade of blown-out windows and burnt and splintered doors.

George follows his eyes. 'Incendiary struck it last week...'

In the large but shabby kitchen, George introduces him to Sally, who is preparing a pot of steaming hot coffee and laying out a vast plate of biscuits.

Sally explains that he will be sleeping in their daughter's room at the very top of the house. 'We sent her away the day after next-door was hit. They picked it bare you know?'

Bill is confused. 'Who?'

'I tried to stop them but there were too many. There's nothing left now.'

George plonks himself in front of the biscuits. 'Enough about that, darling; you'll scare our guest. There's been a lull in the bombing, anyway. I've not heard the sirens in days. Please, Bill, sit down and tell us about your case. I'm quite interested in the law, you see.'

'Well I don't know about the legal side of things. I'm just here to state my case.'

'Well that's the thing, isn't it, Bill. The Act doesn't define what conscientious objection is, so they have to make it up as they go along.'

George's accent is hard to place: aristocratic but with commoner mannerisms. While he nibbles the biscuits with his remaining teeth, Sally parts thick blackout curtains and watches the trees swishing in the back garden.

Bill bites into a biscuit without much enthusiasm. The last thing he wants to do is discuss his case with a hobby lawyer. He yawns and stretches. 'Thanks for putting me up.'

George answers, spraying crumbs everywhere, 'We've had three or four comrades stay here. It's the least we can do for the cause.'

Without turning from the window, Sally says, 'Let him go, George. He needs to get his rest before his appearance.'

'Quite. Yes. You need your rest.'

Upstairs, Bill curls on their daughter's bed, feet poking over the end. Even though they have told him there has been a lull in the bombing, every gust of wind and twitch of the night sounds like the Luftwaffe. He imagines thermite incendiaries the shape of milk bottles dropping silently towards the roof.

He thinks of the burning figure running towards the Tyne. What must it feel like when your flesh is on fire? He wishes away the thought but when he closes his eyes he sees the man tearing and raking at himself in terror and desperation. Sleep is impossible, so he draws some of his papers from the bag. He can't remember the last time he slept well. In the gloom he starts rehearsing the speech he plans to make tomorrow.

The morning bus trundles down the street, turning here and there to avoid small craters in the road. Neat piles of rubble, wooden joists and glass shards lay outside shattered buildings waiting to be cleared by gangs of demolition men. Telephone and trolleybus wires dangle from wavering poles.

The passengers appear indifferent to the dusty remains of

their city: they read newspapers, mutter about the cold or stare blankly at the floor. Bill studies two women opposite: their clothes are dirty and worn; there is plaster dust on their shoulders and in their hair. One catches his eye; he smiles, in what he hopes is a friendly way, but she frowns at him.

'Bugger off, mate. I don't want your pity.'

Percy doesn't even look up. He is engrossed in Bill's papers: his statement from the tribunal, annotated with Thomas's scribbled notes, is on the top.

Bill rests his head against the glass. On the end of a terrace, someone – probably one of Mosley's mob – has painted JEWS OUT and someone else – probably a Communist Party member – has painted DEEP SHELTERS NOW and a messy blob supposed to resemble a hammer and sickle.

They pass an unstable-looking brick public shelter at a cross-roads. Two drunks stand swaying at the entrance. They are arguing with a warden. As the bus pauses at a stop, the smaller of the drunks headbutts the warden. He crumples in handfuls of blood. Bill cranes his neck; the other one pulls his leg back as if he is about to strike a football and unleashes a ferocious kick to the warden's head. Still Percy doesn't look up. The other passengers continue as if nothing had happened.

Bill was sceptical of the wireless reports of plucky East Enders facing down the Luftwaffe. But this is much worse than he had ever thought: the people are mad and traumatised, blundering around in a wrecked city. And this is only the start of the age of the air war. Where would it end?

Percy holds a page up to the light and says, 'What did this chap Brown say to you at the very end?'

'That I should appeal.'

'That's a good sign, Bill. It means he thinks you have raised some important points.'

'This isn't about points of law. This is a war that's destroying everything. Look outside, man.'

Percy rolls his eyes dramatically. 'Quite so. But I want to keep you and other socialist COs out of jail.'

The air in the smart brick building near the Parliament Square is warm and close. It has the comforting feel of a cave buried deep below the city. There is no indication of the turmoil and chaos outside. Bill and Percy take their places at the front. There is a typist and a few people, whom he doesn't recognise, in the chairs reserved for the public and the press.

Bill tries to focus on the task ahead but the typist reminds him of Florence. She has similar freckled cheeks and a similar white dress. His mind flashes with memories of her skin and curves – if only he could lose himself in her softness and warmth.

Percy hands Bill some documents bringing him back to the present. He shakes his head violently as if to drive her from his thoughts. She has no right to be there anyway; she has abandoned him.

Percy frowns at his odd behaviour. 'Explain yourself as you did in the tribunal. Don't be sidetracked. Just focus on your arguments. The chairman, Stafford Page, is a highly educated fellow, a Cambridge don I believe. Don't let him tie you up in knots.'

'You don't need to tell me how important this is, Percy. I've been preparing for months.'

'That's the spirit, old chap. Now, if there's anything you are confused about or don't understand, stay silent and I'll chip in.'

Bill doesn't like being talked down to. 'I'm not stupid.'

'I mean on matters of law. Trust me, Bill. I know I'm not a coalminer but I'm not the enemy.'

Bill turns his shoulders and reads through his notes: there are rows of figures and quotes from history books. He attempts to calm down; he knows he needs to keep his cool if he wants to walk the streets of Gateshead.

'I'm sorry, Percy. I appreciate that you are here to help me.'

The tribunal members file in without any fanfare. Stafford Page, a thin athletic man with glasses and closely trimmed grey hair, takes the chair in the middle. The two others sit on either side of him.

'Well, good morning. Thank you for making it in so promptly. The current condition of our great capital makes travel, amongst many other things, very difficult.'

The typist leans over and begins tapping the keys; her hands move at an incredible pace, almost blurring in the dim light of the room.

'We have much to do today, and as we know these hearings are liable to be interrupted. I trust you have all familiarised yourselves with the exits and nearest shelters. Good. Let's begin at once. Our first appellant today is Mr William Rowe of Gateshead. Is Mr Rowe with us?'

Page lifts his round glasses and inspects the room.

'I am, sir.'

Page shuffles some papers. 'You say in your original statement that you oppose this war because it is an imperialist war. This implies that you would fight in a different sort of war. Is that correct, Mr Rowe?'

'Aye sir. This war...' Bill stops midsentence.

Nobody moves; even the typist stops and looks up. Mercifully this time his hand does not shake. He lifts his head and surveys the tribunal. They stare back at him; three pairs of expressionless eyes. There are some coughs and uncomfortable sighs in the public area as if they can feel his angst.

'Mr Rowe? We do not have all day.'

Bill closes his eyes and recalls his studies in the library. 'This war will lead to ever more war. The last war was supposed to end war and look where we are now? I'd fight if I thought for one minute that killing men from other countries would lead to a peaceful, more co-operative world. But it won't. War in one form or another will return, just like the end of the last war laid the basis for this one, until men...'

'Be that as it may, Mr Rowe. We are not here to provide you with a platform for your views. We are here to determine if you have been wrongfully excluded from the register of conscientious objectors.'

The man to Page's left snorts. He has fine white hair and mottled sun-browned skin. Percy whispers in his ear that it is Lord Douglas Smith, the headmaster of a distinguished public school and former naval commander.

Page takes not the slightest bit of notice of him. 'So what is a conscientious objection? The act doesn't define it but in common parlance it is I think a deeply held, consistently applied conviction. A Christian pacifist for instance, who is opposed to all killing, must be able to show that he would not resort to violence whatever the provocation or circumstances. Neither can it be just a temporary conviction that has been cultivated to avoid putting oneself in danger. That is just cowardice and this tribunal will not help those too scared to fight, especially when good men have and continue to make the ultimate sacrifice defending this country.'

Percy stands up. 'May I interject, sir?'

'Yes, of course. But keep it brief.'

'My good friend, Mr Rowe, has just such conviction. He believes this war is wrong. He believes that it's not being fought to end tyranny. He believes it is a squabble between imperialists – and he doesn't wish to take sides.'

A voice calls out from the back, 'Shame!'

Percy is unruffled. 'Now, whatever one might think of these ideas there can be little doubt that they are profound and sincere. He has come all the way to London. He has lost his home. He has lost friends. His family has disowned him.'

Lord Douglas signals with his hand. Page sits back and allows him to respond.

'Are you saying Mr Rowe's political views are as profound as

Christian convictions? These men reject all violence and display it in their everyday lives – they literally would not step on a fly. They often come from families who have for centuries held the same convictions. But I dare say Mr Rowe has developed his opinions only recently and has no doubt been coached on how to present them by his friends in the ILP.'

Percy frowns angrily and attempts to interject. But Lord Douglas, who is clearly enjoying himself, carries on. 'They don't like it, you can see that, but only yesterday the *Daily Express* exposed this very practice.' He waves a newspaper in the air. 'The headline for those with bad eyesight, like me, reads: "CONCHIES LEARN THE ANSWERS – MOCK TRIBUNALS TEACH THEM WHAT TO SAY". So can I ask, Mr Rowe, if he has practised his answers?'

Bill shrugs his shoulders. 'Aye, but no more than any...'

'There you have it.'

Percy finally gets to speak. 'I fail to see what relevance this has to anything. Like anyone else Mr Rowe has of course thought about what he was going to say.'

Page smiles as if he has indulged a well-meaning but drunken uncle at the Christmas dinner table too long. 'Thank you, gentlemen. If we can get on track, I've some more questions for Mr Rowe. You say in your written statement that you object to this war because it's imperialistic like the Great War. But do you know anything about the Great War?'

'Aye, my Da fought in it.'

'But have you studied it? Do you know its causes, its twists and turns, its outcomes and implications?'

'I've read about it—' Bill flicks through his notes '—I know that at the end of all of the bloodshed Britain ended up with three hundred and fifty thousand square miles of Egypt, three thousand and six hundred square miles of Cyprus, three hundred thousand square miles of South West Africa, three hundred and eight thousand square miles of German East Africa, one hundred thousand square miles of Togoland and Cameroons, one thousand square miles of Samoa, ninety thousand square miles of German New Guinea and Islands, nine thousand square miles of Palestine and one hundred and forty thousand square miles of Iraq.'

'That's all very impressive and I'm sure – as has been indicated – this is the sort of thing you practice with your colleagues. But my question was really about your understanding? What would you have done in the face of the onward marching armies of the Kaiser? Written poetry? Produced a strongly worded pamphlet denouncing imperialism? The Germans I'm afraid would have won. The very basis of this country's prosperity, which you proclaim to care so much about, would have been destroyed.'

Bill decides to continue reading; if only he can make them aware of the cost of war. 'Between 1914 and 1918, eight million people were killed and sixteen million people were wounded. And for what? ... For this. All this.'

For the first time Page looks riled. He presses the palm of his hand with his thumb – roughly, in circular motions.

'I can see you have rehearsed well, Mr Rowe. But you haven't demonstrated much ability to answer our points. Would your representative like to add anything before we make our decision?'

Percy springs up; he is not going to miss the opportunity to perform on a stage as grand as this. 'I'd like to stress that nowhere in the National Service Armed Forces Act does it state that conscientious objection be restricted to religious or humanitarian grounds. I think therefore that it is perfectly possible to accept a political objection.'

Page regains his composure. 'Neither does it state that we are duty bound to accept such objections.'

'My point is that you...'

Page cuts him off as if to suggest what he was about to say

was painfully obvious to all but an idiot. 'Thank you, Mr Williams. Your points will be taken into consideration. We will now leave to determine our decision.'

They return in the same manner in which they arrived: Page at the front and the other two following loyally behind. Page seems to be in a rush and wastes no time with a preamble.

'Conscientious objection must be consistent and deeply held. I'm afraid yours doesn't meet those standards for three reasons. Firstly, we are not convinced that the arguments you made were your own. We detect left-wing rhetoric in them. And as you yourself admitted, you have rehearsed your answers. This suggests you are not sincere. Secondly, your views are incoherent because you cannot say what the alternative to the current war is – or indeed what you would have done in the summer of 1914. This isn't the sign of someone who has carefully considered all the evidence and come to a deep moral belief. Thirdly, society cannot be undermined by those who choose for whatever reason to ignore rules they do not like. You must be and will be subject to the same laws as everybody else.'

Bill can take no more: he flings his notes to the floor. The pages flap and glide across the tiles. All eyes in the room fall on him again.

Percy tugs at his sleeve but he flicks him away with ease.

'Get off me.'

Percy whispers through his embarrassed grin, 'This will only play badly for you, Bill.'

Page glances at his watch and then indicates to the constable at the door that he may be needed in a moment.

Bill is not sure what he wants to say but he knows he cannot let this judgement pass onto the record books without some sort of a protest. He has been led to believe they would consider his arguments in a fair-minded way but they have shown no interest in the points he was making.

'How can you sit there and in all honesty determine if my beliefs are genuine? You do not have access to the inner workings of my mind. You cannot see my conscience. You cannot see my thoughts. You are not gods. All you have is your manmade prejudices.'

The constable's heavy hand lands on his shoulder; his fingers push into his collar bone and brush against his Adam's apple.

'That's enough, son.'

Bill allows himself to be dragged away as he has said what he wanted to say. The constable pushes him headfirst into the entrance hall. The double doors scrape against his scalp as he is thrust forwards, and then clatter into his back and legs.

A smartly dressed woman talking to a man on the far side looks up; she frowns in annoyance then returns her attention to her companion.

The constable forces Bill down on a seat and says, 'Calm down, mate, or this could turn ugly.'

Bill is furious and feels he has little to lose; he whacks his arm away. 'Fuck off.'

The door swings open and Percy appears clutching papers to his chest. 'He has done nothing wrong. He has committed no crime.'

'He assaulted an officer,' says the constable.

'Nonsense. Give me your details and I'll take this matter up with your superiors.'

The constable brushes by Percy as he returns to the tribunal. 'Look, your lover boy is all upset.'

'Bill?'

'Get me away before I lamp someone,' says Bill panting.

Percy hails a cab outside and they jump in quickly. Bill thumps the faded upholstery as they head towards the Thames. Why on earth had he bothered to read those books and gather those figures? They had made their minds up before he even stepped in the room.

'I don't think they had any intention to listen to what I had to say.'

'Quite, Bill. They were emotional rather than rational. But let's try and keep our heads,' says Percy, nodding towards the humming taxi driver's head.

Bill doesn't care anymore about his reputation or what the taxi driver thinks of him. 'Did you see the contempt in their faces? They expect peasants like me to follow their orders.'

'Please, Bill.'

The taxi driver sways his head to an imaginary tune; he appears to care little about Bill's views. They pass Smithfield meat market and plunge into the East End. The taxi arrives at the Greenwood's at midday.

George welcomes Bill and Percy with an unwanted bear hug. 'Bloody well done, Bill.'

Bill grunts. 'It was a waste of time.'

Sally is sat at the kitchen with another man; he is tall with swept-back hair. He puts his cigarette out and goes to shake their hands. He looks like a man on a stroll along the promenade at Blackpool: he is wearing baggy white trousers, a tight-fitting waistcoat and brown slip-on shoes.

'Pleased to meet you, Bill.'

After the man releases his hand, Bill strides towards the stairs as he is no mood for conversation.

However, the man rests his hand on his arm as he brushes past and gently turns him. 'I've heard all about your case. I'm James Maxton.'

Bill eyes widen as he recognises him. 'I saw you speak in Newcastle.'

Maxton's voice is every bit as rolling and rich as it was in the meeting. 'You look like you have had one hell of a day. Would you like some coffee?'

'Aye,' says Bill, forgetting his troubles for a moment.

They return to the table and George pours out the coffee while

Maxton lights up again. He puffs a few times and then drapes his hand along the arm of his chair, letting ribbons of smoke drift upwards.

'Tell me about the tribunal.'

Bill breathlessly recounts the whole experience as Maxton listens patiently. Once or twice he stops, waiting for Maxton to tire of his voice but he just puffs and signals for Bill to continue with the story. Bill relaxes and explains how he spent hours working on his speech but they made no effort to even respond to his arguments.

Maxton stubs his fag out. 'We are hearing that the tribunals are sometimes very good and sometimes very bad. It is the luck of the draw, which can be no basis for justice. I may well raise this in the house.'

Percy, keen to join the conversation, adds, 'His perfectly reasonable preparations were used as an argument to ignore his points. They claimed he had just copied it all down from ILP crib sheets.'

A smile forms on Maxton's long face, and his thick eyebrows arch. 'Had they copied their arguments down from my dear pal Churchill's crib sheets? But don't worry too much about the iniquities of the process, Bill. The most important thing is that you have stayed true to your principles.'

Bill sighs gratefully; his frustration with the tribunal is beginning to subside. Thomas was right; there is something admirable about Maxton. He could have become an establishment bigwig with his talents but he chose a far more difficult path; to fight for the poor in this country.

'I do my best, Mr Maxton.'

George grins, exposing the rotten tips of his teeth again. 'I'm glad you two could meet, even if it is under these difficult circumstances. Now, it's getting rather late – would you like anything to eat, gentlemen?'

Sally speaks for the first time. 'We don't have much because of all the restrictions but I've managed to lay my hands on some sausages?'

Bill and Maxton and Percy exchange excited smiles.

Maxton answers for everyone, 'Aye, that would be grand.'

George adds hopefully, 'I could open a bottle of wine as well?'

Bill is intrigued; he has never seen a wine bottle, let alone tasted any.

Maxton, however, scowls. 'For God's sake, George, I've spent my life fighting the liquor trade.'

As George disappears into the dark pantry, Bill's thoughts turn towards the future. 'What happens next?'

Percy leans forward. 'You will receive a call-up notice soon, and if you choose to ignore that then you'll find yourself in court and then I'm afraid, possibly, prison.'

Maxton pours some more coffee and lights another cigarette; he smokes more than just about anyone Bill has ever met before.

'They imprisoned me during the last war because I spoke out against it. They can't stand a man who thinks for himself.'

'What was it like?'

Maxton pauses. 'Hard. But do you know what, Bill? It ultimately showed them up for the cowards they are – they couldn't contain my ideas except by locking me up, and even then it didn't work. I came out unabashed and within a decade I was elected to parliament to represent the people of Glasgow.'

Sally pauses by the blackout curtains like she did the night before and peers out through a crack. 'I can see someone in the trees, George? It looks like Mr Towers? Maybe he's come back to see his house. He'll be all upset. I'll go out and fetch him.'

George snatches at her wrist as she runs towards the back door. He laughs shrilly and says, 'Darling, it's just the foxes. You said the same last week and there was nobody there.'

Maxton and Percy fall silent as she glares at George. 'Well I must be losing my marbles then.'

'Go and have a rest, darling. I'll finish off the cooking.'

They listen to her clump up the stairs as the sausages start to spit and burn.

Percy shakes the pan and says, 'She's been like that ever since the bomb hit next door. She keeps seeing them in our garden. The firemen and the APR wardens couldn't find any trace of them. I think they are buried in the rubble or—' he lowers his voice '—blown to pieces. But she thinks they wandered off and have nowhere to go. She phones the councils and shelters and hospitals every day. But there's no record of them.'

Maxton waits for him to turn from the range before replying, 'Don't be too hard on her, George. You never know, she might well be right. They are plenty of bombed-out families without roofs over their heads in the East End.'

'They are dead and gone,' he says sadly. 'I'll take her some food once everything is done.'

Later, as George mashes the spuds, Percy attempts to move the conversation on to more political matters.

'I represented a man who lost his house and had to wait months before anything was arranged for him. No one – not the borough council or the ministry – would take responsibility. The system is a complete mess.'

Maxton lets smoke pour from his nostrils. 'We've written to the Home Secretary about this very issue. Herbert needs to make landlords declare their empties so homeless people can make use of them. There are plenty of them around because London's well-to-do classes have relocated to spa hotels in the Lake District or sun loungers in California.'

George delivers three plates loaded with mounds of mashed potatoes and sticky brown and black sausages to the table. As they tuck in he takes a tray with a plate and glass of milk to Sally. They hear a muffled conversation through the threadbare carpets and plaster above their heads.

George returns some time later in a better mood. He pulls up a seat and starts talking about the Ack-Ack guns in Victoria Park.

'It's the only bit of greenery some of the locals have ever seen. Now it's full of guns and shells. That's progress for you.'

After the clock in the hallway strikes twelve, Bill leaves Maxton talking with Percy and George. It is remarkable the difference a full belly and good company can make: he feels more at peace with himself. Of course he feels sorry for Sally but he hasn't the energy to dwell on her predicament, except mentally to note, for the second time that day, that the bombing was making the city mad. He gets into bed and falls into a restful sleep.

Victorian terraces, ivy-covered warehouses and leafless parks slip past in the hazy winter sun. Bill places his head on the headrest as the train engine builds up speed out of neat suburbs of North London. Opposite him are a woman and her three children. The youngest boy keeps getting up and running along the corridor.

'They are excited about seeing their father. He's is on leave from the army.' She glances nervously towards a War Office poster behind his head urging the public to travel less. 'We're only going to meet my husband because his time is so limited.'

Bill worries she will ask him why he isn't in uniform but she leaps up after her son. He closes his eyes and listens to the children's happy babble and petty squabbles.

As they reach the Hertfordshire countryside, one of the children brushes against his knee. He opens his eyes as the woman gently scolds her son.

'It's no bother,' he says, with a wink at the boy.

'I can't handle them without Philip,' she says rubbing the boy's arm. 'He so looks up to his dad.'

Bill thinks of Da for a moment and wonders if he has any interest in what has happened to his son. 'Aye, fathers are important to boys.'

The boy looks at Bill with a thoughtful expression and then his mother. 'Why's he not in the army?'

The woman blushes a little and waits for Bill. But he doesn't know how to respond; he feels his throat drying up. The boy gazes at him in the way only very young children can; clear-eyed without any shyness or awkwardness. The other children stop and stare as well.

Bill wets his lips and considers pretending to be hard of hearing, but he suspects the boy will just keep on asking. Why can't he tell them the truth? After all, he had explained himself to two tribunals and his family. His name had even been published in the local paper; thousands maybe more, knew of his choice.

'I'm a farm worker,' he says avoiding their eyes by looking at the muddy fields beyond the glass. 'I'm needed on the farm where I work so I don't have to join the army like your Da.'

The boy isn't satisfied with Bill answer and doesn't move. 'Why can't father be a farmer?'

The woman shakes her head. 'That's enough questions, Alfie.'

The boy starts to sob so she pulls out a picture book and starts reading to him. Bill curses himself silently. He wants to stop fathers leaving their families to fight in far-off lands; his message might have been well received. Closing his eyes once more to avoid any further lies, he listens to the woman's voice until sleep comes. The train rocks and the tracks click pleasantly.

He wakes as they pull into the curved platform at Newcastle. The woman and the children are gone; crumbs and a single woollen glove are the only evidence that they were sat opposite him. Groggy and a little confused, he takes his bag and heaves open the carriage door. The wet sooty air in the station brings him round quickly.

His pockets are empty so he decides to go on foot. It is late afternoon but there is just enough light to make it back to Gateshead. As he crosses the city, he thinks some more about the tribunal. There was no point reasoning with the establishment; they did not respond to rational argument – they used their power to intimidate and bully. They had made him afraid of speaking the truth to a child.

Thomas is reading in the living room when he gets back. He glances up and indicates he is busy, but Bill is keen to tell him about the tribunal and his encounter with Maxton.

'Do you know where I've been?'

'Of course, Bill. I'm sorry. I've got a lot on.'

'They rejected my appeal.'

'The bastards—' Thomas thumps his fist on the table and almost starts weeping; his lip shakes and he rubs his eyes '—how could they do that to you?'

Thomas is often angry but Bill has never seen him in such a state. 'Is there something the matter, Thomas?'

He clears his throat as if the tears were the result of a physical ailment, not some inner turmoil. 'I've a terrible cold, Bill.'

'I'd like to help.'

'I told you everything is fine,' he says angrily. 'I'm just trying to finish an article for the *New Leader*.'

'I'm sorry.'

'Now if you would excuse me, I need to type this up.'

Bill sighs to himself as Thomas heads up to his typewriter. The deadline wasn't behind his mood; perhaps had something happened to Len or Florence? He picks up Thomas's discarded book on the history of bombing and starts to read.

Before the last of the afternoon light goes, Lizzie gets back. She embraces Bill and he recounts his experience in London for the second time. When she has finished asking him about the tribunal and Maxton, he says, 'Is Thomas okay? He seemed a little strange when I got back.'

Lizzie checks Thomas is still upstairs and drops her voice. 'He's not been himself for months. He has not heard from Len since his last letter. And then there's Florence. She's still refusing to speak to him.'

'He's a good father, Lizzie. Len will be in touch, and Florence will come round sooner or later,' he says with hope rather than conviction.

They both know Len could well be trouble and Florence is as stubborn as her father.

Lizzie nods and goes to fill the kettle. With her back to him, she remarks, 'I don't know what to do, Bill. He's not working that often and the rent is due soon.'

Bill has not heard her worry about money before; he vows to do what he can to help. 'He'll perk up when he hears from Len.'

'You're a good lad, Bill.'

'I'm still owed money from Daniels. Tomorrow...'

Her face flushes with colour. 'There no need to go giving us your earnings.'

'I want to pay my way. That's all.'

'Thanks, Bill.'

Dark shapes glide above Tyne Bridge. Bill hesitates before going under the green arches; he feels his muscles stiffen even though he knows the shapes are too small for planes. He forces himself forward as he does not want to return empty-handed. Each step, however, brings back memories of the man in the yard. He focuses on the pavement ahead amid screams and thuds. He tells himself they are just the sounds of the docks.

On the other side he rests against a wall and looks back: gulls drift on the breeze and ships cut through the river. It is peaceful and calm. He allows himself a smile of relief and sets off to the workshop.

There is no sign of Mr Daniels. Usually he arrives early to make sure his engineers turn up on time. Bill settles down to wait just as an Austin saloon turns into the road and comes to a halt in the yard.

'Mr Daniels,' he calls, as the driver climbs out of the front seat.

'Who are you?'

'I work for you. I'm early for the workshop.'

Mr Daniels beckons him over with a generous grin, which fades quickly as he realises it is Bill. 'I thought I'd never see you again'

'I've come about my wages.'

'Your work here is over, Rowe. The men don't want you back. We don't employ traitors.'

'I just want my money and I'll be off.'

Mr Daniels waves dismissively and pushes past him. Bill rests his hand on his shoulder.

'Get your hands off me,' Mr Daniels shouts, baring rows of small white teeth.

Bill's old friend Dermot appears at the gate. 'What's going on?'

'This man is trying to rob me,' roars Mr Daniels.

'Mr Daniels, it's Bill. He used to work here.'

'He's threatening me and asking for money.'

'I'm owed money.'

Mr Daniels shrugs Bill off; he is surprisingly strong.

'Get him out of here before the workshop opens, Dermot. Or I'll be forced to call the police and—' he pauses dramatically and says with satisfaction '—reconsider my decision to make you foreman.'

Bill knows that the police would take Mr Daniels' side so he allows him to go. He is left facing Dermot, who is cowering slightly under his cap.

'I had to. My family needed the money.'

Bill feels pricks of sadness in his stomach; his comrade had been bought by Mr Daniels. But he doesn't have time to argue, he needs to help Lizzie.

'Can you help me get my wages back? I need to pay something towards my rent.'

Dermot's head stays down. 'You heard him. You haven't got a chance. There's nothing I can do to change his mind.'

Bill groans and walks away. 'We all need his buggering

money, Dermot, but some of us don't abandon our pals.'

The house is empty when he gets back; he hopes Thomas has found some work because he has nothing for Lizzie. He goes to warm his hands by the smouldering fire and notices an unopened letter addressed to him on the mantelpiece. He tears it open to find a smudged appointment for an army medical. It must have been hand delivered.

Although he has prepared himself for this moment, he flinches at the thought of prison. Yet there is no going back now, he has lost everything apart from his principles and he is not about to shed them like Dermot. He holds the letter over the fireguard and relaxes his fingers, letting it drop onto the white coals. The paper rests there a while before it yellows and darkens. Then flaming holes appear and grow until only charred scraps remain.

*

Wrists cuffed behind his back, Bill is led towards a Black Maria in a tiny walled yard behind the court. A bearded officer with a large marbled nose leans close as he clambers aboard.

'What did you get then, son?'

'Twelve months.'

'What for?'

'Failing to attend an army medical.'

His breath carries the sour whiff of cheap scotch. 'You stupid bastard. They are going to beat you black and blue if they find out what you done.'

'How will they know?'

'Don't fucking talk back to me, son.'

The officer follows him into the van and bolts the door. Once the engine shudders into action, he takes a swig from a silver hip flask hidden in his coat.

'This country will be defenseless if we get more like you. There will be bloody anarchy.'

Bill stays silent as instructed.

The officer peers at him. 'Answer me, son?'

'But you said...'

'Don't get fucking clever with me. This ain't a la-de-da debating society.'

'Sorry, sir.'

The van turns a corner abruptly and Bill slides off the seat and catches his temple against the metal bars lining the blacked-out window. The officer grips his hair roughly and drags him upright.

*

Wet night air rolls over Bill's naked body. The infirmary window is ajar and his bedsheets are on the floor. He lies there shaking, feeling his body's remaining heat drain away. Is this how he will die: alone in the dark with no one holding him? He feels a childlike terror rising in his gut.

'My...my...'

Basso's hunched, sleeping form, stirs. 'What's happening?'

'My... my...'

He collects the sheets and drapes them over Bill's body. 'You must have kicked them off.'

Bill feels a sudden need for company. This might be his last night and he has no family and friends to call on. 'Would you please stay with me until I sleep?'

Basso rubs his eyes. 'I'm here. There's nothing to worry about.'

'Thank you.' Bill watches as the Italian's head begins to fall. 'Tell me how you came to be here?'

He stirs again. 'England?'

'Aye.'

'My father came a long time ago. He had money troubles. He

figured the lenders would never look for him here. One morning he pushed his old market stall into Naples harbour and left. We were meant to follow but he never wrote or sent any money back. We gave up on him, but when he died, my name was in the will. A letter with an English stamp arrived one morning – I inherited an ice-cream parlour.

'I saw that he had given me the chance to make new life for myself in England. But when I got here I found it was falling down. He had let the place go to ruin to pay for his gambling.

'I worked day and night painting and repairing. I brought it back to how it used to look. Then I taught myself to make gelatos. I tell you, they flocked to my parlour. On hot days they queued down the road.

'I married one of my waitresses, Alice, and she gave me a little boy, Tito. We were happy back then – the happiest I'd ever been. Nothing bothered us. Work. Money. War. Nothing.

'One night I came home and found two constables waiting. They were standing outside our door laughing. When they saw me, they quietened down. They said I'd been listed as a Mussolini supporter and had to come with them. I said it was a big mistake. But they said it could be cleared up later. I begged to see my son and wife but they said there would be time for that afterwards.

'They took me to this half-built housing estate with big barbed-wire fences. They gave everyone a sack full of straw and told me to bed down for the night. I had to sleep in a house with no roof with twelve other men.

'I told everyone I was not a fascist but they kept saying I was a member of the Fascio. But I only joined so I could see my mother. I was planning a trip. The Italian embassy doesn't help you unless you are a member of the Fascio.

'I missed my boy so much. I went crazy. I stole a small knife from the camp mess and hid it in a bush. In the night I climbed out and got the knife. Then I got over the first wall and under the outer fence. But a solider saw me and grabbed my leg. I stabbed him again and again in the arm. He wouldn't let go. So I kept on stabbing him.

'More of them came and they got me out. I was covered in his blood. I'll never forget that. It was on my skin and under my fingernails.'

Basso is shaking with the effort of telling his story. Bill moves his hand from under the damp sheets to his shoulder.

'It is up to me to atone now,' he says quietly.

*

Through the van's small side window, he can see the thick gates of HMP Durham. The oak is stained black from decades of lashing peaty rain. A miserable-looking guard waves them on and the doors creak open. Bill checks his drunken companion; he is snoring loudly, hip flask dangling from his hand. The vehicle comes to an abrupt halt in the yard; still the officer doesn't stir. Bill can hear the driver chatting to another man outside.

'Jim, you got some baccy for me pipe? What's the hold up with getting this bugger inside?'

'There's a hanging going on. There aren't enough officers to attend to us.'

'Oh aye.'

'It's that seaman who was in the *Chronicle*. He strangled that whore. Don't you remember?'

'He didn't like the price?'

'Nah. Everything is going up.'

Both of them snigger.

*

Basso is carrying a pile of folded, starched white hospital sheets. He puts them down and smiles warmly at Bill. 'How long have you been awake?'

'Not sure.'

'Can you sit up a bit so I can change the sheets?'

'With some help...'

Basso wraps his thin arms around his chest and sits him on the edge of the bed. 'Are you feeling better?'

Bill clasps the metal headrest for support. He glances at his withered legs and feet hanging in the void. 'I wish everyone would stop asking me that.'

Once Basso has removed everything, he lies Bill down again. 'That should be more comfortable.'

The fresh cotton feels dry and crisp. 'Thank you.'

'It's nothing.'

Basso returns to his seat and they watch clouds the colour of pale eggshells gather in the sky. As noon approaches there are cracks of thunder and a heavy rain begins to fall; droplets drum on the slate roof above them and water surges through the guttering.

Bill listens with something approaching pleasure to the storm. It reminds him of lying in bed with Ma and Peggy, safe and happy, listening to rain pound the cobbles outside.

'This might sound strange but I'm pleased I'm still here to listen to this storm.'

Basso is confused. 'What do you mean?'

'I thought the doctor sent you to spy on me, and maybe he did. But you are a kind person.'

Basso frowns. 'You are forgetting what got me here in the first place. I'm no saint.'

'But you shouldn't be here, Basso. The politicians who lock up men because they carry the wrong travel documents, and send planes to bomb cities every night should be here.'

Basso shrugs his shoulders. 'Maybe we should all be here.'

The storm passes by late evening and a hot sun makes steam rise from the garden. Flying insects – butterflies, bees and midges – suddenly fill the air. Bill loses himself in the flitting, darting and buzzing outside; he forgets the soreness in his chest and the ache in his sides.

Basso, for his part, seems content with his own thoughts. Bill is glad because he hasn't the desire to talk at the moment. He is at peace with the world and has no wish to talk about the past or the future.

As shadows grow in the garden, Bill wiggles his toes in the bed and yawns. This is the longest he has managed to stay awake since he arrived. Basso starts snoring in the chair: he sounds like a train stopping in a station. As he contemplates joining him, the door swings open and the doctor strides in with a package.

'Mr Rowe, have you been awake for long?'

Bill ponders for a second. 'All afternoon.'

'Well that's marvellous. Can I have a listen to your chest?'

Bill loosens his shirt and Neave places the cool metal head of his stethoscope against the ridges of his bony chest. He squints and draws his lips in as he listens.

'What is it?'

'Nothing to worry about – your body is mending itself,' he says a little too quickly for Bill's liking. 'How are you feeling in yourself?'

Bill smiles thinly. 'Calmer.'

'Well, I suppose you had better have this then.' He brings the package to Bill's side and awkwardly rests his hand on his arm. 'You'll know that the guards have to read all prisoner mail...so it often takes a long time to get to the recipient.'

Bill's face drops. 'Have you kept this from me?'

Neave takes his hand back and heads for the door. 'Procedure I'm afraid.'

Bill examines the already ripped-open package carefully: the postmark is a few weeks old. Inside there is a short letter and a bundle of letters tied together with a red ribbon. The handwriting is small and familiar: it is from Peggy.

Dear Bill,

Ma told me never to speak to you after you got mixed up with them conchies. She says you lost your right to know about us when you left us to shame and poverty. But I need to tell you about Da.

I know you didn't always see eye to eye but he was found outside The George this morning. I went down there with Ma. He was as cold as a stone; I reckon he had been there all night. The constable patted me on the head and said he had gone to heaven. Ma wasn't having any of it, mind. She started shaking him and cursing him for drinking himself to death. The constable had to pull her off and carry her inside the pub.

This may sound evil, Bill, but I'm glad he's gone. He hated his life. Drink made it bearable for a bit but he always had to wake up in the morning. It is over now.

There were other sides to him though, Bill. After you got carted off to prison he told me he still had all these letters he had written in the war. He never posted them because he didn't want to upset Ma. He said they were disloyal. When he came back he hid them under that creaking floorboard in the hall.

He made me promise to send you them if something happened to him. I had a quick flick through. I think he was more like you than any of us ever thought.

Yours P.

With a strange calm, Bill unties the ribbon. He should pause and take in the news but he doesn't want to lose control. Not yet. He needs to know about Da's war. The paper is thin and coated in a layer of sticky dust. Turning it over in his faintly shuddering hands, he can still see blobs of silky wax and dirty thumbprints. Some pages have been nibbled by mice or woodlice.

Dearest Annie,

We marched to a place called Ypres today. There are so many fires burning that us lads on the flanks had to push into the middle to get away from the heat. It burnt the hairs on me arms and it made me eyes water something rotten.

The people who used to live here are long gone. All the buildings are smashed to pieces. There are only dogs and dead mules left. It's a vision of hell, Annie.

I've even started to miss that shithole Etaples. You can say what you like about those French boys begging us for chocolate and baccy and selling their little sisters for five francs a night but they took our mind off the front.

The others keep saying they are sick of waiting, mind. They want to have a crack at Jerry. But I'm not sure I'm up to it anymore. I know I shouldn't say this in a letter but all that stuff about King and Country rings a bit hollow when you can't get any kip 'cos you are thinking about all the bodies you've seen outside the field hospital.

The only one I can talk to is that Hexham lad I told you about, Victor. They say he's a stupid clot 'cos he's always falling over and can never seem to get anything right, whether it is cleaning his sodding rifle or putting his belt on. But he's got a good heart. He helps me with these letters and doesn't mind me stutter.

Supper is nearly ready so I'd better sign off. It's bully beef. There's no bread, so it's biscuits again. I could murder one of your stews, Annie. I miss you.

Your husband, Joe.

Dearest Annie

I'm supposed to be getting some rest in the dugout but I'm shaking like a leaf. Jerry shells are dropping all around. Them bastards have got to have ten buggering artillery guns for every one of ours.

We were meant to be relieved after eight days but we are still here – twenty days later. Captain Bray comes round with a tot of rum every night to keep our spirits up and says he is trying to get reinforcements. The lads all like him because he makes time for a game of cards and a chat. But I don't trust him. He only cares about his own kind. I can see the way his nose wrinkles when he gets close to us. He's revolted by us.

Victor is only seventeen. I found out yesterday. He says a lad his age shouldn't be here and I agree. I don't mind saying it in this here letter, the minimum age is nineteen not bloody seventeen.

Listen to this story, Annie. He says he was walking through Hexham with his pals when this well-to-do lady bold as brass pushes a white flower into his face. He says he wasn't old enough to fight. But she says he's lying and calls him a disgrace. People start crowding round to see what all the fuss was about. Then this vicar comes up and says Victor should get down the drill hall and prove the lady wrong. They signed him up that very day. Didn't even ask for a birth certificate.

I must go now. Bray wants me outside. It is my turn on the fire step.

Your husband, Joe.

Dearest Annie

Made it back to rest camp. Some Irish lads came in and relieved us yesterday. I should be blissfully happy. The others are out drinking and dancing with the village tarts. But I'm in the padre's tent 'cos something God-awful has happened.

Before we left the trenches, Bray asked for volunteers to cover over the shit hole and dig a new one. Well nobody wanted that job. The smell of them buckets mixed with the lime chloride makes you want chuck your guts up. Bray ordered Victor to do it 'cos he missed all the patrols last week; I told you Bray was a nasty piece of work. Anyway Bray said the others risked their lives for him so he should cover up their shit. Well the lads liked that one. There was lots of laughing and pushing and poor old Victor ended up in the mud.

I found myself a shovel and went to help him. But by the time I got there he'd nearly done it – he ain't the shirker they make him out to be. Then out of nowhere this big Jerry shell blew up. I blacked out. When I came round Victor was lying next to me with this big grin on his stupid face. He said get up you lazy sod. This confused the hell out of me; I smiled back but then I saw this dark blood coming out of his ear. It looked like black snot or ash washed out of a range. Right away I called for the body snatchers. Bray popped up from the dugout and ordered me to get back into the trench. I couldn't leave me pal Victor so I tried to drag him. He looked up at me and said in this odd sort of whisper that he needed to rest. Then he asked me if I could get him a blanket 'cos he was getting a bad chill. I put my coat over him. Bray kept shouting at me but I just ignored him. What's rank matter when a man is breathing his last? Victor kept saying he was cold, so in the end I lay on top on him. I think I must have fallen asleep. When the snatchers arrived they pulled me off him. They said he's dead, chum. Leave him. There's nothing you can do for him anymore.

Joe.

Dearest Annie

I haven't slept a wink since it happened. I try to make it all go away by thinking of your face. But it has been too long, Annie. All I can see is Victor's bloody ear and that stupid grin of his. I don't know if you'll want me back anyways. Me nerves are shot to pieces and me mind is gone. I'm not the man you kissed goodbye to all them years ago.

Joe.

Dearest Annie

The order has come down, we are going back to the front. I begged the padre to let me stay on in the camp but Bray caught wind of it and said he would horse whip me in front of everyone and then have me court marshalled. He said I ought to take out my problems on the Hun bastards who killed Victor. But I've got this bad shake in me hand and I can barely hold a rifle, never mind fire it.

Joe

Dearest Annie

Bray's gone and put me in the same dugout as before. At night I hear Victor saying things and crying. I said this to the others and they said I've gone dingo. That's what they here call mad here. I don't know what to do, Annie.

 Pray for me, Joe.

The last sheet of paper is an official document: the military record of Joseph Rowe. It lists his age, height, chest measurements, distinctive marks, next of kin and children. The final entry under a column titled History is a description of a German attack.

On 9 May 1915 Private Rowe inhaled the gas and collapsed. Stretcher bearers managed to get to him when the wind changed. Rowe was treated at a field hospital in Ypres and transferred to Etaples. His medical notes indicate there is a distinct weakness in his lungs and an uncontrollable shaking of his right hand. Rowe also displays a certain mental infirmity. He claimed on two occasions to hear the voice of a dead soldier. Discharged as medically unfit.

Bill realises he has been holding the letters so tightly his knuckles are white; he relaxes, letting them drift down towards the polished floor. A draft carries them a short distance before depositing them the near the wheels of his bed.

A kaleidoscope of memories swims in his head: blood on the hearth; Ma sobbing in a heap, small body trembling; a singed book on dirty floorboards; Da face down in the street, pockets turned out and belt unbuckled; Peggy coughing; Ma counting out the last of her coins in the grocery shop.

Da was a heartless brute. But he was made that way by civilised men in uniforms and suits and dog-collars; by officers and generals and politicians and clergymen. The bitterness was now almost gone; he could admit to himself that he loved him. He lets tears of relief as much as sadness swell in his eyes. His chest rises and falls like a fishing boat on a rough sea.

Basso comes to life in his chair. He rubs his face and wipes a line of dribble from his chin. 'What's the matter?'

Bill brings his breathing under control; he likes Basso but doesn't want to talk to him about his father. 'Just chest pains.'

Basso pauses. 'I must have worn myself out in the garden. I hope the doctor didn't see me like this.'

'No,' he lies.

'Can I get you anything? Water? Food?'

Bill wipes his eyes and nose with a fist full of sheets. 'Get me the doctor.'

Neave comes straight away; he must have been hovering in the corridor. He looks uncomfortable but disguises his feelings with the brash indifference of a public schoolboy.

'Is everything in order, Mr Rowe?'

Bill looks at Basso. 'Give us a few moments alone.'

Basso holds his hands up as if to apologise.

Bill fixes his glare on Neave but says nothing until the door is closed. 'Why did you keep that letter from me? Did you know what was in it?'

Neave strokes his moustache. 'You were not able to read. You were in and out of consciousness. The fact is, I didn't want to harm your recovery.'

Bill snorts dismissively. 'I thought this—' he sweeps his hand over his shrunken torso '—was for nothing. I thought that I'd wasted my youth opposing the war because no one was listening. That's why I wanted to die. But it does matter. Even if my stance changes no one's mind – it is better than fighting and killing—'

'I'm sorry I don't understand.'

'You should have given me these—' he stabs his finger at the letters on the floor '—rather than those pills. I didn't need sedating. I needed waking up. And I'm awake now.'

'I still don't understand...'

'My father is dead, Doctor Neave. They found him outside the pub where he drank every buggering night. Face down in the gutter. But do you know what? He may as well have died in France. That war killed his spirit.'

'I see.'

Bill's chest spasms and blood sprays the white cotton. 'How can I trust anything you say again? You kept this from me for two weeks.'

'I'm your doctor. I was trying to help.'

Bill's tears mix with the blood in the corners of his mouth. 'You said my lungs were mending themselves earlier. You said there was nothing to worry about. That I'd get better. Were you withholding the truth then?'

Neave sighs with exacerbation. 'I know you've had a terrible shock and you have my deepest sympathies, but I'll not give up on you.'

Bill yanks the bloody sheet from his body and thrusts it in the direction of the doctor. Then, with as much anger as he can muster, he roars, 'Blood!'

Neave's voice falters. 'You may die. You are very ill.'

Bill falls silent. He looks out at Basso collecting apples in the garden. *You may die.* Neave's words boom in his head. You may die. It is true he had once desired death, but to hear it from the mouth of the doctor was something else entirely. *You may die.* He imagined Da's body outside The George. Then he imagined his sparsely attended funeral.

This time his voice is calmer; calculating and firm rather than aggressive. 'I want to see my family and friends before...'

Neave pulls out his notepaper but his pen slips from his fingers and spins on the floor until he stoops to collect it.

'Give me their names and I'll have telegrams sent,' he says, kneeling on the floor.

Bill had misjudged him; telegrams are expensive. 'Thomas Weaver and Lizzie Weaver of Coldwell Lane, Gateshead. Peggy Rowe of Rawling Road, Gateshead.'

'And what should they say, Mr Rowe?'

'Bill Rowe is sorry. Now in hospital. Please visit HMP Durham.'

Later, Basso comes in from the cold with a basket of Russets. He cuts one up into tiny pieces, yet Bill has almost no appetite and can only manage a few mouthfuls. Their tart flesh reminds him of raiding orchards in Gateshead.

'I used to steal these when I was a boy.'

'Where did you grow up?'

'Bensham, Gateshead.'

Basso takes a bite himself and grins. 'Is that why you ended up here?'

Bill smiles half-heartedly. 'Apples. Nah. You must have heard the rumours.'

He swallows and locks eyes with Bill. 'The doctor said you were a principled man.'

'I refused to fight in the war.'

'And they put you here for that?'

Bill coughs up a lump into his hands. 'Aye.'

Basso hands Bill a rag to clean himself.

Bill wakes in the night with a salty taste in his mouth. His chest heaves and he sprays blood all over his sheets. The tiny drops spread into roses and poppies on the white sheets. He watches them settle and dry before wiping his mouth with the back of his hand.

As Basso snores in the chair, he worries that the telegrams will take too long. He doesn't want to die without making peace with his past. He starts to compose apologies to everyone: Peggy, Thomas, Len, Lizzie and Ma. Even Florence gets a mention.

Under his breath he mutters and whispers to himself for hours. It helps him order his thoughts and sooth his conscience.

'I had to leave behind my old life to get by in here but I love you all the same,' he says to the darkness. 'I love you all the same.'

In the morning he wakes before Basso. As soon as the Italian stirs he asks him for a pen. However, his hand is too unsteady to write and the ink runs across the page in long meaningless wobbles. Basso persuades him to get some rest and try again after lunch. Sleep overcomes him before too long.

He is roused in the late afternoon by footsteps in the corridor. It is murky and wet outside and a cold bowl of potato soup sits untouched beside the bed. Basso's chair is empty. The doorknob twists and the doctor comes in clutching a piece of paper.

'We've had a response—' he adjusts his glasses '—from a Mr Thomas Weaver.'

'Thomas,' Bill mouths in delight.

'He wants to visit tomorrow. I'm afraid there's been nothing from the others yet. But I'll make sure the messengers keep trying, Mr Rowe.'

Bill catches Neave's eye before he leaves. His behaviour is very curious. He had nothing to gain and in fact a lot to lose from helping a war resister. 'Why are you doing all this? It is more than any normal doctor would do.'

Neave cranes his neck into the corridor; Basso is nowhere to be seen. 'Well, if you must know, my father was an objector in the last war. But I'd do this—'

Bill interrupts. 'What happened to him?'

Neave circles the bed looking up at the ceiling; he locks his hands together behind the small of his back.

'He was a great scholar. He loved to read and discuss literature—' suddenly he sounds softer, more human, without any haughtiness or briskness '—I've never seen someone with so many books. They needed two carts when they came to take them all.'

Bill feels like he is finally making sense of Neave. He probes some more. 'What do you mean?'

He stops and inspects Bill; his eyes glimmer like wet, dark pebbles on a beach.

'The bastards...I'm sorry, Mr Rowe, but there's no other word for them. They gave him a penal sentence when he refused to parade. He had to labour in a slate quarry in Wales. It was the first time he had worked his hands. He died not long after I was born. Look, I may not agree with your stance against this war but I believe society must treat its dissenters kindly – because it is right to do so, and also because dissenters are society's alarm bells. They remind us that our side might be wrong.'

Bill feels like hugging Neave or at least shaking his hand, although he is probably not a man who likes or knows how to be comforted. 'I had no idea, Doctor. I'm sorry.'

Neave clears his throat and straightens his white coat. 'There's something troubling, even hypocritical, about locking up men for their beliefs, however distasteful we find them, in order to wage war against a totalitarian state. Isn't that what totalitarian states are supposed to do?'

'I appreciate you helping me, Doctor.'

'It isn't for me to say if your stance is worthwhile, Mr Rowe. Except perhaps to ponder what would happen if there was no one to question authority?'

Thomas is as Bill remembers him: bald and stooped. As he sits down, Bill notices his neck is dotted with clumps of wiry black and grey stubble. He has the air of a man on the run. Yet he seems more shocked by Bill appearance.

'Bill, you are so thin?'

'It's TB.'

'Dear God.'

'I'll be fine.'

Thomas studies the white walls for a while. 'Why didn't you reply to my letters?'

Bill hesitates. 'I didn't know what to say to you.'

'I understand, Bill.'

Bill waits for more but Thomas is unforthcoming.

'I'm sorry.'

Thomas frowns in confusion. 'For the letters? They don't matter, Bill. I just wanted to you to know I hadn't forgotten you.'

'Has Len been writing?'

Thomas squeezes his hands but he cannot keep them still. 'He's in a bad way.'

Bill throat tightens – he feels bad for making no effort to contact his pal and comrade. 'Why?'

'It seems that an officer took exception to his refusal to take part in military activities and…'

Thomas blinks and his breath quickens; Bill worries he is about to keel over.

'I thought he was in the non-combatant core?'

'Aye, but they were making him move bombs about. He said he would not "help kill conscripts" and sat on the ground. They dragged him by his hair into what I think is called the icebox.'

'Icebox?'

'A freezing cold cell. He was left without clothes and bedding. They threw water on him and opened the window. When they opened the door the next morning, he was laying there: limp and blue.'

Bill rubs his brow with his thumb letting his palm cover his eyes for a moment. The shame is too much. 'I should have…'

Thomas reads his mind. 'You have nothing to feel guilty about, Bill.'

'How is he now?'

'They got an army medic to bring him round and now he's back in the camp. He says the officer who did this is going to kill one of them sooner or later.'

'Christ.'

Thomas moves his bad leg into a different position. 'The truth is I'm to blame for all of this. You and Len. All of this.'

Bill gathers his thoughts; there was a time when a confession like this would have pleased him but he can take no pleasure in it now. 'The government put Len in the icebox and me in this bed. Not you.'

'It is kind of you to say that, but if I'd never met you then you would not be lying here, taking your last breaths in captivity. And my son...'

Bill follows Thomas's eyes as they drift around the room in search of relief from his decaying body. 'Perhaps I'd be lying on an army stretcher in a field hospital or gleefully butchering German conscripts. Would that be better?'

Thomas's gaze lands finally on the floor. 'I don't know anymore, Bill. Maybe there are differences between the Allies and the Axis after all. Maybe it is a different matter when a war starts.'

For the first time since they met all those years ago in Len's front room, Bill sees only despair in the deep lines on his face. It unnerves him because he never imagined that Thomas would end up doubting himself and his beliefs.

'War destroys people, Thomas. It destroyed my family.'

'I'm sorry, Bill.'

'I'm doing this for Da so that others don't end up like him.'

Thomas doesn't react as Bill hopes – instead of slapping him on the back or cheering he lifts himself carefully from the chair.

'Please drop by for a cup of tea when all this is over. Lizzie would love to see you. And I'm sorry about your Da. I read about it in the *Chronicle*.'

'Thomas?'

As he hobbles out of the door, it strikes Bill how very old he looks.

'Goodbye, Bill.'

As the night draws in and the prison falls quiet, Bill reflects on his meeting with Thomas. How different the erstwhile villain of his imagination seemed in reality; how small, how human, how frail. He had never for one moment dreamt that Thomas would lose his conviction. He had been preparing for this war all his adult life; determined to avoid the mistakes of his generation. Still he could not have prepared for how it would feel to stay at home whilst his son suffered and for his daughter to abandon them all.

Basso interrupts him with a bowl of steaming soup. Bill sips a little but Basso doesn't even look at his own. Bill wonders if something is wrong because he is normally ravenously hungry.

'Are you ill?'

He bites his bottom lip. 'This is my last night.'

Bill musters a grin. 'Are you going free?'

'No, the governor is unhappy about the way the hospital is run. He says the doctor treats us orderlies too well. He said a man like me should not be gardening in the sunshine every day when men who have committed lesser crimes are stuck in their cells.'

'So what's going to happen?'

'I've got to go back to the wing in the morning.'

'I'm sorry, Basso.'

Basso rests his head and hands against the cool glass dividing the room from his beloved garden. 'I don't want to think about it. Can we just watch the sky?'

'Aye.'

He is gone when Bill rises at dawn. He waits hours for his breakfast before two men turn up with a trolley. The younger one comes from his old wing; his red skin looks sore and dry. The older one is from a different wing. He has greasy hair and a throaty laugh.

'Here's your grub, pal.'

'Has Basso gone?'

'Who? You mean the Macaroni? Back to his cell.'

They turn to go.

'Aren't you going to do anything about the mess? Basso used to change the sheets.'

The old one looks at the young one. 'Go on then, Bert.'

'I ain't touching that bugger's blood. It's infectious'

The older one laughs. 'Sorry, pal. '

Bill brings up more blood as they edge out the ward. 'Can you get the doctor for me?'

'He'll be round later, although you look like you need an undertaker.'

Bill sleeps on and off until midday without the doctor making an appearance. He starts to wonder if the governor has got rid of Neave as well. Then at about lunchtime he comes in flanked by the new orderlies; it is almost like he is being frogmarched by them.

Neave smiles although he looks particularly ill at ease in their company. 'I've some good news for you, Mr Rowe. You have another visitor. She's waiting to come in.'

Peggy? Lizzie? Bill tries to fold the sheets over to hide the blood. 'Could you change the sheets, Doctor? I don't want them worrying needlessly?'

The younger orderly, Bert, smirks. 'Do you want to impress your little gimmer?'

Bill ignores him. 'Can you help, Doctor?'

Neave shakes his head. 'I'm sorry there isn't time. The governor wants all mercy visits to be halted by the end of the week. Can you show her in gentlemen.'

Bert opens the door and winks. 'Come on, pet. He's ready and waiting for you.'

Bill longs for the strength to climb out of bed and slam his fists into Bert's pockmarked head. That would show him the kind of war resister he is: a man unafraid to side with the weak against the strong. Instead he has to make do with the fantasy and the snarl of his upturned lip.

'Oh look, your lover boy is all upset,' says Bert.

The young man puts his hands on his waist and thrusts his groin forwards but Bill's guest steps deftly round him without making any contact; it is Florence.

She is wearing trousers and her hair is tied up; her lips break into a half-smile. She is a woman, not a girl anymore.

The older orderly cups his hand over his friend's ear and says at a volume loud enough to be heard by everybody in the room, 'What you do reckon? I wouldn't mind if you scrubbed the cow shit off her.'

Doctor takes his arm gently. 'Well, this is really too much. Let's get on with the rounds. We'll be back in an hour and then I'm afraid you'll have to go, Miss Weaver.'

Florence waits until the door closes. 'I appreciate I'm not who you were expecting. Can I sit?'

Bill notices her quickly take in his withered torso and arms, which are visible above the folded bedclothes. She tries to hide her reaction but he can see the disgust and fear in her eyes. He pulls the sheets up as best he can, but that only reveals more blood and mucus stains.

'Bill, I'm so sorry.'

Bill eyes her warily; he is suspicious of her motives. 'Who told you I was here?'

She presents him with an oily scrap of paper; it is Lizzie's telegram. 'She gave it to me and told me to make my peace with you before...I think she knew all about us.'

Bill is still resentful that she could not bring herself to tell her parents about him; he was the ugly secret she had to keep from them. 'And Thomas – did he know as well?'

She hesitates – perhaps doubting the wisdom of coming to see her former lover. Bill doesn't, however, intend to make it easy for her. She had abandoned him and her family in desperate circumstances.

'I haven't spoken to him since I left for the farm. I meet Lizzie in a tearoom in Hexham once a month. That's when—'

Bill cuts her off mid-sentence. 'Why didn't you write to me?'

She ignores his question and peers at his hands. 'You're so bony, Bill.'

'I'm on the mend,' he says although he can tell she is not persuaded. 'Please don't go on about it.'

'I can go,' she says curtly.

A tense quiet holds for what seems like five or ten minutes. They exchange glances as wasps feast on rotting apples outside and a moist autumn breeze lifts and drops the blinds.

Bill detects the same indifferent look in her face as when she shut the door on him in the snow. 'Why did you shun me when I needed you most?'

'And what did you do in my hour of need?'

'What do you mean?'

She rubs her belly. 'Our bairn.'

Bill grips his bed. It had never occurred to him that she might have been carrying – they had always been so careful. 'Bairn?'

She holds his gaze. 'I was a few months gone when I tried to tell you. You remember that night I stayed at your digs? You wanted to get your hands on my tits but I just wanted you to hold me. Then in morning when you heard the news about Poland you dashed off because you were keener on martyrdom than listening to a woman.'

Bill doesn't hear her slights. 'Am I a father?'

'I got rid of it, Bill,' she says with what appears to be relish.

'Why?'

The pleasure drains from her face. 'Look at you, Bill? What kind of a Da would you have made?'

'So what did you do?'

She prepares to leave. 'This is a waste of time. I don't know why I came.'

The doctor's words fill his mind again. *You may die.* 'I'm sorry, Flo. I want to make my peace with you.'

She drops her voice until it is little more than a whisper. 'I ignored it for months, hoping the odd swig of whiskey would...but it just grew bigger. In the end I told my friend Sarah. You know she works in a chemist. Well she said she would get me some women's medicine. We both knew what that meant.

'One evening she came round with a little blue bottle; it was called bitter berries. I swallowed it in one go and went up to bed. In the night I woke up and threw up over my bed clothes. But nothing came out down below.

'Next weekend she brought round a box of laxatives. I took as many as I could and this time I got these terrible stabbing pains in my sides. Blood started leaking out of my underwear. I was in such pain that I had to drive my nails into my palms to stop myself crying out.

'Just before midnight, I went to get some water and a...thing fell onto the towels I'd spread on the carpet. In the morning I dropped the lot in the Gut. It bobbed around on the current before sinking. I'll never forget it – it looked so small. I didn't want to see you after that.'

She is trembling from the telling of the story.

Bill curses himself for thinking only of his own predicament. He sees her lying in his bed curled in sleep in his digs and the moment she nearly threw up in the stairwell. He should have realised. 'I'm so sorry. I could only think of stopping the war. I should have...'

'Stop saying sorry. I need some air.'

He pauses. 'There's a garden out there. I believe you can get to it through the corridor.'

She leaves quickly, avoiding eye contact. Bill wonders if she will come back but she leaves her coat on the chair. A moment or so later she appears in the garden. She picks her way through the fruit-drunk wasps and leans against the trunk with her back to him.

The breeze lifts the blinds again, filling his nostrils with the whiff of mushy apples: cider and caramel. After about twenty minutes, she turns and looks at him through the glass.

'Come in,' he mouths to her. 'We don't have long left.'

She nods and retraces her steps. He prays she doesn't run into the new warders or the doctor for that matter. Once safely back in her chair she reaches towards him and begins stroking his wrist; her touch is soothing.

'We both followed our hearts. There is nothing more to say.'

The line in the poem she underlined comes to him: *fear not the future, weep not for the past.* 'Aye.'

She moves up his arm. Despite everything he responds to her touch; it is as though he is back in her yard shovelling coal in the rain, or lying on a grass bank, or following her up the stairs to her bedroom.

'Are you okay, Bill? Tell me if this is too much?'

'I'm pleased you came to see me.'

Bill closes his eyes; he can feel the world slowly drifting away from him. It is as if he is caught in a very gentle current taking him out to sea.

He says, 'Where are you living?

'Black Farm. It's near the Roman wall. It's a beautiful around there and far from all the bombs,' she says. 'I delivered some calves last week because the vet was late.'

He blinks himself awake and follows the tanned stretch of her forearms; chestnut-brown freckles and fine hairs are burnt white from the sun.

'Have you met anyone?'

'No, but the other lasses and the herders carry on like it's the end of days. They have no shame and who can blame them.'

'But not you?'

She smiles; her awkwardness appears to have given way to something approaching normality. 'I told you no.'

'I'm sorry. It's just I wish I was there with you.'

She leans over and kisses him gently on the cheek. 'You feel cold. Shall I close the window?'

'No, I'm fine.'

Another pleasant lull. They linger in each other's eyes with the familiarity of former lovers. Could it be longing? Or just curiosity?

After a while she says, 'What did Thomas seem like?'

'Old. Very old.'

'I haven't seen him since I left. He could never understand my choice.'

'He can be a hard bastard, but he loves you and Len.'

'I suppose you know about Len?'

He nods. 'I wish I could have been a better friend.'

The breeze ruffles some stray brown curls that have escaped her hair clips. Bill wishes he could run his fingers through them one last time.

'He will pull through. I know he will. He's desperate to get on with his life when all this is over.'

'You know about Aiden?'

Her eyes narrow. 'Of course I do. Thomas and Lizzie still think he is a woman though.'

Bill laughs a little.

'It's nice to see you smile, Bill.'

'Thomas told—' Bill lurches forward suddenly and his mouth fills with blood the texture of lumpy porridge '—he told me he felt responsible.'

She notices his discomfort. 'Are you okay?'

'Aye.'

'I can see you are holding something in, Bill. Are you going to vomit? Shall I get the doctor?'

Blood spills out of his mouth. Florence stiffens and stands.

The chair falls and clatters on the floor – it all happens in faltering, slow motion, like a jammed film reel at the pictures.

'Oh my—' her voice is strangled and high '—shall I get someone?'

Bill holds his hand up as his cheeks fill again. 'I'll be just fine in a moment. It's nothing to worry about.'

She spreads her hands over her mouth and nose to hide what could be terror or revulsion. She looks from side to side as if she cannot bear the sight of him anymore.

'Why did you have to take it so far? To satisfy my silly father?'

Bill gulps it back down and wipes his chin with the sheets. 'It was my own decision. I'm the one to blame.'

'I can't blame you.'

'But I would do the same again.'

'I know that. You are as stubborn as me.'

Bill smiles, his teeth stained red.

She cannot look at him. 'I wish this war had not come between us. I...'

Coughs overpower him; dark blobs land on the floor and her shoes.

'There's blood everywhere, Bill!' she cries.

Bill splutters and coughs again. 'What were you going to say? I want you—'

The door opens; it's the older orderly. 'Lovers' tiff?'

The exertion of coughing has been too much. He tries to speak but he hasn't the strength. Instead he makes a terrible groaning and gurgling sound.

The orderly screws his face up as if Bill is speaking in a foreign tongue. 'What did you say, pal?'

Doctor Neave pushes past. 'This visit is over. You need rest, rest, rest. Not shouting matches.'

Florence removes her coat from under the upended chair. Her eyes are bright and burning like hot coals. 'I was just talking to him,' she says slowly.

'Just go, please,' he says firmly. 'If the governor hears of this I'll be for the chop.'

Bill prepares to plead with them both but his throat is too tight. Helplessly he opens and closes his bloody mouth.

She kisses him as Neave holds the door for her. This time her kiss is stronger; he feels the warmth of her core on his skin.

'I'll come back tomorrow.'

Neave shakes his head impatiently and guides her out of the ward. 'Move him to window so he can get some fresh air.'

Bill is left with the orderlies. They unlock the wheels on his bed. He is too sleepy now to think about Florence or the war or Da or Ma or Thomas or Len or Lizzie. A cool numbness spreads from his toes and fingers across his body until he can barely feel his heart beating.

'What's he in here for anyway? Do you know?'

'No,' says Bert.

They position the bed next to the window. The breeze has dropped and the garden is subdued and restful. The last rays of evening sunlight are filtering through the bronzed leaves on the tree.

'Some lad on the wing said he was in for cowardice, like?'

'Cowardice? What's that?'

'He was too scared to fight.'